JUMPSHIP HOPE

ADRIA LAYCRAFT

JUMPSHIP HOPE

ADRIA LAYCRAFT

TYCHE BOOKS LTD.

Jumpship Hope
Copyright © 2019 Adria Laycraft

Published by Tyche Books Ltd.
Calgary, Alberta, Canada
www.TycheBooks.com

Cover Art by Niken Anindita
Cover Layout by Indigo Chick Designs
Interior Layout by Ryah Deines
Editorial by M.L.D. Curelas

First Tyche Books Ltd Edition 2019
Print ISBN: 978-1-989407-03-5
Ebook ISBN: 978-1-989407-04-2

Author photograph: Erin Laycraft

This book was funded in part by a grant from the Alberta Media Fund.

Government

This book is dedicated to Erin:
"No matter what..."

CHAPTER ONE

JANLIN WOULD GO dirtside, SpaceOp restrictions be damned.

Her fingers flew over the keyboard as she did her best to convince the orbital's security system to let her book out a Shunter without authorization. She wished she could ask Gordon for help. Or her dad. But Gordon would tell her to wait for SpaceOp to save the day, and her dad was missing.

Her stomach ached.

The fungal spore from the now-abandoned Luna base had ripped through their crops, starving out plants just as they would starve if they couldn't fix it. Such a nasty way to die.

So she made up her mind to steal a ship, get Ursula some uncontaminated green life, and get out, storms be damned. As a pilot, this was her only way to help, and she was one of the few who could actually pull it off. So what if she wasn't willing to wait for the proper channels of authority to approve her flight? They would dither until it was too late.

First, she needed a Shunter, and that wasn't going well.

Janlin's comm buzzed. She touched her earlobe. "Go ahead."

"Ursula wants to show us something. You got a minute?"

Janlin stared at her botched attempts to hack the orbital's systems and sighed. "Yeah, sure."

She stepped out of her quarters to find Gordon waiting for her. At nearly six and a half feet, he dwarfed Janlin's lanky five foot four and caused all kinds of hassles for SpaceOp's cockpit designs.

"What's this about?" Janlin asked as they fell into step

1

together. His long face was more drawn than ever, and kinda grey. Just another thing to drive her.

Gordon shrugged. "Not sure. Ursula probably wants to experiment on us again." He stared straight ahead as they walked the corridors, face tight, broad shoulders hunched. "Blimey hell, but I'm sick of being hungry."

Janlin wanted to tell him, wanted to ask him for help with her plan. But he knew the restrictions were in place for damned good reasons, and he tended to respect that. "We need a new damned planet," she muttered. Gordon gave a humourless laugh and agreed.

They strode along the corridor linking the thousands of pods that made up the orbital station. "Any word from Mars?" Janlin asked. That was the other place her dad could've gone, maybe to plead their case, maybe to negotiate more settlers, maybe to beg some fresh plant material to work with.

"After their response when the Luna base went under, they can blow it out their arse."

Janlin had to agree with her Brit friend.

"Do you think my dad's gone there?" she said, unable to keep her voice steady.

"Maybe," Gordon allowed, but he did not back it up with any further hope.

They entered the growhouse, where thirty pods were joined into one large area filled with rows of hydroponics. A lone soul moved among the plants, her lean figure clearly female but her face obscured by an old rebreather mask. When she noticed their approach, she tugged the mask off over what was left of her blonde hair.

"What have you got, Ursula?" Janlin wrinkled her nose at the smell of rotting foliage and stagnant fungus underlying the green life.

Ursula blinked, her eyes ringed with dark circles of exhaustion. "All I can figure to do is preserve as much of the crop into food as I can. Hopefully it will be enough to sustain us until we receive help. But once it's gone, it's gone. None of the new seedlings survived." She lifted her chin, but fear shone bright in her eyes. For all her calm logic and belief in science, Ursula's despair ran deeper than Janlin had realized . . . which left Janlin feeling a deep-set terror.

Gordon laid an encouraging hand on Ursula's shoulder, and she slipped closer to lean into him.

"What have you cooked up, luv?" Gordon asked.

"It's in my lab," she said, straightening and waving them to follow.

Ursula led them across the corridor to another pod, the door opening to a room stuffed with machines and equipment. A smell like sun-baked hay overpowered the place.

"This is mat-grass," Ursula said, presenting them with a small plate of flat, green squares. They each popped one in their mouths. Blue eyes wide, Ursula gave Janlin a look of appeal. "It utilizes every part of the plant to create nutrition, albeit lacking in taste. I don't know what else to do."

Gordon winced, chewed, and swallowed. Janlin quickly swallowed her own square, wishing she had a drink at hand. "Have you started new seedlings?"

"Sure," Ursula said, but Janlin caught the shadow that crossed the scientist's face. "We have a dozen different trays in containment that I'm testing different solutions on."

"How long can we last on these wafers?"

Ursula's look begged Janlin not to ask.

"We need to know," Janlin said, squeezing Ursula's arm in useless comfort. "How long?"

"The mat-grass wafers will last eight weeks. The seedling trays won't be ready for three, four weeks, and of course that only gives us baby plants, not full-grown crops." Ursula looked away, giving a little shake of her head. "If all the seedlings are clear of contamination, I could make more of this mat-grass out of some and let the rest mature . . . but we still have at least a hundred days until harvest." She gave them a look of desperation. "That's about fourteen weeks. We're short by six weeks, and that's only if these crops make it."

"We've sent for help, Urse," Gordon said, giving Janlin a murderous look over his wife's head. "SpaceOp will have to send those new bio-engineered plants they've been using on Mars."

"If Mars doesn't respond, then it's official. SpaceOp has abandoned us," Janlin said with quiet vehemence. "It's like they have no clue what we're really up against. Why else just shut us out?"

"Those blokes haven't gone hungry, not like we have," said

Gordon. "And they're scared . . . for good reason." He took another tiny square of green and turned it over and over in his big fingers, but he didn't make any move to eat it.

"Kulturkampf," Ursula said in a mild voice as she poked a tray of the dried plant material.

Janlin tipped her head at the German. "Culture-who?"

Ursula smiled. "It's a 'culture struggle' . . . this is what we have here, don't you think?"

Janlin nodded. "Yeah, I guess so. Mars is its own culture now. But they're not really going to let us starve, are they?"

"I've done what I can . . ." Ursula began.

"Of course, you have, Urse. It's certainly not your fault." Janlin stared at the pile of green squares on the plate. "The mat-grass is . . . tasty."

Gordon sputtered, tossing his square at her. "Janlin Kavanagh, don't you lie to my wife!"

Janlin caught the tiny morsel and pulled her face into the best look of wide-eyed innocence she could muster to try and lighten the mood. Gordon shook his head. Ursula just looked sad. Janlin thought of how they were when they first came up to the station, how they would eat together in the lounge, laughing and talking late into the night shift, playing off each other's humour and basking in the glory of being involved in such an innovative program.

The goal had been to become independent of Earth support, a functional, closed system. There wasn't much hope from that quarter anyway. The numbers wiped out by famine were staggering, and when the growing storms had made Earth a no-fly zone, it got real . . . and they had met the challenge. Now, however, one little spore could end it all, starving them slowly as they circled the innocuous but unreachable blue marble . . . one nearly as inaccessible as Mars at the moment.

They were all suffering. Ursula's fine golden hair looked even sparser than Janlin's darker hair, and her already lean frame now seemed frail. Gordon hid his hair loss by simply shaving his head, but it pained Janlin to watch his muscular bulk dwindle away. When her own auburn hair started falling out in clumps, Janlin took to wearing a hat, which only brought it home harder at the end of the day when the hat held more hair than her head seemed to.

"We have to find something to start over with," Janlin insisted. "We could take a Shunter down, just me and Ursula, and you could scan for us. All we need is a few plants or seeds, right?" She held Gordon's gaze, daring him to take this chance. She scrambled for some leverage with her rule-abiding friend. "If we could get the gardens producing like they once did, maybe they'll let you have kids, too."

Something hollowed in her as she watched the look of pain and longing pass between her friends.

"If they'd only open up another dome on Mars—"

"But they won't," Janlin said, cutting Gordon off. "Not until it's too late." Too late for them, anyway, but she didn't need to say it. They knew.

Besides, a new dome would take years to establish. And the growing population on Mars might simply move in, leaving them struggling back in Earth's orbit, stranded while they watched Earth being torn apart by storms and drought. The joke was that Earth scoured itself clean of humanity.

It didn't help morale that applications for Mars were no longer being accepted "for the safety of those already in place." Janlin couldn't blame them. Every attempt at decontamination before abandoning Luna Base obviously hadn't kept the nasty mould spore from travelling with them to the station.

"They should help more, send more supplies," Gordon said, persisting. "Their gardens aren't as dodgy as ours. I can't believe Diona would let it go so far as to let us starve."

"Well, she *is* Stepper's sister, and she's had control over the entire space-faring population since Earth collapsed."

"But they could send something unmanned . . ."

"Again, that would be too little, too late. Look, our gardens did just fine until this infection spread. If we could just get some fresh soil and a plant or two, start again . . ." She could see Ursula's wheels turning, but Gordon still shook his head.

"It's too dangerous dirtside," he said. "And we'd never get permission."

Janlin swallowed and looked away, unable to admit she would go without it. She always was more of a rebel than him. Thankfully Ursula took up the fight with what she knew best— scientific logic.

"New material could give us a fresh start, Gordon. If I could rebuild with a completely clean system, and somehow keep the spore out . . ." Ursula paused, tapping her chin. "Perhaps if I created pathogen inoculums before we bring anything in, that would do it."

Janlin and Gordon exchanged their usual blank looks at Ursula's scientific jargon, but Janlin held on to the small hope. "All I know is, we need fresh plants, and we need them soon. It's worth the risk."

She'd fired something up in the biochemist. Ursula confronted Gordon. "Love, you told me the other day that there are growing pockets of calm between storms. Perhaps it *is* worth the risk."

Gordon frowned. "Those pockets are brief . . ."

Janlin waved off his protest. "You know a Shunter can take it, and you know I can fly it."

"I still don't like it. Why risk both of you?"

The words stung Janlin to silence for a long moment, a moment where Ursula explained how her bio-chem equipment and storage cells for proper decontamination weren't something she could just teach Janlin to use overnight, and Janlin was of course the best choice to get them there, seeing as they would need Gordon on the scanners while Janlin piloted.

But if Janlin could get what was needed without putting Ursula at risk, that would suit Gordon better.

Janlin never felt as alone as she did in that moment.

"We have to do something," Janlin said, ignoring the sting. "We can't rely on SpaceOp to rescue us."

"You're not even going to try and get this cleared first, are you?" he asked, and Janlin grimaced.

"We'll all be long dead if we wait for that."

"Stepper might—"

Janlin stopped him with a look, and the close quarters suddenly became uncomfortable.

"Let me look at the latest weather charts first," Gordon said, and Janlin grinned, knowing he'd given in.

CHAPTER TWO

As EARTH'S STORMS grew deadly and never-ending, the three orbital stations helped house those in transit to either Luna Base or the Mars Colonies. These stations then became lifeboats when Luna's gardens failed and the spore became too lethal to breathe. Despite all efforts to eradicate and sterilize against it during the evacuation, the spore followed them in a milder mutation that now devastated their food production and prompted Mars to shut them out.

The stations held just over seven thousand survivors. As Janlin stared out a small visual-check window in the C-bank corridor, she wondered just how many people held on down below.

It wasn't much of a gene pool, which was only one of the many arguments against any population growth at first. Yet the Mars project had experienced enough crop success that the ban on conception was lifted for qualified applicants. This pulled big objections from those left behind, especially when SpaceOp shut down the applications for migration to Mars.

Despite her anger at this injustice, for Janlin it didn't really matter. She had no partner, hadn't for a long time. For Gordon and Ursula, however . . . well, two people that loved each other that much deserved children. As the station turned, generating gravity for its inhabitants, the planet slipped out of sight and left her with nothing but a view of pinpricked blackness.

She sighed and continued along the narrow corridor to the

open door of a work pod. She let out a pent-up breath when she found it empty. A datapad rested next to a steaming mug of Vita-tea. She wrinkled her nose at the acerbic smell of the helpful but disgusting drink and bent over to tap at the screen.

Gnawing at her inner cheek, Janlin searched for the flight request Gordon had hacked on the console. She found what she needed, logged her name as the pilot, and put in what she thought as a reasonable lie regarding an emergency bio-chem meeting for Ursula at the New Horizons station for the next day. Janlin selected Shunter Green as the mode of transport, a quick two-seater ship enabled for both inter-orbit shuttling and surface landings. She filed the doc just as sounds of approach echoed down the corridor.

When the tech entered, Janlin lounged in his chair with a look of boredom.

"Hey, Brighton." She rose and let him reclaim his seat.

"Hey yourself, Kavanagh. What's up?"

"Can you check for a flight request? Ursula said she put it in, but we haven't heard anything."

Brighton grinned up at her, teeth white against ebony skin and spine rounded from so many hours at his console. He bent his dark curly head over his datapad.

"Yep, you're up tomorrow first thing on Shunter Green."

Janlin nodded. "Perfect. I'd rather be out flying than just sitting around starving."

"True enough." He tapped a few more commands and sat back with a sigh. "There, you should have release codes uploading now."

"Thanks." Two steps to the door, but her gut was burning, and she couldn't leave without at least checking.

"Any word—"

Brighton was already shaking his head. "Sorry, Kavanagh. No news, no messages. I can't dig up a thing on your father or the *Renegade*."

Gordon hadn't been able to find any record either, and with his hacking skills, she should've known Brighton wouldn't do much better. Janlin ducked her head to hide her dismay. "Right. Catch ya on the re-fly, then."

The only clue she had was the mysterious *Renegade*, a ship that appeared briefly on the docket and left with no records logged—no passenger list, no destination, nothing—at the same time her father went missing.

Seventy-five days had passed since the *Renegade* left the orbital. Her dad hadn't said goodbye, hadn't left a message. After the way Stepper left her, the abandonment hurt double, especially coming from her only remaining family. She wanted her dad to be in trouble just to explain why he'd do this to her . . . but not too much trouble.

Janlin returned to her living quarters to wait. Despite the small square footage, she rattled around like a lonely marble in a tin can. She took the time to dial up the release codes for the Shunter, just to be sure, and gulp down her evening dose of Vita-tea. Too bad it did nothing to ease the ever-present hunger.

She slid the door open, wishing they swung so she could slam it, and followed the hall lined with other pods. A quick right, then left at the joiner to the next pod over. She found Gordon studying the latest scans.

"I've got the flight codes. Have you found an excuse to shut us down yet?" she asked, collapsing into the one-seat lounger crammed into the space between his console and the window. The view, mostly of the next pod, still fascinated her with sun and shadow, and she let her head fall back to stare into the shifting patterns.

"Moody much?" Gordon said. Janlin struggled for a smart-ass reply, but she couldn't speak around the knot in her throat. She fought back the tears that threatened to spill.

"Ah, bloody hell," Gordon said softly. His hand landed on her shoulder for a quick squeeze and a little shake. "Your dad's going to be fine. Rudi's not the kind of bloke to take off without good reason, I swear."

"I know. There has to be something to this, but not knowing is killing me. I just hope he's okay."

Gordon nodded. "Maybe you're right, and the *Renegade* is on a mission to help us out. Your hero will appear, your knight in shining armour."

Janlin snorted and turned back to the window. "Too bad it's my dad, and not Stepper being who he really could be, if he had a heart."

Gordon let out a long sigh. "Look, I agree Stepper's a wanker, but he's faced more than his share of trouble in life and you know it."

"Fine, drop it already," Janlin said, turning away to hide her hot tears. "What've you got?"

She heard him inhale, as if ready to pursue the painful topic further. There was a pause while he reconsidered. "There are small quiet spots. But you're going to have to watch for survivors, too. Even the noise of the Shunter coming in might draw unwelcome company."

"Do you see signs of habitation?"

"Not really, no, but I'm worried they've gone underground. That'll make it bloody hard to tell what's in the area." He gave her a hard look. "They'll be desperate, you understand?"

Janlin pulled her jumper straight, scrubbed her face, and lifted her chin. "Yeah, I understand. And maybe it's good if they're underground."

"Good?"

"If they're underground, there's a better chance they won't hear the Shunter come in."

"Right," he said with heavy doubt. "Look, you're not on some suicide mission, are you? 'Cause you can leave Urse out of it if that's the case."

Janlin reeled, at first astounded, then stung, then incredulous. Then, just plain angry, which brought her to her feet. "God dammit, Gordon, we're *starving* in case you haven't noticed, and I'm trying to do something about it." She pushed her way past Gordon's chair, wishing she could run endlessly like she did as a teen in the wide-open spaces of southern Alberta.

"Janlin—"

She didn't give him a chance, swinging out into the hall and bouncing down every joiner she could find until she'd put some distance between them.

With some horror, she wondered if he was right. She shook the doubt away. She'd never do anything to hurt Ursula or Gordon, and she wasn't suicidal. They simply had no one to turn to for help anymore, and her gut told her not to wait for something that might not show up.

She hadn't told them about her plan to land near Dad's old lab though, and that said something. He could be anywhere, and dirtside seemed the least likely. But she had to check. If he'd gone to Mars, there would be no reason to keep it secret.

Movement caught her eye and her heart leapt, but it was only a Shunter coming in from another station. Every day she held hope that he would return with the *Renegade* full of exactly what they needed for a fresh start, and the mystery explained away.

Too many days had passed, and her hope had dwindled. The idea that he might need help, might be waiting for her somewhere, that was the motivation she clung to now.

They had to take care of themselves, and as a pilot she was one of the few that could get what they needed. If she had a side mission at the same time, that was her business.

She stopped at another porthole and pressed her forehead to the cool plate while she waited for the station to give her a view of the planet below. When it did, she found herself staring at a superstorm over Africa, its whirl of white destruction obscuring the surface. From here, it was silent and beautiful. On the surface, she knew the planet's topsoil churned in the air, whipped into massive dust storms by the intense winds that rarely let up.

What was she thinking, heading down there? Every other mission that had tried, died.

Janlin straightened and drew a deep breath. She had no desire to risk her life, but circumstances left her little choice. Besides, she was done being hungry.

Maybe, just maybe, there was a way to reduce the risk.

CHAPTER THREE

HUNGER NIPPED AT the edge of her attention, always there, always demanding what wasn't available. Janlin adjusted the thrusters, punched in the stabilizers, flicked her gaze over the controls and back out the windows. Just then the clouds broke, and she could make out the land below through the yellow haze. She straightened out and scanned the flooded plains.

Beyond the water lay a wasteland of rock and dust that marched over foothills and off into the Rockies. Some slopes still bore macabre forests of blackened trunks and scorched earth, but most were washed clean by the harsh storms and frequent landslides. With each visit more land disappeared, eaten up by the rising sea levels.

Earth looked more like Mars used to everyday, and Mars had become the new oasis. How ironic.

Smoke from worldwide fires and the smog-thick air vied for dominance, swirling grey and brown, bringing a welcome respite from the view of the ground. Janlin wrinkled her nose, already anticipating the stench and the pinch of the necessary rebreather mask. The cloudbank thinned, the view returned, and she could see the area she once called home.

High-rise remnants of Calgary studded the water below. Floating jetsam rode the waves, the debris of a broken civilization. She flicked switches, checked the fuel cells to see if they were charging the lithium batteries effectively, and entered commands with her right hand to program the NECS.

"They're called Nano Electrochemical Systems, and someday they will enable us to create faster and more efficient space craft. In fact, they may eventually perform miracles, like allowing us to fold space and Jump to other systems." The voice of her instructor echoed through her head, and she shook off the memory. Where were the miracles now? Jumping to a new planetary system would certainly solve some problems.

She came in fast, headed for the foothills west and north of the flood basin. Janlin cut one set of thrusters, fired another set hard. The ship dropped, losing altitude and speed fast. Wind gusts reminded her of the good old days of piloting aircraft, and she fought for control with a joyful intensity unlike anything she'd felt in a really long time. She might be scared, but this was flying old style, and she missed it.

Below, swaths of rippled sand ran from the edge of the water right up the slopes of the foothills. Janlin checked the readouts, searching for just the right GPS position. Away from the high-rise remnants, the area below held few landmarks of times past, but satellites still circled, many performing their ongoing functions despite a lack of response from below.

Her earcell let out a burst of static, making her flinch. "Orbital to Shunter Green, please come in."

Janlin winced and considered ignoring it, but Gordon might have data she would need. Might as well get the tongue-lashing over with.

"Shunter Green to Orbital, go ahead."

"Shunter Green, you are a blasted idiot! Going down alone is not the answer—"

"I'm just doing what needs done. I'll be back so fast you won't have time to miss me."

"Bloody right I won't miss—"

Janlin tapped her ear, severing the connection. He would be livid, but at least she wasn't risking his wife's life, right? She'd get what she could, and Ursula would just have to deal with whatever she brought back.

The Shunter's integrated aerospike engines whined, a sound that put a thrill through her again. In space, there was no atmosphere to whistle through your jets, no wind to rock you, no sensation of flying at all. This—this was flying, and her heart rushed with it.

Below, the water's edge passed and the ground rushed by. While great swaths of land had become barren, not even holding enough life to warrant being called a desert, this area still had standing forest. It also happened to be where her family's cottage once stood.

Janlin prepared for her big finish, her hands rarely still as she ran the descent protocol. Could she convince the computers to let her cut engines and glide in silently?

She sent the command she'd carefully programmed. Alerts lit up across the console. She grappled with the sudden loss of stabilizers, urging the digital nanoelectronics to just let her take over.

Her chosen landing site approached fast. "So far so good," she said, patting the stick. She calmed a few of the flashing alarms, letting the smart machine know she was aware of what was happening. It seemed to work.

She brought the Shunter into a mild turn, heading northwest of the old city. Calgary. Alberta. Canada. Names like that didn't matter anymore. Neither did borders, although the survivors eking out a living down here might still care. Janlin doubted it . . . on both counts. The biggest pockets of survivors still left were in Europe, where biodomes had allowed for some crop preservation. Those domes were long gone now, but the descendants of those builders lived on. Before Luna's devolution there'd been much talk of bringing them out despite SpaceOp's strict protocol against any new emigrants from Earth . . . again for the "safety of those already in place." Sometimes SpaceOp, which meant Diona Jordan, tended to be a little forgetful of what it was to be human.

Janlin banked in to make a run at an old strip of asphalt highway, a relic of the days of metal cars and combustion engines. From here, it didn't look long enough by half.

The winds twisted, gusting hard, and the forward thrusters suddenly kicked in, screaming with force. She cursed the noise, but she could see how necessary they were. Janlin let the ship drop, determined to leave a nice patch of highway ahead of her for take-off. Turning a Shunter around was a bit of a pain in the ass, and mucking with a straight thruster take-off in full Earth gravity and high winds was simply asking too much, even for a good pilot like Janlin. A good old-fashioned strip landing and take-off would work just fine.

Touchdown rocked her in her seat, but otherwise went well. As soon as the Shunter stopped, Janlin unbuckled and checked systems status. She hit the switch for the hatch. Moments later, in tandem with the red signal warning on her console, Janlin's nose flared at the pervasive smell of smoke. The clang of the unlocking hatch followed. Janlin rotated her shoulders, took a deep breath before it got too bad, and got back to her shut-down procedure.

The smell of smoke meant death in space—here it never went away. With another deep breath for good measure, she slapped a rebreather over her face. It took some effort to get out of her seat, and she staggered under the pull of Earth gravity on her space-weak body. Already the dry heat engulfed her, and in mere seconds sweat soaked the shirt inside her jumpsuit. She pulled at the zippers and clips, angling the top down off her arms and tying it around her waist. Her pale freckled skin might burn, but the vitamin D couldn't hurt.

To the east lay plains of grey, and further out a shimmering horizon, yellowish in the haze of contamination. Where once ran the rolling hills of prairie and farmland, now dead water evened the score. Few fish species survived, and those that did carried enough toxins to be inedible. The floodplains stretched south, disappearing under roiling clouds of a brewing storm system. Janlin frowned at the dark mass.

Against the cloudbank, and lit by the rising sun, the skeletons of Calgary's downtown stood hollow and black, an echo of the forests she'd seen from the air. They protruded out of the water, ghostly spires of a lost city in the strange light. Behind her the Rockies still stood proud, if dry and barren. Despite the sunrise here, she'd been awake for nearly half a day-shift.

She touched her earcell. "Gordon, you read?"

"Oi, now she wants my help," came the answer. "You've got some explaining to do, lass."

"Later. I don't have time."

"How's it look?"

Janlin grimaced and adjusted her rebreather. "The place just isn't what it used to be. More importantly, tell me about the weather forecast."

"It's a bit dodgy, that, so no pissing around. Get some plants, and get gone."

"Will do." It was a small enough lie. The cottage was just up over the rise. Wouldn't take long.

Janlin ducked into the Shunter and swung up Ursula's pack she'd snuck along with her. She may not know exactly how to use all the fancy biochemist gear, but she could at least fill the chambers.

"My God, this thing weighs a ton!" Earth gravity was enough to deal with without adding twenty kilos to her back. She adjusted the pack for her shorter stature as she set the ship's seal.

She turned and faced the steep hill that led up to the trees. Each step kicked up little drifts of dust. The soil, if you could call it that, looked empty.

Then she looked closer. Ants crawled here and there, and a beetle scuttled out from under a rock. Bugs whined around Janlin's head, making her flap her hand to ward them off.

Some life did survive. Too bad they couldn't eat the spore that ate their plants.

Fifty-odd steps brought her to the top of the ridge. Trees rose up, welcoming her with shade. As she strode into the relative cool, the smell of soil struck her. It was faint compared to the wave of moisture and mustiness in the growhouses, but it was here.

High on a ridge, this area was bordered by a dry riverbed, an expanse of field, and two old highways, putting this tiny pocket of life in direct contrast with the charred area around it. She wandered under the trees, many of them limp and yellowing, but to her scorched eyesight they stood like vibrant beacons of hope. Janlin ran her hand down the smooth bark of a slender aspen, marvelling at the shocking whiteness of its trunk. Still, it stood bare of leaves despite the late spring season for this area. She knew she needed to bring either seeds or a whole plant with living roots. Leaves from nearly dead trees weren't going to cut it.

Colour flashed in the shadows. "A wild rose!" Janlin scrambled through tangled deadfall to reach it. With a little exclamation, she fell to her knees to examine one shrivelled rose hip standing out as a shock of red on the otherwise barren bush.

Janlin had a sudden memory of being at her grandmother's acreage as a child, crying because a rose's thorns had scratched her legs. Her grandmother had pointed out the beauty of it, how it was covered with delicate pink blossoms and serrated leaves as well as thorns.

She reached out, half lost in memories, and touched the precious rose hip. It came free in her hands too easily, revealing the plant's true state. Still, a closer look gave her pause, and she pocketed the rose hip to investigate. A few withered leaves pushed out from the stem, not exactly green, but not exactly dead. Staring at the surrounding skeletons of bushes, Janlin wondered how such a little survivor managed to make it. She shrugged off the pack and took out a small folding spade, determined to bring this valuable plant home.

The wind chose that moment to whip up, clogging Janlin's rebreather with dust and throwing grit into her eyes. She crouched forward, using her arms to shelter the tiny bush instead of her face until the blast subsided.

With some struggle, and not a little cursing, she dug up the rose bush, retaining as much of the root structure as possible, and encased it in one of the chambers Ursula had prepared. The wind gusted and tugged, and then seemed to settle, teasing at her hair and clothes but not driving quite so hard anymore.

Janlin's stomach growled. In response, the distant sky growled back.

The wind had a cooler touch all of a sudden, and shadow and light interchanged quickly as the clouds scuttled overhead. Janlin studied the sky as she hoisted the pack up with a grunt. Getting trapped by a storm wouldn't up her odds of success.

She scanned the area, hoping for another miracle.

That's when she saw the footprint.

Fear gutted her worse than the hunger. The boot print stood out where the soil was sandy and loose. She looked around, wondering how many other signs didn't register on the hard-packed ground. It was no consolation that the print was roughly the same size as hers. Man or woman, any survivor down here would be desperate and willing to do anything to fly out of here. Janlin scanned the surrounding woods for any sign of movement.

Her earcell buzzed, and Janlin tapped the switch in her

earlobe. "Go ahead," she said quietly.

Static was her only answer for a few seconds.

". . . looking beastly," came Gordon's voice. "Your area will catch the edge of it. Bugger the plants, Kav, you need to knock off and head back. Even a minor storm down there is still a right bit unpleasant."

"Perfect," Janlin said under her breath, hoping he didn't hear her through the crackle. She winced when the static's volume rose. Then the connection cleared again, bringing Gordon's voice back.

"You still there?"

"Yep. I'm on my way," she assured him. "I've come across a fresh footprint."

The bit of silent airtime seemed to ring with a cockney "bloody hell." She knew Gordon far too well not to hear it.

"Right, then, get out of there *now*," he said out loud. "You'll have to hurry in order to lift before the storm. You could shelter in the Shunter and wait it out, but the dust will clog the systems and might make her a flight hazard." Janlin heard Gordon's false bravado, and it chilled her worse than the cooling breeze. He said more, but the static chopped it up. The wind pulled at her constantly now, tearing away bits of soil from the ground. Shadow engulfed the landscape, then sun, then shadow again.

Light. Shadow. Light. Shadow . . .

Then the light didn't return.

Janlin began to run . . . in the opposite direction of the Shunter. The pack and the gravity pulled at her, but she pushed on. The cottage that held her dad's laboratory had a fine root cellar that would protect her if the storm came on too fast.

And if she came across people?

She swore at the thought, knowing full well what desperate people were capable of.

She stumbled into the clearing, memories warring with reality as she stared at the flattened building and the debris scattered everywhere. A quick check revealed the root cellar open and empty of any tools or supplies, which wasn't that much of a surprise, really. A further look inside made her sure the place stood abandoned.

She'd been a fool. Nothing would bring her dad back here. And with little or nothing to eat, not even survivors would be here.

The wind whistled through the fractured structure, forcing her into action. She half staggered, half ran back to the Shunter, plunging out of the tiny forest and sliding down the long slope. A light sprinkle fell, drying quickly in the fierce wind, and then the wind shrieked and rain lashed her face and arms. The muggy temperature had plummeted abruptly, and with the heavy pack on she'd never had a chance to pull her jumper back over her arms and shoulders. The rain stung her skin and soaked her clothes.

Above all, she'd forgotten how much she hated the wind. It sucked at her breath, tangled her hair—

"Wait! Please . . ."

Janlin spun as the thin wail reached her over the storm's anger. A young girl in jeans, hiking boots, and a severely distended t-shirt rushed headlong down the ridge.

Janlin stared with horror and wonder.

"Space me . . . she's pregnant!"

CHAPTER FOUR

JANLIN STOOD STUNNED. The girl slid her way down, throwing up dust that hadn't become soaked yet.

Janlin wiped rain from her eyes to look again. The girl's face, her movements, told Janlin she was more than anxious, she was frantic. Was there—?

A shout, deeper this time, followed by the crack of a gun being fired. Janlin ducked, cursing. A hole in the Shunter would take time for the nanites to repair, and storm or no storm, it was time to go. Of course, a hole in her gut would be worse.

Janlin turned, her back tense with imagined imminent impact, and keyed in her code. She twisted around as the hatch cycled, trying to gauge the situation.

A man stood at the top of the ridge. A moment later, three more figures joined him, and together they plunged down the slope after the girl.

"Oh, this is not my day," Janlin said through gritted teeth. She ripped off her rebreather, uselessly clogged with wet sand now, and continued bringing the Shunter live. If she could bring the hatch a hair's breadth from open . . . If the girl could win this race . . . If she could take off in this wind without being battered back against the ground seconds later . . .

There were a lot of ifs.

She should be locking herself in and letting the lot of them work their own problems out. Her brain screamed at her to just go, save her friends on station. She couldn't do anything for this girl if they were starving anyway, right?

She couldn't chance opening the Shunter until the last possible second. The sheer amount of dirt flying through the air would be as harmful to her systems as a bullet hole. Janlin watched the tiny screen on the side of the hatch, watched the girl stumbling down the slope, watched the men barrelling after her, all of it through a barrage of rain and wind and dirt.

The girl wasn't going to make it.

Janlin hesitated. She should just get in the Shunter, close the hatch, and get gone. The storm's power grew with every passing moment. Men with guns bore down on her position. And the girl wouldn't be any better off if Janlin couldn't take off.

Besides, space didn't have much of a life to offer anyone anyway. Did she really want to bring two more mouths to feed?

The girl floundered in the buildup of grey dirt at the slope's bottom, giving the men a big advantage. They would be on her in moments.

"Ah, hell." Janlin dropped the precious pack and pushed into a run. The girl glanced behind her, overbalanced, and fell, her mouth opened in a soundless cry of agony and fear. Another crack echoed through the roar of the storm, and Janlin leapt sideways as the mud and water sprayed up in front of her from the bullet's impact.

She pushed on, fighting the wind and rain and gravity. The girl managed to get her feet under her again. Janlin watched the man with the gun, grateful that it was the only firearm she saw, grateful that he was too busy shouting orders to fire it at her again.

When Janlin was just twenty paces away, one of the men caught the girl, grappling with her to hold back her flailing arms. She screamed and fought, but another man joined the first and pinned her easily.

The other two caught up, stepping just past the struggle to face Janlin where she stood exposed and trembling in the downpour. They looked no better; worse, in fact, with matted unkempt hair and beards, and tattered clothing, to say nothing of the wild look in their eyes.

One man leered and made a comment Janlin couldn't hear. The two holding the girl laughed. The man with the gun didn't.

"This isn't your business," he shouted. Janlin could tell the others, especially the jokester, were disappointed. "Get lost,

SpaceOp scum."

"Get her food stores first!" the jokester protested.

Janlin took a step forward. "What food stores?" she shouted back at the jokester. "We're starving, you idiot. Why do you think I'm here?"

The leader frowned, but the jokester laughed. "You expect us to believe that?"

She took another step forward. "What are you going to do to her?"

Now the jokester really did grin, his face suffused with a grim pleasure that chilled Janlin. "She's dinner, sweetheart. I can't figure out why you shouldn't be breakfast."

Janlin covered her mouth with her hand. Was he serious? A glance at the twisted expression on the leader's face seemed to confirm it.

"Why would you do that?" she cried. "You're so hungry you'd eat an innocent girl and her unborn child?"

The jokester laughed again, grating on her, but it was the leader who answered.

"She's no innocent. She ate my brother."

Janlin swallowed hard. She held herself still with some effort—the idea of turning her back to them didn't seem like a good one, but the idea of staying was worse.

She looked at the girl, whose defiant eyes now melted in guilt. "He told me to," she screamed. "For the baby, for our baby!"

Grateful for once of her empty stomach, Janlin took another step, and the leader raised his gun. "Just go," he said. "This is none of your business." He waved his free hand, and the men holding the girl began to back away.

Janlin raised her hands, palms out. "I'm unarmed," she assured the leader. The others now fought to hold the girl while she kicked, screamed, punched, and twisted. "Can't we talk about this? Killing her won't bring your brother back."

"No, but it will feed all of us for days." The calm leadership melted away, becoming feral. "This is your last warning."

Janlin stood, wavering, stunned by the power of their hunger and her raw need to help this girl. The leader started to back away.

"Wait! What if I did have food? I could trade for the girl . . ."

She took another step. "Or maybe I have something you could use?"

The leader laughed at her. "You're too skinny. I don't think you lied about the food."

The jokester leered. "Let's eat her just for that," he said, laughing again. Janlin recoiled from the sound. He drew a huge hunting knife from his belt and moved forward.

"No," the leader said, holding his arm out to block the jokester's path. "If we do that, we'll start a war we can't win." He tipped his gun at the sky. "Our ammunition dwindles . . . what do you figure they can fire at us from above?"

All the men looked up. The girl saw her chance, kicked out at one man's knee so hard it cracked, and struck at the other while the scream still rang through the air. Janlin surged forward, ready to join the fight, but before she'd taken two steps the leader moved, and Janlin found the gun pointed at her face.

The jokester's knife rested on the girl's throat.

"No," Janlin screamed, and the storm surged again as the knife slid across flesh, opening a gruesome wound that flooded red down the front of the young woman. She tried to echo Janlin's scream, forcing blood to bubble from her mouth.

The leader pushed Janlin backwards, his face lined with grief and despair. "Go now, before I can't hold him back anymore."

She fled.

CHAPTER FIVE

JANLIN SHUDDERED, SWALLOWING hard to avoid retching again.

"Okay then, luv," Gordon said. He handed her a cup of Vita-tea, which she waved away. "What happened?"

"I don't—you don't want to know," she said, refusing to meet his insistent gaze.

"You're a dammed fool, Janlin. I'm right pissed with you for going alone."

"I got a plant—that's all that matters." Janlin curled her body tighter.

"There's no plant, no pack, and two of the tanks are missing." Janlin jerked upright, denial flooding through her at Gordon's words. "What you found, you didn't bring back."

Janlin moaned. "It has to be there." She tried to remember the last moments, her headlong run for the Shunter, the storm maddening, her tears worse. The takeoff had been out of some crazy nightmare of sightlessness, a faint grey patch of old highway too short for a proper runway, and buffeting winds that threatened to crumple the Shunter like a station hit by an asteroid.

Did she pick up the pack she'd abandoned? She must have. *Please, don't let it still be sitting down there.*

"I can't go back," she whispered. Gordon made soothing sounds, but she rode over his words, grabbing his arm to make sure she had his attention. "Earth is a wasteland of despair, and I'm not ever going back." Janlin's voice cracked.

"Kavanagh!"

Gordon's shout brought her out of it. She stiffened, sucked a deep breath, and then gave her head a shake.

"Thanks."

He nodded. "There's more."

Janlin closed her eyes for a long moment. Of course, there was more. "Might as well get it over with."

"Stepper's back."

Janlin hissed, and her heart turned over. She hid her face in case the rush of emotion showed. "On the *Renegade*?" she managed to get out.

"No. He's flying a Shunter."

Janlin turned back to him, glad for the new focus, glad for the redirection of her clamouring emotions. Gordon knew just what to do to pull her around. "So, what're people saying? Have you hacked into his file?"

"Everyone's speculating, but there's no meat to it. And I can't find bugger all about why he's here in the system."

"Seems fishy. SpaceOp usually at least leaves you something to find."

Gordon nodded. "The talk is that Stepper is leading some big experiment, no outside contact allowed. So maybe he didn't leave you for just any old promotion."

"He still slept with Fran," she said, the old rage returning. "I don't know what he saw in her. Her shoulders are square, and she's got no hips at all . . ."

"Janlin!"

"What? It's true! And I haven't even got to her personality yet."

Gordon just shook his head. "Whatever the case, he's called a meeting for a chosen few, and we're on the list. I was worried you wouldn't make it back in time and it'd come out you'd gone dirtside without authorization."

Janlin shuddered, the memories flooding back. She mentally pressed them down and put them away. Nothing could change what had happened. "Maybe he's got news from Mars." She gripped his arm. "Maybe they're ready to let us move out there. When does the meeting start?"

"Right about now," Gordon said, helping her up.

"Let's check it out."

They walked in the side door to find the briefing hall nearly full. In the front row sat the upper echelon. Tyrell Gregory was there, but the moment he saw Janlin he ducked his head, his inky black curls hiding his bronze face.

"What's with him?"

Gordon pulled her to one side of the door so they could scan the room before finding a seat. "Not a clue. Looks like he'd rather shag the carpet than talk to us."

People were climbing the steps, finding seats.

"Where's Ursula?"

"She wasn't on the list," Gordon said, and for the first time that day Janlin came right out of her own worries to recognize another's.

"But—"

"This looks like a crew briefing," Gordon said before she could question further. Janlin studied the attendees, noting that there were doctors, engineers, even nanotechnology specialists, which meant she was looking at top physicists she only recognized from news vids.

Most people looked puzzled, curious, except for that front row. Some sitting there looked excited, others nervous. Tyrell still avoided her gaze.

"It's a ship crew all right," she replied. Her scan froze on Stepper as he entered from the far side of the room. "Shit," she said under her breath, struggling to smother the rush she felt at the sight of him. It had been months. She turned to look up at Gordon. "I really don't want to fly with him."

Gordon snagged her arm. "We're just here to find out what's going on. We haven't agreed to anything yet."

Janlin grit her teeth and let Gordon lead her up the risers to a back-row seat amongst the other latecomers.

Stepper mounted the dais and faced them. The room fell silent. Janlin wondered why he wasn't in his SpaceOp uniform, the black and gold one he was so proud of. She'd once loved how it complimented his dark looks, the gold picking up the hazel in his brown eyes, the black matching his hair. He had handsome features that hinted at traces of Italian in his bloodline, and skin that always looked tanned beside hers. She flinched from the memories.

"Thank you for coming." He stopped, staring down at his

databoard. Janlin and Gordon exchanged a glance. Stepper finally looked up and, after a deep breath, began again.

"Three months ago, we completed construction on the first ever Jumpship."

The room caught a collective breath, and then exploded with sound. Jumpships were the biggest urban legend of the SpaceOp society.

"Bloody hell," Gordon said. He and Janlin glanced at each other again, trying to take in the significance of the news.

"Should've known there was some truth to it all," Janlin said. "Just never imagined we'd ever find a way to Jump for real, NECs or no NECs."

Stepper waited for things to calm down, and Janlin thought he didn't seem as triumphant as he should be with his insider information. In fact, he looked older, his face lined and his eyes sunken.

"This first Jumpship travelled to a solar system pegged as having two planets within the life zone. For the mission we assembled a crew of the best—"

"Wait a goddamn minute." Janlin was on her feet. Heads turned. Gordon spoke her name, tried to pull her back to her seat. Stepper stared at her, his mouth pulled tight, not challenging her or ordering her to sit down. Not like she was going to shut up now anyway.

"I just risked my life dirtside . . ." This brought a gasp from some, and a groan from Gordon. ". . . where I was nearly shot and eaten by desperate men, and I watched helplessly as a pregnant girl was brutally murdered *as dinner*, for Christ's sake, all in an effort to find some fresh plant life for Urse's failing crops . . . and all this time you have a way to explore other solar systems?" Janlin threw off Gordon's forestalling hand and glared at Stepper, wanting answers fast.

"The first Jumpship was named the *Renegade*," was all he said.

Janlin's rant diffused at this revelation, and she struggled to catch her breath. Then new hope rushed through her, and she choked on conflicting emotions. Her dad would've been so proud to fly the first Jumpship, so thrilled. Why didn't he tell her?

"Here's the thing," Stepper said, and she sank into her seat, focusing to be sure of what he said through the rushing blood in her ears. "They Jumped, but they never came back. Now we've finished a second Jumpship so we can go find out what happened. Her name is *Hope.*"

Janlin gaped, her vision blurred. What did he mean, didn't come back? She watched Stepper, desperate for more. Stepper didn't disappoint.

"I want you to be her crew."

CHAPTER SIX

JANLIN WAITED JUST out of sight, and caught Stepper as he left the briefing room.

"Why all the secrecy?" she demanded, startling him. "What the hell is really going on, Stepper?"

It had clicked for her when Stepper swore them all to secrecy "for the safety of the mission." Tyrell, the young helmsman, knew something, and she needed to find out what. So afterwards she'd sent Gordon to find Ursula, knowing there'd be no secrets kept there, and pulled the young helmsman aside.

"Your dad refused at first, see," Tyrell had admitted, squirming under her glare. "I was supposed to go instead, and then I got a stupid head cold, got pulled from the mission. Those medics, you know how they are about germs and all that. They swore me to secrecy, threatened to take away my sister's place in the next ship out to Mars if I didn't keep my mouth shut. I can't imagine what they threatened him with if he didn't stay quiet about everything." Then he frowned. "My sister made it onto the last transport Mars took in, so I guess it was worth it."

"Bastard!" Janlin punched the wall, making Tyrell squeak. Janlin knew Gordon was on his way to tell Ursula . . . would that jeopardize his place in the mission? No, something still wasn't right about all this.

Tyrell, smart kid that he was, quietly dismissed himself. Janlin let all her anger fill her as she waited. There was no way

Stepper was getting out of explaining some things to her.

Now, to her satisfaction, Stepper did look nervous. He pulled her into the now empty briefing room. Her skin burned at his touch. She shook him off and crossed her arms.

Stepper rubbed a hand over his forehead. He really did look older, and it took him a long time to speak. She held her ground, fighting her impatience, and studied him. No uniform, but he still looked fantastic, even if his favourite button-up shirt was fraying at the edges. It did still sit open at the collar enough to make her catch her breath.

"This is not SpaceOp's deal," he finally said.

She let out a low whistle. "How is that even possible?"

"We've had a lot of help, but most of the crew of the *Renegade* were unaware my sister didn't back this. When I brought it to SpaceOp officially, they said it would never work, it was too risky. And Diona simply scoffed."

"Yeah, and look what happened."

Stepper scowled. "Diona has put all her eggs in the Mars basket. She didn't think something like this was necessary because that's the plan . . . but her plan doesn't include the Orbitals because we actually endanger them, and she'll never risk that. She also doesn't plan on doing anything to try and repair the Earth but ignore it in hopes it will sort itself out. But I'm here trying to save us, Janlin. And I made it work!" Excitement replaced his stress for a moment, taking the years off to reveal the face she had once loved so much. "We built in secret. She can have Mars . . . we'll find our own damned planet to colonize, thank you very much. Live free or die trying, I say." Then he seemed to remember she stood there. "Wanna tell me about going dirtside without permission? You say I take too many risks . . ."

"I had to try something!"

"And so did I," he countered. "Rudigar supported me in this. And we couldn't have done it without his genius."

"Why wouldn't you let him tell me?"

Stepper rolled his eyes. "It wasn't me. Why do you always blame me? He didn't want you involved, said there were too many risks in such a new technology. Said you would demand to go."

"Well, he was right, wasn't he? How long have they been

gone? Why haven't you done something sooner?"

He reached out. "Listen, Janni . . ."

"Don't call me that," she said, stepping away. "I don't care what he said, you should've told me. And you should never have let him go on the first run."

"Someone had to," he said, and again his face sagged.

She wanted to throttle him for his thoughtlessness, but that was nothing new. She focused her anger in a less personal direction. "Why did you make Tyrell think SpaceOp was threatening his family?"

At least Stepper had the decency to blush at this, but his explanation was all the usual single-mindedness. "Do you really think they'd come on board otherwise? They'd never trust something this big and groundbreaking if it didn't have the big money of SpaceOp behind it."

Janlin groaned. "Oh, Stepper. Did you ever stop to think there's a good reason for that? This is the wrong way to go about it."

Stepper shrugged. "Again, I had to try something. Things are going from bad to worse, and my sister has left us out in the cold."

"Us? What happened to the loyal family employee? Isn't SpaceOp the corporate teat that you loved more than me?"

"Don't be stupid, Janlin," Stepper said, his voice full of scorn. Janlin sucked in her breath.

"No, I was only stupid enough to love you once," she said as she headed for the door. "I won't make that mistake again."

"Janni, I didn't mean—"

"Stuff it," she said, cutting him off. "Oh, and by the way, Gordon is bound to tell Ursula about the mission. Why the hell isn't she on the docket anyway?"

"If anyone can keep this place alive, it's Ursula. I can't pull her."

Janlin turned and stepped close until she was in Stepper's face. "You'd better not even think of splitting them up."

"Are you threatening me?" Stepper's face bunched, anger making it ugly.

"No, I'm telling you something important. I'm going to talk Gordon out of this."

"What? You can't—"

"Stepper! You can't possibly think to send only one of them on a mission that dangerous!" His eyes rounded a bit, but he didn't argue. "Just leave them be, okay? It's not like they're going to run off ratting on you to SpaceOp."

For once, Stepper seemed at a loss for words. He blinked a few times, then nodded. Janlin knew that was as good as it would get, and left him before she gave in to the urge to strangle him.

She made her way to Gordon and Ursula's, buzzing the door when she arrived. They called her in. Ursula looked shocked and pale, but she still smiled and hugged Janlin. "I'm so sorry about what happened," she said. "See, now we will be okay, and no one will need to go dirtside."

Janlin didn't share her optimism. "Except the *Renegade* didn't come back. I don't think Gordon should go."

Ursula spoke over Gordon's sputtering. "This is a great opportunity, Janlin. I can't hold him back from that."

Janlin looked from Ursula to Gordon, and back again. "What if we don't return?"

"What if he stays and I don't find a way to beat this bacterium?" she countered. "No, this is our hope for a better future, whether it is in this system or another. And Rudigar and the others must need help. No one can decipher communications equipment like my Gordon can. Das beste is gut genug—the best is good enough."

Janlin had to give her that. Gordon had a way with electronics that was downright spooky some days. "Are you aware of the fact you're not supposed to know about this?"

"Oh, bollocks on that," Gordon said, his voice booming in the small space. "I won't deceive my wife, and Stepper knows it. Piss on SpaceOp and their rules."

Janlin debated the wisdom of sharing her new knowledge with them. Didn't seem like it would change anything, so she let it go. "Just be sure to keep it to yourself," she told Ursula. "From everyone, even SpaceOp officials."

They both frowned at her, and she scrambled for a way to change the subject. She stuffed her hands in her pockets, and her fingers found a little kernel of hope.

"A rose hip!" The look on Ursula's face made the whole day worth it. "I will plant the seeds in quarantine from the others."

"I'm sorry the bush I dug up didn't make it."

"Bugger the plants. If this Jumpship works out, we're quids in," Gordon said.

Janlin shook her head. "How does he manage to keep those horrible sayings alive after all these years?" she said in a not-so-quiet undertone to Ursula. Gordon snorted, but at least she'd managed to get Ursula to smile a little.

"Sheer stubbornness," Ursula said. "I thought you'd be quite aware of that trait by now."

Sure, she knew how pig-headed Gordon could be. Sometimes she thought he spoke like that just to be different, though Ursula loved her German phrases, and they'd caught Janlin with her own Canadian sayings and pronunciations too. The fact that they all spoke a working version of English didn't erase their heritage, though . . . and really it shouldn't.

Janlin left, allowing her friends the privacy they deserved to prepare for their separation. For her, all that was necessary was to pack her kit and go for her briefing with Stepper. She wrinkled her nose.

In her pod, she sorted through basic issue nano-nylon shirts and pants, trying to focus on the moment at hand. Each crew member was allowed a small personal kit of five kilos. Everything else would be waiting for them.

Janlin rummaged for her favourite undies and heard something clink at the bottom of the drawer. Pushing aside the soft socks that made her boots almost comfortable, she found a small silver disk.

"Well, well. I forgot about this." So thin she had to get a nail under it for leverage, she lifted it to the light. Barely two centimetres across, and less than a millimetre thick, a quick spin around the circumference with her opposite hand's finger brought the device to life.

The first holo showed her father, Rudigar Kavanagh. Janlin's breath caught. She activated the file, letting it play on the nano-speaker within the device instead of through her earcell.

"Happy Valentine's to my little girl." The hologram of his handsome, clean-shaven face, square jaw, and calm gaze melted into a bouquet of roses that twirled and sparkled, each perfect bloom lit with dewdrops.

She sniffed and dialled up the next file. Gordon and Ursula

smiled at each other. This one contained the two performing a karaoke duet of an old love song called "Bridge Over Troubled Waters." Janlin shook her head at the memories, a fond denial of how much they meant. If she wallowed too much, she'd end up a bawling mess.

She spun the dial again, and there stood Stepper in full SpaceOp regalia, ready to receive his promotion to captain.

Janlin flipped the nano-recorder into her hand and squeezed, shutting it down. She stared at it for a long time before clipping it onto her neck chain. She'd delete Stepper's file later.

CHAPTER SEVEN

AS JANLIN APPROACHED Stepper's office, Gordon emerged.

"How did it go?"

Gordon shrugged. "Same old," he said. He leaned in. "Don't let him rattle you, Janlin."

Janlin gave a dry laugh. "Not a chance." Gordon punched her lightly on the shoulder and walked off, leaving Janlin no choice but to enter the captain's office.

Stepper sat at a functional workstation piled with report datasheets. He rose when she entered.

"Janlin."

"Captain."

Stepper sighed at her formality. "I'm so sorry about Rudigar," he said.

"Screw you."

Stepper gave a nod of acknowledgement. "I'm just glad you're willing to do this."

She clenched her fists—did he think she'd refuse? "Why have you waited so long? Anything could've gone wrong, they could be—"

He held up a hand. "They knew the risks, and it's taken some time to finish the second ship. Remember, we're doing this all on our own." Stepper leaned forward and smacked his fist into his palm. "Something happened out there, and it's finally time to go find out what. We have to go get our ship and our people back."

They regarded each other. Janlin wondered which he worried about more—his precious ship, or the crew he sent off without care for their well-being. "If we can get back," she said, breaking the uncomfortable silence.

"I still don't think it's a technical problem. Every test and simulation came out perfect. That's why we're arming the *Hope* with new shuttles and a fighter pilot or two." He indicated her file sitting before him.

"What, you expect some big bad aliens are holding our people hostage?"

"We really can't know, and so we'll go in as armed as possible. That way if we have a fight on our hands, we'll be prepared. Between you and Gordon, we'll have the best pilots on station."

Janlin rolled her eyes. The compliment sounded so empty, and of all of the scenarios she'd run in her head, meeting some kind of alien antagonist seemed so . . . well, Hollywood. She'd completely discounted it. That said, she wasn't going to argue with any reason that would get her onboard. Her theories saw the *Renegade* floating adrift with some unknown malfunction, or caught by a comet unawares, or . . . the accident scenes in her imagination were endless.

"But you're sure we can return," she asked.

"The technology is sound. You're just going to have to trust me on this."

Right. "Trust is an ongoing issue between us," she reminded him. He dropped his gaze, shuffled his docs, and changed the subject.

They carried on with details, all business from there. Janlin did sit when asked, but once they were done, she stood again, ready to leave. It was her way of letting him know that he had her full cooperation as pilot, but nothing more. She certainly looked forward to testing out the sleek new Seraph ships.

"Can I get an upload of the Seraph's specs?" she asked.

"Sure. I'll have to send it to your pod's system."

Despite knowing the reaction it was bound to cause, she pulled out her neck chain from under her shirt and dangled the nano-recorder in front of him. "I'd rather have them with me."

"You kept it," he said in a surprised and wistful voice.

Janlin shrugged. "It's useful," she said, handing it to him. Stepper stared at her until she looked away. He sighed, swiping it over his console and selecting the file for exchange without further comment.

She had almost cleared the doorframe when he spoke in a much different voice than that of captain to pilot. He said just one word, an old nickname that sent fire through her.

"Jannilove."

She stepped into the hall and let the door whoosh closed. Some things never changed, and Stepper was one of those things. He didn't know how to let go five years ago, why should now be any different?

She stumbled to a full stop a few paces away and leaned on the wall, arms wrapped around herself. If she was honest, she hadn't let go either.

Janlin took a deep breath and carried on. *What's done is done*, she told herself, and all she could do was keep moving forward.

"WE SHOULD ALL have a call sign, like in Earth's Air Force," Gordon said.

They stood in a huge room once used for SpaceOp parties and tours. Now taken over for use as a simulator setup, it was one of the largest open areas on the station.

Despite the fact that the corporation owned everything out in space, SpaceOp—as a good way to maintain discipline and create a solid chain of command—had adopted many military traditions. Gordon applauded this idea, being an old Royal Air Force communications officer.

Janlin sometimes regretted that she'd never had the kind of formal training the military offered. Instead, she'd learned most of her technique from her father, a talented pilot instructor in his own right. Both her father's connections and her aptitude as a pilot got her into SpaceOp only a few years after her father joined up. She had hoped for a future that didn't include people killing each other.

Janlin grinned up at Gordon. "Call sign? Thanks, but no. I've had enough with bad nicknames. Besides, I'm not so good at flying this thing. It's pretty dammed powerful."

"I don't know . . . that last sim was pretty smooth."

Janlin blinked at him in surprise. "I destroyed the flyer on landing and ended up in a simulated med-bay."

Gordon grimaced. "Right, but anyone else that's tried it can't even get out of the Jumpship without crashing full on into something, including me. You'll get this sussed out."

Janlin peered over at the console to check on Tyrell's progress. The talented young helmsman eased the virtual ship through the debris of a computerized asteroid belt encountered directly out of Jump. He somehow dodged every obstacle and sent the Jumpship sailing into the inner solar system.

"Wow," Janlin said.

Gordon grinned. "He's good." He turned to face Janlin again. "You're good too, Janlin. You deserve a call sign." His encouraging smile turned into more of a smirk. "How about 'Bouncer'? That's about what your flyer did on that last run."

Janlin gave Gordon a smack on the arm. His laughter rang around the training room, making heads turn.

"I like it."

They both turned, Gordon snapping to attention out of habit from his old military days. Janlin did her best to copy him.

"At ease," Stepper said, waving them down and rolling his eyes. "I don't expect this on mission, you two." Janlin recognized something in the brightness of his eyes. He had news.

"Sorry, Captain. Old habits die hard."

"And it looks like you've been training up the civilians," Stepper said, nodding at Janlin. Then he smirked. "Bouncer."

Gordon roared with laughter, but Janlin didn't want Stepper to think he could be part of this circle again. She remained at attention, staring at the opposite wall. She would've left, if it weren't for the desire to know what he'd come to tell them.

Gordon gave her such a wallop on the back she couldn't hold her stance. She growled at him. "I'll get you back for this, Spin." She used Gordon's old call sign like an insult. She continued to ignore Stepper.

Gordon still laughed. "I'm sure you will, Bouncer. I'm sure you will."

The sims in progress had ended, and the crowd in the hall swelled as people emerged from different training booths. Stepper moved to the display at the head of the room. When he turned back, Janlin sucked in a breath at the hurt on his face. He caught her looking, and quickly stiffened up, his expression returning to business.

Janlin replaced any sense of chagrin with one of haughtiness. He deserved every nasty feeling she could give him.

"All right, folks, here's the deal. No more sims; tomorrow we leave for the launch site. You will fly the real thing within a couple days."

They responded with cheers, but Janlin worried for Gordon. He would have to leave Ursula behind. The room quieted. There was more.

"We Jump in a week, so get in what time you need, and make sure you're ready to do your job."

CHAPTER EIGHT

"LEBEN SIE WOHL, Liebchen," Ursula whispered to Gordon. Janlin didn't know the translation, but it could only be a farewell, one full of love and worry and hope. Janlin stepped away, embarrassed to be sharing in that moment of intimacy. She'd already said her goodbyes, impatient to be finally on the move.

"Suit up, folks. Let's make this happen!" Stepper walked through the room, already in his own suit. Others were in various stages of readiness, and the general bustle threw Janlin into a nervous excitement.

Finally, they were away to the hidden base. Finally, she would fly the fancy new Seraphs. The sims suggested a sense of power and swiftness unlike anything she'd flown before, making her anxious to try them out long before the Jump. If she were needed in some unknown emergency, she wanted to be in full control of her craft.

A week later, she did have that confidence, and a new passion for the latest technology. The Seraph's SEMs performed well beyond the Shunter's, allowing for nearly on-point turns and powerful thrusts. Above all, the Seraph had the latest in nano-technology, giving the ships the strongest hull ever known.

The new Jumpship brought that entire line of advancement one step further. She was a marvel to behold, sleek with a nano-tech hull casing and the best hydrogen fuel cell system, with modifications for the Jumpdrive computer the naked eye couldn't see.

"This is a great moment in human history," Stepper said as they gathered for the final boarding. He straightened his crisp SpaceOp uniform, Stepper's only deceitfulness in this gutsy game. At least, she hoped it was.

"You may not be the first, but you are the ones that will bring our loved ones home, and open worlds of opportunity to all humankind. Today, we will live free, or die trying!"

This garnered a few cheers, and a few frowns. Janlin shook her head. Stepper referred to getting out from under SpaceOp's thumb, forgetting that these folks were not aware of the hush-hush nature of this enterprise. His mouth pinched as he realized, and he pushed on with important updates and final announcements.

Janlin smirked at Gordon. "He needs to work on his PR skills, eh?"

Gordon puffed his cheeks. "He's a nutter for even uttering the word 'die' at all," he said.

Still, excitement pervaded the crew as they moved through the well-practiced start up procedures. Soon the *Hope* disengaged from her construct station as system checks and headings were reviewed, and reviewed again.

The physicists had expressed worries over some faulty after-Jump readings—which proved to be only a small system glitch—and the way folding space would affect the human physiology. Small Jumps to the edge of Sol's system and back had produced nothing more than mild headaches and a brief sense of confusion. Janlin wondered aloud to Sandy Beckett, one of the physicists, if a longer Jump would acerbate the effects.

"It shouldn't," said Sandy with a little shrug. "Folding space is folding space, this much or that. The distance involved shouldn't matter at all. However, we do have the ship set to fly on autopilot for the first few moments." Sandy had helped create the Jumpdrive for both ships, and been on one of the test runs of the *Renegade*, so Janlin took comfort from her words. The physician's reports agreed that the after-effects of Jumping didn't appear to hold any health hazard.

A bigger worry was the inability to send probes to scan the system before travelling there. While they took every possible precaution available to them, folding space required manual on-the-spot adjustments, and robotic tests had failed every time. So, Jumping blind, the crew of the *Hope* prepared for anything and everything.

Everyone who could find an excuse to be there crowded into the control room for the big moment, except for those like Lead Mechanic Candice Young, who kept an eye on things in the launch bay along with her second, Weston Clark. Grateful that Stepper had changed his mind about her riding the Jump in her Seraph, Janlin gave her tiny disk a little kiss for luck before tucking it away under her shirt and strapping into a seat.

Stepper tapped at his console. "All right, folks, this is it."

Tyrell eased the ship out of the construction girders and into open space. Since they folded space instead of firing huge booster rockets, it could be done within close proximity of the base.

"Communication test, please copy in commanding order," said Gordon through her earcell.

"Copy that, Comm-tech," Stepper replied.

"Copy," said Tyrell, and on down the line they went.

Janlin's mind wandered as she listened to voices she'd known for years run down the pre-Jump check. In reality, Stepper was being a good man by going in himself to rescue those he sent before, the ones that didn't return.

Thoughts of what they were about to attempt would not be ignored. Earlier the creators of this breakthrough technology had said to the new crew, "The quantum physics involved go beyond simple explanation, other than the age-old idea of folding space." She pictured the demonstration once again, the paper's edges being pushed together, the excess looping up between, so that the distance became nothing between points.

JUMP

Folded? More like compressed, Janlin decided as reality took a whole new shape. It was like existence hung in suspension while being flattened, rolled out, and stretched thin, all while being blown through a straw.

And then, it was over.

Trouble was, Janlin couldn't see. She thought she heard moans . . . was it her? She struggled to regain her equilibrium, to focus her thoughts in a way that made sense, but instead her brain floated in ambivalence, sounds made no sense, colours darted across her vision. This last resulted in shocking pain radiating through her brain core, and she tried to cry out with no success.

A terrible sense of *wrongness* pervaded everything. Sounds roiled in discord, echoing in her head like the cry of a million tortured voices singing out of key. Was this hell? Were they all to be trapped forever like this?

Time must still be suspended. Or maybe they still Jumped.

Or maybe this is what happened when you tried to fold too big a slice of space.

Janlin had no clear idea of how long this sensation persisted, only that when the dissonant sounds retreated, her vision cleared and the headache receded a little. Everyone else seemed to have experienced the same effects. The clock showed that the pre-set autopilot had run for nearly two hours, scanning and collecting data while the crew sat stupefied.

The control room reverberated with silence as they all gaped at each other, brains still confused and fuzzy.

"Status?" came Stepper's choked command. Janlin heard someone heaving, and Janlin gritted her teeth in an effort to make the headspins stop before she joined them.

"Telemetry shows we're in the right place," called Science Officer Jari Lovell. He held his head with both hands while studying the screen, as if that would help somehow.

"Computers are operating, though we're seeing some glitches," said Sandy.

"Clean them up. Helm?"

Tyrell didn't look up from his own console. "We're on course, heading into the system."

"Scans?"

"The system has two, maybe three planets in the life zone. Once we're in closer we'll know more," said Gordon.

"We did it. Well done, everyone."

Janlin's heart swelled at the sound of Stepper's pleasure in his crew. They'd all braced for the worst, but the Jump was done, and they'd survived.

Stepper tapped his earcell. "Medbay? I need to know if we've suffered any major repercussions from being out of it for so long. Start down there and then move up to the control room.

I'd like everyone examined."

People undid their seat straps. Crewmembers hugged, and Janlin hugged back. They all looked as bemused as she felt. Controlled pandemonium ruled the room as more scans came in. Janlin hovered over Gordon's shoulder, watching and waiting for any sign of the *Renegade's* signature.

Stepper appeared at her side.

"It worked," he said, his voice incredulous. Him, the one that had assured her and everyone else that the Jumpship worked without any doubt. "We're in a new solar system! Once we're in orbit of that fourth planet, we'll see what we can see."

Janlin frowned. "What about the *Renegade*?"

His attention shifted to her, and at first, he seemed puzzled. He blinked, straightened, and answered. "That's where they're likely to be, if they've been out here so long. Right?" He leaned in closer to her. "Imagine if we find a liveable planet, Janni. Imagine!"

"Don't call me that," she muttered, but someone called him and he missed her protest. Gordon gave her a small smile of encouragement and directed her attention toward the middle of the room. The holograph machine whined, and an image sparkled to life, coalescing into a 3-D image of what the scanners had recorded so far. There, just as the astronomers had promised, spun eleven planets, three well within the life-zone of the orange-ish star, two close in like their own Mercury, and further out the standard collection of gas giants and frozen rocks.

Janlin wondered if her father walked on one of those planets, waiting for rescue.

Something moved on the peripheral.

"Bring scanners onto that movement," Stepper ordered.

"It's a ship," Gordon said into the sudden quiet.

"The *Renegade*?" Stepper's voice broke on the inflection. Janlin stared at Gordon's screen, already knowing the answer.

"She's so big . . ." Gordon said in a soft voice of awe.

Janlin squinted. Her eyes couldn't seem to focus. "We're in trouble," she whispered. The exhilaration from the successful Jump turned to a stone in her gut.

"Stations!" Stepper snapped out the word, breaking everyone out of the shocked denial that froze them.

"What's their bearing?"

"Straight for us."

Stepper growled. "Tyrell, prepare for some fancy flying. Gordon, send the first contact communication."

"Done," said Gordon a second later.

"And?"

"No reply," he admitted. "Wait! Something . . ."

"Stepper, my board just went down."

"Mine, too."

"We are losing computer systems, Captain," said Jari.

"Dammit, don't we have better protection than that?" Voices shouted back and forth, meaningless in her confusion.

Aliens? Really?

She glanced over to see Gordon's fingers scrambling over the keyboard.

"Do we have helm?" Stepper roared over the pandemonium.

Tyrell rattled his controls, his face pale.

"No, sir. It's all locked up, nothing is responding."

Stepper spun around, saw Janlin standing there rooted to the floor.

"Man your Seraph!" he shouted at her before turning away again.

Gordon stood from his board. "It's a virus of some kind—one that knows our systems way too well."

Stepper cursed. "Go with Janlin," he ordered, taking over Gordon's board. "Restart the Jump system, get it up and running. Engineers, find a way for us to fly this thing without computers. Prepare for return Jump—"

Janlin heard this last line as she and Gordon ran out into the corridor and slid down the ladder-stairs to the flight deck. They couldn't go back without looking for the *Renegade* first! Besides, could you fly a ship without computers? How would they program a Jump without the computers to take the codes and the NECs to do the calculations?

Candice and Weston emerged from a side corridor, confused faces full of questions.

"What's going on? Everything seemed fine . . ."

"Ready the Seraphs, we're heading out," Janlin said, turning Candice and giving her a little shove forward. "There's a huge alien ship bearing down on us, and it's given us a computer virus. Can you get those bay doors open without computers?"

Candice's face drained of colour. "There's a manual override function," she said.

"Good. Get us ready as fast as you can," Janlin said as she and Gordon struggled into flightsuits. The babble from the control room continued on in Janlin's ear, panic building as the engineers tried to explain the impossibility of Stepper's command.

The Seraphs stood with lids open to accept the pilots, level with the flightdeck floor as they sat in the launch trench. Janlin fought down her panic as she struggled into her helmet and mounted the ladder down into her ship. She'd just switched over to the flyer's comm-link when the babble in her ear chose that moment to cut out.

"Candice? Weston?" Janlin flicked a few keys, switching her broadband earcell link over to the Seraph's. "Gordon?" She punched the comm-link button twice, then flipped open a panel and fumbled with the connections. Her hands shook so badly she nearly tore the wires from their slots.

Candice appeared at her side and gently blocked her hand from the wires. "No one has communications," she said. Her chin trembled, but her voice stayed steady. "Is this what happened to the *Renegade*?"

"Doesn't matter right now," Janlin said. It came out more abrupt than she meant it to, but she had to keep Candice focused. "Can we fly?"

Candice was signalling to Weston in the flight booth. "The Seraph's flight system is separate from *Hope*, so they just might fly, but—"

"But?"

"We can't open the flightway doors. Not one system is responding, even manual override functions. It's a very thorough virus, apparently." A jolt rippled through the ship under them. Her wide eyes stared at Janlin. "We're all going to die, aren't we?"

"Get off the deck," Janlin ordered. "Make sure you seal the hatch."

Candice opened her mouth, then shut it again, hesitating only another second before climbing out of the flightway gulley and running for the uncertain safety of the booth.

Janlin thought about her options.

The Seraphs didn't have Jump capabilities. Good thing, or she'd have Candice climbing in here with her. Janlin punched the comm-link button again, with the same lack of results.

She stretched up and pulled down her lid, and engaged the manual start-up. Seconds ticked by as she prayed to a god she didn't believe in, and then the ship fired to life.

She glanced over at Gordon, who gave the thumbs-up and went about doing the same thing.

Janlin stared at the flightway doors. She willed them to open. That or Stepper's voice in her ear telling them to stand down. She continued to reset her earcell, hoping the broadband signal would return.

Another, stronger, jolt rang through the ship, and a voice did speak in her ear, but it was not Stepper.

"This is Fran Delou, previously of the *Renegade*."

"That bitch was on the *Renegade*, too?" Janlin said. Her gut churned with old anger. Fran's voice cut hard and bitter, and for all the relief Janlin felt knowing that someone from the *Renegade* was alive, she was not happy. What the hell was going on?

"For our sakes, please don't resist. Each action of resistance you take, one of us will be punished."

Another shudder rocked the ship. Janlin met Gordon's gaze across the flight deck floor. Janlin tried the comm-link again, but it was completely dead.

"Dammit, Stepper, what are we going to do? We can't just go down without a fight!"

There was no answer. Some rescue mission this was. Again, the *Hope* rocked under her, and that decided it for Janlin.

Her fingers flew over the board. She would fly out of here, open doors or not. On the display her text message app popped up, and she completed the post to Gordon's Seraph. She sent a silent word of thanks to whoever decided the Seraphs' computers would be on their own network.

She looked over and watched Gordon as he read the message. He grinned at her like only Gordon could under such stress, then looked down at his own board.

Sounds like a desperate idea.

No kidding, she typed back.

Don't off yourself.

Janlin grimaced. He would have to say something like that. Still, if they were under attack, then their freedom could make all the difference.

Once I'm through, I'll send the all clear and you can follow my lead, she typed.

Right, then. Good luck.

She took a deep breath, powered up her Seraph, and began the take-off sequence.

Would it be worth putting a hole in the side of the *Hope*? She'd better make it worth it, or Stepper would have her head. Alarms popped up on her display, one after another, finally scrolling there were so many. Janlin shouted in defiance at them all and popped the clamps that held her in the gulley.

Once she had a steady hover, she aimed carefully and nailed the button on the gunnery.

Before the explosion was done, she sent her Seraph forward at full launch speed—straight for the flightway doors that were now obscured in smoke from her barrage.

"Seraphs have hulls proportionately thicker than a Jumpship," Janlin recited. The walls of the launch gulley flashed by. "They are designed to withstand the hardships of outer space, re-entry, and hazardous landings." The cloud billowed out, rushing at her, or she at it, she couldn't tell. "Flyers have withstood all the tests—"

Every muscle tensed for the moment of impact. Janlin closed her eyes a split second before her body was thrown against her seat straps. Metal shrieked and groaned as she punched her booster for more power, her mind straining for hope as much as her machine strained for freedom.

Janlin opened her eyes to see the bent and jagged steel of the inner hull passing her by. Next would come the outer hull. She fired another round, hoping Candice had prepared for decompression as she'd told her to. She knew Gordon would follow if he could.

Her Seraph struck the outer hull, groaning under her. Suddenly she was pushed into her seat as the ship broke through and accelerated. Bright lights pierced her eyes and she blinked away tears as she eased off the thrusters. She glanced at her scanner. It told her she was still inside the *Hope*. She smacked it with the heel of her hand and gave it up for useless, peering out into an undefined brightness.

Janlin tilted her head back and forth, trying to discern where the light came from, and which way she could fly to freedom. Nose up, it was hard to see, so she let up on the speed, started a turn, and saw the wall she was headed for far too late. No amount of directional thrust was going to prevent impact, but she slammed it on anyway as the wall sped towards her.

"Dammit, no!"

Impact. The crush of steel on steel pierced her ears. Gravity pulled at her too, and at her Seraph. A second impact rattled her teeth, and she knew she'd dropped onto something very solid.

A glance out the other side of her cockpit revealed the *Hope* sitting on a huge expanse of flight deck, surrounded by machines she did not recognize, with a Seraph-sized hole leaking atmosphere in her side.

Stay put, she typed to Gordon, sending just as her systems crashed and the flyer's power died. Janlin groaned, rotating a sore shoulder. Then she punched the dead controls with a curse.

Bracing her mind for just about anything, she glanced out again. The mist coming from the hole she'd made dissipated, and a different movement caught her eye. There, on the other side of the *Hope*, massive hangar doors ground shut. The darkness of space on the other side slowly disappeared.

CHAPTER NINE

JANLIN WATCHED HELPLESSLY, immobile in her crushed flyer. Adrenaline ebbed, and dull pain took its place. She flexed, confirmed nothing broken, but the control panel pinched her legs. She removed her helmet and wriggled free of her suit, wincing at the pain that heralded the bruising to come.

She crouched on the seat to peer into the massive bay. Should she try to get out and hide? But already she could see people entering the huge flight deck.

No, not people. Their heads were sunken between their shoulder blades, their bodies thick and broad, their skin a deep yellow shade.

Aliens.

Some rode machines while others marched on foot toward the *Hope*. A few were on their way to her. Janlin stared, unable to move, her brain unwilling to consider the consequences of what had happened.

As they closed the distance, Janlin assessed the creatures, reeling with the thought of first contact gone wrong. The aliens stood between six and seven feet tall, some even more, and despite twisted features, they had more similarities to human faces than differences. Two eyes, a nose of sorts, a mouth that obviously spoke. Hair. Two arms, two legs. A group approached her flyer, and they called back and forth, pointing and—could it be?—laughing.

A bang made her jump, and she twisted around to see one of

the aliens perched on the flyer. He peered down at her with a scar-lined sneer, his lip curled to reveal teeth within. Close up, she realized their yellow skin was scaled, reptilian. Janlin wondered if she could simply stay in her flyer. It was sealed, strong, impervious even to their mighty fists or machines, right?

The alien called to someone below, and a machine arm came into view. It looked like a huge steel jackhammer, and Janlin hastily pushed the release to open her hatch.

The hiss of air made the alien flinch, and he grunted angry sounds in her direction. The jackhammer still hovered as she climbed up to stand on her seat. He stared back with hard eyes.

"Hi," she said for lack of better ideas. "My name is Janlin."

"Janlin Kavanagh," came a voice from below. Janlin leaned over to see Fran walking up. "Still as useless as ever, aren't you?"

Janlin bit down on her first reaction, though the second thought wasn't much better. "To think I was glad to hear you were alive."

"Well, I'm not glad to be alive. Soon you're gonna wish you hit that wall a little harder."

Janlin opened her mouth to demand an explanation, but Fran turned to the alien beside her and began to gurgle and grunt at him. The alien replied in kind. Janlin stared. Of course, Fran the linguist using her skills to make sure she came out on top. Just as she did when she slept around command to ensure her place on Mars. So, what the hell was she doing here?

A ladder of sorts appeared at her side, and Janlin scrambled down it to face Fran. For her part, Fran was listening closely to the orders she received, and before Janlin could speak Fran waved her to follow and took off at a run towards the *Hope*. It was either follow or remain with the hulking strangers that alternately leered and snarled at her. Janlin chased Fran, her boots thumping on the steel floor of an alien vessel.

Her crewmates streamed from the hatchway. Armed aliens escorted them. Stepper led the way, an alien weapon aimed at his head. Fran was headed straight for him.

Janlin pumped her legs harder to catch up with Fran, grabbed her arm, and spun her around.

"What's going on? Are the others alive? Do you work for these brutes? Where's my—"

Fran wrenched her arm away. "Shut up, Janlin! You have no idea what you're dealing with." The aliens closed a circle around them, herding the crew of the *Hope* together.

Gordon appeared and laid a hand on Janlin's arm, but she shook him off and lunged at Fran with her fists bunched. Fran caught her flailing fists and yanked her forward, throwing Janlin off balance and onto her ass. Fran backed around, watching with a raised eyebrow as Janlin scrambled to her feet, shaking with rage.

"She's a traitor," Janlin cried. "She works with them, speaks their language. I saw her! How could you?" She threw the question at Fran.

Silence fell, and Janlin felt the bay floor tremble beneath them.

Fran crossed her arms. "I do this to protect what's left of my crew," she said. "You have no idea—"

A whine cut the air. Fran paled. Janlin felt the hair on her arms stand on end, and she swore softly. Following the sound, she saw bolts of electricity crackle around the end of the short stick one of the aliens held. A smell like a soldering iron made her nose twitch.

A gurgle came from the alien. Fran nodded and turned so she faced the crew gathered at the base of the ramp.

"Listen up, all of you," she said, pitching her voice so all could hear. She pointed at the humming device. "I've danced with those a few times now. They work a lot like a taser, only worse. It's better not to resist."

Janlin choked. "You're telling us to just give in?"

The whine rose to a higher pitch, and Fran glanced sideways at it. "We call 'em nerve whips. They hurt right down to the bone without ever leaving a scar. First, you'll piss yourself, and then you get to lay in it for a while, since you won't be able to move for a few hours, despite still being able to feel the excruciating pain."

The crew stood silent. The aliens watched, some wearing green and black uniforms equipped with what could only be weapons at the waist, others in plain, if dirty, coveralls. The latter had abandoned all pretence of work and stood staring at the spectacle. Most had what Janlin could only interpret as a pleased expression. They were huge, and their lack of necks left their heads sunk down in a permanent shrug. A few here and there had a faint reddish slash along the side of their heads, below what seemed to be an ear, but most didn't. Red tinge or not, they all looked mean. Even the ones without nerve whips didn't look like good playmates.

"Those who require the whip too often become useless, unable to handle the physical work. They, and others, are taken away and never seen again."

The tableau held for a long moment before grunts and gurgles forced Fran into motion again. "Just go with it," she said, waving Stepper to follow her.

"You're not really going to—"

"Janlin, shut up." Stepper turned and followed Fran.

Janlin ground her teeth while they were herded through some sort of scanning machine. Stepper and many others were stripped of side arms, belt tools, pocketknives, and the like. Janlin turned so she faced Gordon.

"Cover me," she said. She unclipped her nano-recorder from her chain and popped it into her mouth, tucking it under her tongue.

"Blimey, Janlin, did you just eat that?" Gordon asked.

Janlin shushed him as they went through their own processing, reminding her of a security clearance station at a launch site. Everyone wore ID tags on chains, SpaceOp's version of the military's dog tags, and the aliens were collecting all of them. Janlin handed hers over and walked through the scanner, barely breathing until she got through without an incident.

On the other side of the scanner ran a narrow passageway. Fran directed them through and into a holding room. More aliens stood against each wall, all holding nerve whips, and there was only one way in or out. Soon they were all there, and Janlin angled over to where Fran sorted them into groups.

"What the hell, Fran?" she started. Someone grabbed her elbow hard, and she glanced back to find Stepper there. He squeezed again and gave her a warning look meant to shut her up, but she hadn't asked about Rudigar yet.

"It's good to see you alive, Fran," Stepper said. Fran just shook her head.

"You'll change your mind soon enough." Her eyes shifted sideways to the waiting guards, and she moved along to group more people.

"Are there other survivors?"

Fran spun on him. "Stop following me. Here, Gordon, take care of these two, will ya?"

"Great to see you too, Fran," Gordon said. He wore a strange grimace and flashed worried eyes.

"Right. Look, I'll try to get you some intel later. Once we leave this room we aren't supposed to talk. Let's not push it right now."

Janlin exchanged a glance with Stepper. Fran moved on with her sorting. "Fran!" Janlin called, wanting to ask that one all-important last question, but Fran hissed over her shoulder to stuff it before she got whipped.

Janlin turned back to her group. "No talking . . ." she began.

"Means no planning," finished Gordon.

"We'll find a way out of this," Stepper said. His forehead furrowed as he watched Fran, and Janlin thought his assurance sounded empty.

"We should've fought harder," Janlin said. She knew she sought a release for her anger and fear.

"No, don't fight," Stepper said. Janlin gave him an incredulous look. "Let them take us in so we can find out what happened to the *Renegade* and her crew."

"Does the boss even know what you did to the ship yet?" Gordon asked. He elbowed her in his usual daredevil manner, but he also watched the sorting with careful consideration. "Maybe your call sign should be Crash."

"Gordon!"

Stepper turned on both of them. "I am aware of what happened. Candice and Weston were both injured when you blew through the hull. They'd be dead if we'd been in open space."

Janlin felt her stomach drop. "No! I told her—"

"Candice fell, hit her head. Weston was tending her. He knew nothing of your plans." Stepper gave her a hard look. "I know you were trying to do the right thing, Janlin, but now you've got to play it Fran's way. She knows what the hell is going on here, and we don't."

He turned away, leaving Janlin to reel under the weight of guilt. She had tried to take all the risk on herself . . . she never meant for anyone else to get hurt. Worse, it had been all for nothing.

CHAPTER TEN

FRAN STEPPED UP onto a riser and turned to face them. Janlin's angry guilt faded under the desperation of their situation. She wouldn't just sit on her duff while these aliens called the shots.

"Stay in your assigned groups unless told otherwise. Each group will be assigned work on one of three round-the-clock shifts. Once you're done with your shift, return to your bunk. Anyone caught where they shouldn't be gets whipped. Anyone who talks too much gets whipped. Anyone who annoys the wrong Imag gets whipped. It's that bloody simple."

A few words of protest started but Fran stared them down.

"Some things never change," Gordon said to Stepper, but he just shook his head. Something had changed in Fran's demeanour, and Janlin saw that Stepper watched with pity in his brown eyes. Janlin looked away, teeth clenched against the flop of her stomach. Crewmates injured, all of them captured by aliens, Fran running the show . . . it just couldn't get any worse, could it? She held any thoughts of her father away from these musings, unwilling to even consider just how much worse it might get.

"You should be glad I'm here to pave the way for you," Fran said. She looked straight at Janlin. "When we were taken, our only communication with them was by nerve whip."

"What about—" Janlin started, but the Imag moved among them now, splitting them off from each other and herding them out the door. Janlin looked around, wondering how they were taken so easily, why no one was resisting. Stepper wore that determined look, though, the one telling her he must have some idea in mind. Reluctantly, she followed his lead. Maybe now they would be reunited with the *Renegade* survivors. Sick hope wound its way through her gut.

As quickly, doubt and worry replaced it. Her father would never have put up with capture and passive resistance. It wasn't his style.

A blast of heat struck her as they moved further into the ship. The rumbling beneath them also intensified, forming now into regular noise. They walked along a corridor, the heat growing with each step, and the air tasted of hot iron. She could also smell unwashed bodies, sweat and fear and despair mingled in tight quarters.

Flashes of light came from ahead. Janlin craned her neck to see past others doing the same. In the huge area beyond the doorway, misshapen shadows moved against the brightness of white-hot molten steel flowing along blackened channels.

The image stayed on her retinas even as she tried to blink it away.

The heat, the noise, it all came from a huge cavern-like bay. Janlin knew some of the stations built by SpaceOp were large, but to have a working factory on board a space ship seemed a little over the top.

The shadows moving across the bright heat were misshapen because they were alien, she realized. In that moment the significance of what was happening finally sunk in, and it took every bit of courage she had to keep walking.

She worked the nano-recorder out from between her teeth and cheek and flipped it over to the other side. Built with amazing endurance, it should be fine. She would tuck it away somewhere more permanent once they stopped moving. What good it could do, she wasn't sure, but it did offer some measure of comfort to know she'd snuck it in.

Distance muffled the heat and din as they moved deeper into the ship. She had a feeling the noise would always be there, round-the-clock, rising and falling in pitch, but always there.

They entered a long room with rows of stainless-steel slabs jutting from the walls and support struts. Everything was steel— the floor, the walls, the doors that slid into the wall.

Gordon's eyes were round as he sidled up to Stepper. "I saw what could only be an electric arc furnace, and more than one blast furnace." He leaned close, barely sub-vocalizing the words. They were jostled into the middle of the group as the guards crowded them from behind, and Stepper shook his head to quiet Gordon. Ahead, Fran seemed to be assigning people to something.

With a start, Janlin saw people lying on the steel slabs.

"They're bunks?" she said, her voice too loud. Stepper and Gordon both glared at her before looking ahead to see for themselves.

"What's it all for?" Stepper asked Gordon quietly. His voice had an edge of urgency. Soon they would not be in the middle of a crush of people, and it would become even harder to communicate.

"Refining iron ore or scrap metal into usable steel . . . only I didn't see any coke or coke oven battery."

Janlin turned from trying to see ahead to give him a funny look.

Gordon rolled his eyes. "Not that kind of coke. It's a processed form of coal that is super strong and burns steadily. It produces the kind of heat required to get things to a molten stage. How they're doing it without coal I don't know."

"Let me guess—you'll be happy to work here," Janlin said. She laid the scorn on heavy in her tone. She knew Gordon could take it.

Gordon looked bemused. "I mean I'm not sure what we're in for here, but they're refining iron ore into steel in space, for crying out loud. I want to know how."

"And why. But not now," Stepper said in an undertone. Most of the crew stood bunched together, whispering amongst themselves just as they did, and Stepper looked as if he was about to start calling out orders. Janlin reached to forestall him, but the crowd thinned before them and Fran appeared, saving Stepper from the role of drill sergeant.

"What do you people think this is, kindergarten? Pick a bunk and get in it. It's gonna take me a while to sort you all out." She looked drawn out and old, not the confident woman that Janlin remembered.

Janlin nudged Gordon. "If we lay down head to head, we can

talk," she muttered. He nodded, and they moved down the row as Janlin scanned those already there, searching face after face. Some she recognized from Luna Base, and others she'd never seen before. Finally, not seeing her father anywhere, she was forced to take a bunk next to Gordon as Stepper snagged one across from them.

"Thank you," Fran said as she marched up. "Maybe your example will get things moving. I have to keep reminding these idiots that a nerve-whipped slave is useless, although this influx of numbers has them pretty excited."

"Excuse me?" Janlin said, not liking Fran's tone. Janlin liked her prone stance even less as Fran stood over them. "Did you just call us slaves?"

Fran's lip curled. "I sure did, honey," she said. The sarcasm made Janlin tense.

"So, we're expendable," Stepper said heavily.

Fran grimaced. "It hasn't been good," she admitted.

"What about my dad?" Janlin asked. "Is he here?"

Fran shook her head. "Haven't seen him in months. There are quite a few of us missing."

"Missing? Or dead?" Stepper asked.

Fran shrugged. Her eyes flicked to the other end of the hall.

"How much talking is too much, Fran?" Gordon asked.

Fran sighed. "You never know with these idiots. They're as likely to whip you for nothing at all, like big alien bullies really. The ones in uniform are the worst, mostly because they like to whip their own workers too."

Fran moved on to sort out the last few stragglers.

"I'm sorry about your pa." Gordon spoke softly, and Stepper nodded from across the way.

"Missing doesn't mean dead."

They heard Fran ordering others into their bunks with a reminder to refrain from speaking. "I don't want to clean up after you if you get caught," she warned.

Soon she was back between them, stood facing the end of the hall with her hands clasped behind her back.

"What the hell took you guys so long anyway?" she hissed.

"You know how it is, Fran," Stepper said. Nothing more really needed said. "Why do some of them have that red under their ears, and most don't?"

Fran laughed without humour. "Those are females. They don't have a planet anymore, just like us, so their whole population lives in space."

"Just like us," Gordon muttered, sarcasm strong.

"What happened to the *Renegade*?" Stepper asked her.

Fran's mouth pinched so hard her lips whitened. "We are forced to integrate the ship's parts with theirs every day. They don't understand the nano-technology, but their steel is quite advanced, and seems to serve them well enough. Based on what they did to you, they've also studied our computer systems. Once I could, I asked what they were trying to accomplish, hoping to stop the mindless brutality. That started a line of questioning I'd rather not remember. They were pretty shocked when they realized I'd figured out their language."

Gordon frowned. "Did you tell them how to activate the Jump?"

Fran whirled around, her face pale but for two bright spots of red high on her cheeks. Janlin saw a dark shadow in the soul behind the eyes.

"I told them it broke, that's why we didn't simply Jump away when they found us." She spoke through gritted teeth. "I told them that so many times I began to believe it myself."

Now Janlin saw the fear behind the attitude. Now that they were here with another, working, Jumpship . . .

"It's near enough to the truth," Fran continued. "When the Imag came at us with guns firing, we couldn't Jump. We tried. And we were all still so muddled in the head."

"They might've hit something," Gordon said. "I'm sure the *Hope* will still work." Janlin flinched at the desperation in his voice.

Stepper shook his head. "Couldn't they try making friends if they want to learn about the Jump technology?"

Fran grunted a laugh. "That's not the kind of people they are. You'll see." She stalked away, hands still clasped behind her back.

Janlin twisted around to watch Fran speak to the alien posted at the entrance. Fran never raised her head as she spoke, keeping her spine bowed before the alien. Janlin had never seen Fran give anyone such deference. Janlin checked the other direction and saw many other heads peering out, Stepper's included.

They had to get back to the *Hope* before these idiots started taking it apart.

All around them the ship trembled and rumbled. Even here the smell of hot steel overpowered the stench of sweat and fear. Fans and air pumps and who knew what whirred and hummed all around them, and far off machines clanged and roared.

They were about midway along a rack of bunks. As Fran returned along the hall, she reached out to grasp hands with many along the way. Just as often she shook her head, obviously passing on some message. Soon she approached their bunks again.

"If we could get to the *Hope*—" Janlin began, her voice too loud by Fran's flinch.

"Stow it, Janlin." Fran's whisper cut across hers. Her mouth barely moved. "We've all tried to run, and all we got for it was nerve damage."

She made to move on, but Stepper spoke. "It must've been horrible, and now we've been no help at all."

Fran stopped as if struck. She stared at the far end of the hall, her mouth pulled into a tight line, her knuckles white where her hands clasped. Something in her seemed strung tight like a wire that was about to snap. Janlin noticed Fran's hands were rimmed with permanent grime, her arms were abraded and scarred, and three fingers on one hand looked curled and twisted.

"They appear to live, work, and breed on this ship. The other areas are closed to us, but I've heard talk. This part is built like a manufacturing plant. From what I've gathered, they're upgrading this tub into a warship to take a planet from some opposing race."

She made to move again, and again Stepper stopped her with only his voice.

"Security?"

Fran gave him her best "don't be stupid" look. "Like I said, this area is a steel plant. It runs 24-7. There is always someone awake: one crew working, one sleeping, one screwing around. Doesn't matter who you run into, they all carry weapons, and the guards carry the whips."

"Will the whips knock us out?" Gordon asked.

"Oh, no. You're awake for all of it, enjoying the experience of having your entire nervous system screwed so you can't walk or talk or control your own god-damned shithole, yet you can still feel the pain."

"Fran," Stepper said, making her glare at him instead of Gordon. "I'm really sorry all this has happened, but we gotta focus on finding a way out. There's no one else to come if we don't return."

Fran laughed then, the sound hard and bitter, making many of the bunks' occupants look around with wide eyes. "I'm surprised *you* came."

"We have to try something," Janlin said.

"Do what you have to, but my captain hasn't been seen since his fourth escape attempt." Fran walked away from them with a slight limp, still shaking her head.

The former crew of the *Renegade* stared mute and wild-eyed at the newcomers. *What are they thinking,* Janlin wondered, *how badly we'd failed them, or that there was safety in numbers?*

CHAPTER ELEVEN

GAZES TURNED AWAY, and people settled in as time passed and nothing more happened. Janlin nudged Gordon, but he shook his head and turned to the wall. She looked across at Stepper. Dark shadows underlined his eyes, and she knew he struggled with the responsibility of letting his ship and crew be captured. Even more, they struggled with the apathy of the people they'd come to help.

Janlin shifted on the steel slab. There were no blankets, no pillows, no comfort offered to the humans. She stared at the bunk above her, occupied by a *Renegade* crewmate that she didn't know. These were the first people to ever traverse a new solar system, and now this was all they had to show for it.

With a twist of her tongue, Janlin spit the tiny nano-recorder into her palm. How would she keep this safe now?

Janlin rolled again, scanning up and down the hallway. No one moved, and the doorways stood empty. Where was Fran? What came next? Janlin shut her eyes, the recorder still in her hand, but that left her with nothing but her thoughts. Where had the missing gone? And what of this opposing race Fran spoke of? If she could get to Gordon's Seraph, slip away somehow, maybe she could go to the planet and warn them, make friends, and get help.

A loud clang reverberated through the hull. Janlin's eyes popped open, and she looked around for the source. Stepper stared around; Gordon still faced the wall but his back was tense. A few people shifted on their bunks, but otherwise nothing else moved. The noise was apparently something they were used to.

Stepper gave her a desperate look before rolling over, his back to her. Janlin sat up. Her head brushed the bunk above her. The steel flooring would give her away as soon as she set her boots upon it. She reached out, undid the laces, and slipped them off, setting them carefully against the wall. The left boot had a few loose threads in the tongue, and she worked at them until there was a small tear she could slide the device into.

The floor was cool against her sweaty socks, and she welcomed it. She took her first step only to have someone grab her arm.

Stepper pulled her down to his level.

"Not yet, Janlin."

Janlin wrinkled her nose. "Why not, sir?" she asked in a harsh whisper. She let her frustration at him show in the sarcastic use of the title. "If we don't move quickly the *Hope* will end up in pieces just as the *Renegade* did, and we will have even less chance than we do now. Let me go look."

Stepper grimaced. "Willing to have the first go at the nerve whip, are you?"

She pulled her arm free and checked over her shoulder, ignoring Stepper. Many eyes watched her now, but she ignored them too, slipping along the bunks, ready to dive onto one if a guard appeared . . . whether the bunk was occupied or not.

Another clang rang through the ship. Janlin's whole body twitched, and her hip was already on one of the bunks before she could think. A middle-aged woman lay on the bunk, fast asleep, mouth open and trailing drool. Dark smudges marred her cheek where a dirty hand had brushed away overlong hair. She gave no indication that she heard or felt anything; she was lost in the sleep of the exhausted. Janlin stared, her brain searching for a name, until she realized this poor soul was physicist Linder Brown, an accomplished nano-scientist.

Janlin continued her reconnaissance despite her pounding heart and huge misgivings. The idea of returning to her bunk and just lying there, waiting for the bad news to come, was even less inviting.

At the end of the hall she noticed a panel with markings etched onto the various buttons. Below stood a canister that she hoped was a version of a fire extinguisher. It did boast a nozzle and trigger, but she could count on nothing being what it seemed.

Sweat trickled down her sides beneath her shirt. The heat that seemed a permanent state rose as she neared the doorway. Bootfalls echoed from beyond, and Janlin squeezed her body into the tiny space between the last bunks and the wall where the canister stood. The man in the upper bunk stared at her in horror. White stripped away the former blackness of his greasy hair, but intelligence shone from his eyes.

The footsteps slowed as they passed the doorway, but carried on, leaving Janlin's heart thumping loud in her ears. The man continued to stare, and he shook his head slowly from side to side. He reached out an arm, pushing up the fabric of his shirt as he stretched, and revealed a withered arm with curled, claw-like fingers. Janlin pressed her body against the wall, willing him silently not to touch her.

He stared at her, his expression demented, before he glanced out beyond their hallway and pulled his arm back to curl it against his chest. He laid his head down and proceeded to ignore her.

Janlin lowered her body to the floor so that she lay mostly under the lower, unoccupied, bunk. Dragging herself, she twisted until her head reached the doorway. With agonizing patience, she moved forward in hopes that her movements would not alert anyone standing guard.

There was no guard.

Panting in relief, Janlin studied the intersecting hallway. In each direction the floor gently curved up out of sight—far in the distance—solving one of Janlin's curiosities: gravity came from spin, just like the stations at home. Only this place must be huge in comparison.

A slight movement caught her eye, and the sight of what could only be a vidlens made panic pour through her veins. She heaved herself back into the bunk hall. Already she could imagine she heard footsteps of someone coming. She scrambled to her bunk, Stepper watching with questions burning in his eyes.

She was still struggling back into her boots when the alien appeared. He scanned the hall, slowly making his way down to them. Stepper closed his eyes, but Janlin could not bring herself to be blind, instead staring at the bunk where Tyrell appeared to be asleep.

The guard passed, his gnarled and hairless version of a hand—with nerve whip at the ready—going right by Janlin's face.

She lunged, focusing her whole body on that hand, reaching for just *there*, the pressure point on the back of the hand that would render it unable to keep its grip on the weapon. Janlin had her other hand ready to take the whip, and so felt the weapon pulse with power.

It was as if the molten steel they'd seen now poured over her, through her, and she opened her mouth to scream. No sound emerged. Her mouth locked open, her eyes bulged in her head, her hands curled into claws like the man she'd seen on the end bunk.

The hum dissipated; the pain remained. The Imag stood over her. He touched the side of his head, gurgled a few words, and walked away.

Stepper and Gordon appeared in her field of vision. "Goddamn it, Janlin!" Stepper said. He whispered the words, but they still carried vehemence. A new smell assaulted her nose, and she knew she'd lost control of her bladder. Luckily there was little else in her. Once more she was glad of an empty stomach.

The pain didn't ebb, instead soaring through her without respite. She wanted to writhe and cry out, but her muscles were locked beyond her control.

"Get back in your bunk, Stepper. You too, Gordon." Fran's voice cut the air after so much silence. Stepper opened his mouth, then shut it and moved out of Janlin's line-of-sight.

Two uniformed aliens knelt over her. Suddenly she was in the air, only to land on her bunk a second later. Janlin decided it was a good thing she couldn't feel anything other than the waves of nerve pain, based on how quickly she'd travelled from floor to bunk.

Fran looked at her with obvious disdain. "Somehow I knew you'd be first," she said with no satisfaction. Janlin barely heard Fran through the buzz in her head. She wished she could close her eyes. She also wished she could pound the look of despair off Fran's face.

CHAPTER TWELVE

JANLIN COULD WALK by the time they were called for a work shift, but her pants were stained with dried piss and her whole body ached to the bone.

Their team consisted of Stepper, Gordon, Tyrell, herself, and strangely enough, the man from the end bunk. He grinned manically at Janlin and winked. Stepper raised his eyebrows, and all Janlin could do was scowl and look away.

They followed the alien into a factory setting much like the one they'd passed through the day before, Gordon so lost in awe he seemed to forget their situation. Janlin, on the other hand, focused on every passageway, every vidlens, every possible opportunity. She noticed Stepper scanning, too.

They took a lift down, making Janlin think again about the ringed structure of the ship. She'd meant to tell Stepper, but there'd been no chance.

When the lift doors opened, it was to an even hotter stench of fumes that Janlin had no name for. Piles of scrap steel and dark coal reached well above their heads. The Imag pointed at a pile of shovels, then at Janlin and Tyrell. Stepper and Gordon were put to pushing the huge bins and dumping them into the top of the massive furnace that occupied a large portion of the room one level below.

The work was hot, the room was hot, the steel handles of the shovels were hot. Janlin struggled to breathe, uncertain whether it was the sheer temperature of the air or the chemicals that thickened it. She wondered too how the grime could stick with so much sweat running off her.

The shovels were heavy, and it wasn't long before Janlin's arms began to ache. Blisters formed on the pads of her palms, but if she stopped to lean on her shovel the alien guarding the pit would snarl, a hand on the nerve whip at his belt. Even Gordon had to stop peering around at everything and bend to the work.

It seemed like days later when their guard motioned them to stop and led them back to the lift. Once they joined the other groups, all equally filthy and exhausted, they were herded into a room that had sealed glass doors and no vidlens that she could see. Nozzle-like pipes protruded from the walls at regular intervals.

Janlin gripped Stepper's arm. "This looks like a gas chamber," she said in his ear.

"Couldn't be," he said, but he eyed the room. He nudged her and pointed to where trails of water streaked the floor leading to a central drain. "Shower time."

Sure enough, water began to spray from the nozzles, growing in force until the people on the outer edges of the group were crying out and pushing the rest of them into the centre. Janlin wanted to get clean, so she pressed through to the edge.

The water cut her with its heat and velocity. At first Janlin wondered why they weren't required to remove their clothing, but then she realized this "shower" was meant to do double duty. There was no soap, however, and before she could even contemplate scooping some water to her face it was over. Those on the edge of the group were left dripping and red-skinned while those in the middle were still relatively dry and very dirty.

"This is ridiculous," said Gordon. The doors were just opening, the chance to get clean gone.

"I'll bet Fran has her own private shower," Janlin said under her breath, and Gordon chuckled. Stepper gave them a warning look, and Janlin wondered just what he planned to do if they didn't behave as he saw fit. As captain, he needed to take more risks to get them out of there, not be so dammed careful.

It wasn't until they were back at their bunks that Janlin realized Stepper was gone. At least half a dozen aliens wandered up and down the hall, returning one group and gathering the next, so Janlin lay down as if nothing was wrong.

She caught Gordon staring at Stepper's empty bunk. She clicked with her tongue to make him look at her, and shook her head. She raised an eyebrow in question, and he just shrugged.

It was a long time before two guards appeared carrying his limp body. They tossed him onto his bunk, and the acrid aroma of urine wafted through the air. It made her glad they hadn't been fed yet, even if her gut cramped with hunger. With so much demanding physical labour, surely these brutal aliens fed their slaves. Janlin wondered just how long it would be.

She waited, wishing the guards away so she could check on Stepper.

Instead, they came at her.

She crouched, ready to fight, and the brutes both readied their nerve whips. She didn't relish that joy ride again, at least not so soon. Worse thoughts crowded her mind. She didn't want to "disappear" like some of the *Renegade* crew had. Although, what if her father and the others were somewhere else on this tub? Maybe somewhere with lighter security and more opportunity?

She took a deep breath and stood. One grabbed her and bent her arm in such a way she couldn't move in any direction but the one he pushed her in, and the other led the way.

They left the heat and noise of the factory level and travelled through warrens of halls and holds and storerooms. If a ship like this had a proverbial basement, she felt sure that was where they were headed.

She heard a scream cut short, and adrenaline pumped through her. Fran had said they questioned her for details of how the Jumpships worked, and she had insisted that she hadn't given up any secrets. Were they now torturing the new crew for info?

Janlin's lip curled at the knowledge that the only way they could do such a thing was through Fran's translations. Which meant the woman would get to stand and watch her being put through hell.

So, who was in there now? Had they worked Stepper over? Here she'd thought he'd gone scouting for an escape route, and instead he'd been tortured to unconsciousness.

Great.

Another scream punctuated the air as a shielded door dissipated before them, making Janlin stare. The smell of burnt flesh with undertones of excrement struck her senses. Janlin started to struggle, unable to stay brave, and the Imag simply shoved her in and reset the shield.

She threw herself against the shield, clawing despite the electricity that poured through her fingers. Hands grasped her and hauled her backwards, and she became aware that the gibbering she heard came from her own mouth.

Janlin struggled for dignity and clamped her mouth shut. The aliens pushed her into a cylinder-shaped prison that reached her chest. Somehow the unit held her immobile from the gut down. She gripped the edges, fingers scrabbling for any purchase, and surveyed the room.

The smells made her gag, but the view was worse.

In another cylinder stood Fran. At least, she was pretty sure it was Fran. Blood flowed from the woman's nose and crusted around her chin. Her eyes were both black, and her bottom lip puffed out beyond the upper one. Fran held a thousand-mile stare, but one of the aliens tapped at a console, and her neck snapped back. When she straightened again, she focused, noticed Janlin, and laughed.

"Ah, fresh meat," she said, her voice marred by the swollen lip. Her head lolled again, but she pulled it up with a little shake. "Stupid nits, they picked the wrong leverage to force me to talk."

"Fran—"

"Doesn't matter what you say, Janlin. I'll never tell them." She flashed a macabre grin, her teeth stained red. "You can confess all you want, and you will, but I'll never tell, never tell, never tell."

Janlin watched this, her breath coming fast. The temperature in this room was several degrees cooler than elsewhere, yet sweat slicked under her arms and breasts.

"They think if they threaten you, I'll give in. The Imag know now I've been lying . . . at least they're pretty sure." Fran's words thickened, as if she were drunk. "They want to be sure."

"I'm sorry, Fran," Janlin said.

"Fuck you, Janlin," Fran said without any feeling. Her head

rolled, and her eyes blinked again and again. She touched a finger to her nose, grimaced, and turned a hard stare on Janlin. "I wish they'd kill me instead of you. I really do. Don't know what I was thinking making myself indispensable."

The aliens busied themselves at their console panels, ignoring their exchange. "Fran—"

"Give it up, Janlin," Fran said, cutting her off. "They can kill the whole lot of you off before my eyes—I'm never gonna tell them how to work the Jumpships."

"Good!" Janlin said. "I'm with you on that, don't you see?"

"Maybe if you're all dead they'll finally let me die, too."

Janlin stared. How could she just give up? She had power with these idiots; she could use it to lead them astray, build trust and find a way free, or something. Janlin opened her mouth to say so, to shout at Fran until the woman saw some sense, but sudden fire ignited in her legs and groin.

The torture session had begun.

They used both technology like the nerve whips to send agony through her lower body and simple physical blows to the head and face. They twisted her arms and crushed her index finger into a device ironically reminiscent of a medieval thumb press.

It took far longer than she'd hoped before the Imag realized Fran wasn't going to tell them anything new. Janlin bore each blow the best she could, but it wasn't long before she babbled endlessly about home and Rudigar and even the *Hope*. Fran didn't seem to relish the abuse like Janlin thought she would. She kept her gaze lowered and only spoke when they beat her. Janlin wondered how she'd managed to refrain from telling them what they wanted to know.

It seemed like hours before darkness welled up in Janlin's vision, and she welcomed the release of unconsciousness.

CHAPTER THIRTEEN

EVERY FEW DAYS the torture sessions resumed, always random, always brutal. Fran would pretend to question her; Janlin would attempt to engage her in planning some kind of strategy to get free. It all came to nothing, and the aliens were clearly losing their patience.

Afterwards they'd bring warm broth and tend her wounds. Or they'd do nothing, leaving her gasping on her bunk. Always they played with their minds, until Janlin wept with the futility of it all.

Janlin struggled to heal from the sessions while still working the battering labour shifts. At first Stepper nearly went ballistic on the guards when they brought her in bleeding and bruised, but she managed to convince him it would only make things worse. It wasn't like she was the only one undergoing such treatment. He looked as bad as she must. When her head throbbed, she saw the goose egg welt on his forehead. When her eye swelled shut, she saw his shiner sealing away a sad brown eye.

The aliens worked their way through a few others, but again and again they returned to her and Stepper, as if they sensed the antagonism between her and Fran, and the link that Stepper had to it all.

When she couldn't rise from her bunk after one particularly bad time, she'd thought for sure she'd be shipped out the airlock—or maybe to wherever they sent the injured—but they left her alone. She felt relief mixed with disappointment. The idea that her dad might be alive somewhere drove her mind in tight circles. By being one of those "disappeared" she would either find out, or at least be free of the pain once and for all. Yet neither opportunity seemed as easy to reach as she first thought.

She healed, went back to work, and underwent more torment. It was a routine of hell, and she fell into it against her will.

Once, Janlin regained consciousness to find a girl bent over her, prodding a particularly sore spot on her head.

"Ow," Janlin said, swatting her hand away.

"Let her check, Janni," said Stepper's voice from somewhere above her head. She craned around to see his battered face looking at her from his own bunk. "She's only got a few more minutes before the guard comes by."

Janlin looked back at the girl. She held her hands up, palms out, and Janlin grimaced at how filthy they were.

"How many fingers?" she asked. *She is so terribly young*, Janlin thought. Her blue eyes were ringed with exhaustion, and she bore a scar on her cheek that had puckered the skin into a teardrop shape. It made her appear to be weeping.

"Two," Janlin said.

She bent and looked close at Janlin's eyes. "Does your head hurt when you turn it side to side, like this?"

Janlin tried, winced. "A bit, yeah."

The girl glanced at Stepper. "A mild concussion. She shouldn't sleep for more than a couple hours at a time. Not much else we can do, but she'd be better off with some rest."

Stepper nodded his thanks. "You'd best get back. Time's nearly up."

Her lips pressed into a thin line as she nodded back. "Right."

Janlin rolled over slowly. It still hurt. "Who is that?"

Stepper hissed at her. "Shush. We have news, but we have to wait until the next round."

"Aren't the vids watching anymore?"

Stepper gave his click-clock sound with his tongue that he used to warn everyone the guards were coming. Someone was moaning in their bunk, and continued to do so. Janlin wondered who it was, and what the Imag would do about it.

She lay still, fighting to keep her eyes open. She needed to hear what everyone else had found while she was gone. Something had changed, or the girl wouldn't be out of her bunk tending the injured without being whipped and hauled away.

"No! No! Don't take him! He'll be okay, it's just a painful burn. Please, don't take him!"

The voice, close by, keened on the edge of hysterical, and Janlin risked the flash of pain behind her eyes to twist around and look. The man who was moaning, who now cried out as they pulled him off his slab, had a woman wrapped around him. She refused to let go. The familiar whine cut the air, and the woman jerked into spasms as the other guard hauled the man away.

Janlin rolled onto the floor, landing on her hands and knees, but Stepper was faster, pushing past her to face the towering alien. Janlin mouthed a denial, a plea, but to no avail. Stepper took the whip, too, and slumped to the floor, twitching.

The alien looked at her. Janlin stayed down, unable to do more as her head spun. Her fingers curled, scraping against the hard floor as she stared up at her tormenter. He bared his teeth in a grisly grin and followed his mate.

Janlin collapsed onto the floor. Strong hands lifted her, and she looked to see that others were lifting the woman and Stepper gently back to their bunks. She reached up to catch the single tear that slid down Gordon's nose as he bent to lay her on her slab of steel.

Hours later, once the woman regained the use of her limbs, she ran screaming down the hall and attacked the nearest guard. He hauled her to her bunk, unable to reach for his whip as he held off her frenzied violence, but every time he let go, she fought harder, still screaming like a banshee. Just as Janlin, Gordon, and others began to rise to join the fray, more aliens arrived and the nerve whip rendered her silent. Janlin wanted to scream with her.

After the third time, they took the woman away.

In the grieving silence that followed, Stepper watched the door until two guards walked by, and then nodded to Gordon.

Gordon faced Janlin. "Seems we can talk here as long as we don't leave our bunks," he said.

"But the vidlens . . ."

"*Renegade* people told us. For the first few weeks, any movement brought instant reprisal," Gordon said, his eyes dull. "Now that we're beaten into submission, and know how hopeless the situation really is, they won't bother to run in at every little thing."

Janlin stared. Beaten, broken, and hopeless . . . that's what they'd come to. Of course, this news gave them the opportunity to talk, but just then no one was in the mood to do so.

CHAPTER FOURTEEN

JANLIN SAW FRAN occasionally, but always from a distance. The woman's limp was more pronounced, and she stared right through Janlin as if she didn't even know her. That suited Janlin just fine.

Today, however, Fran accompanied her and Stepper on their work assignment.

"We have to take the catwalks," Fran said, her voice as gruff as ever, but Janlin noticed the linguist swallowed hard. "They've given me a communications unit, and I have to translate to you what needs done. Apparently Imag don't like heights much."

Janlin could see why as she stood at the top of a rusty ladder and stared at the narrow walkway high above the factory floor.

"No safety straps, eh?" she said, but both Stepper and Fran ignored her. Far below, aliens moved about their business, making Janlin wonder yet again just how big this station-like ship must be.

They climbed, and worked out what needed done through Fran's translation. After the first dizzying glance, Janlin did her best not to look down.

Fran's limp might've been the cause of her fall, or maybe she decided to try the suicide way out of this nightmare like so many others had. Imag always tried to stop any death, which was one of the arguments for the possible survival of those that disappeared. "We're valuable, maybe we're being sold for something," one *Renegade* scientist had argued.

"Valuable for what, meat?" No one had any better ideas. At first, they were happy to have food . . . now they wondered what it was made of, let alone how any alien bacteria might affect them.

Whatever the case, Janlin watched with an air of detachment as Fran slipped off a canted part of the catwalk and broke through the railing. On the way down, her grasping arm caught in some chain, breaking her fall with a snap. Stepper dove forward to grab the chain before it broke, but he wasn't strong enough to pull her up on his own. She dangled over a five-storey fall, easily high enough to kill her.

Imag down below pointed and shouted at each other, some beginning to run, but they were a long way off.

Fran's grip slipped a bit further, and the whites of her eyes flashed in the gloom.

"Janlin, help me," Stepper said, his breath coming in gasps. Janlin stepped closer, realizing only then that Stepper's wrist was twisted at a very odd angle.

"Janlin!"

If Janlin let Fran die, the torture would stop. They'd have no translator anymore. Wouldn't that be a kindness?

"Janlin, you have to help . . . she is trying to get us on work shifts closer to the hub. We might never succeed if you let her die."

Who cared about some slight chance like that? It would be better to simply end the torture. Janlin knew Fran wanted it, knew it in the way Fran looked at her right now.

Worker Imag climbed the ladders, prodded along by uniformed guards with nerve whips out.

"The only way we are going to have any chance of getting pilots like you on the specialist teams is with Fran's help. Come on, Janlin!"

She could hear his pain, knew he wouldn't let go. Maybe she could pretend to help and send them all to a mercy death below?

She knelt by Stepper, then laid on her stomach alongside him. The steel groaned under their combined weight.

"Grab on and pull!"

Still she hesitated. She stared down at Fran and saw her own bitter hatred mirrored at her.

"She doesn't want saved, Stepper."

"I don't care." His face twisted with agony. The catwalk groaned and sagged further. Stepper slid, and Janlin reached to grab him before she could think about it.

"It's either we both go, or none," Stepper said then, challenging her to either let him go or help him.

With a cry of anger and frustration, she braced her ankle on the opposite railing and grabbed the chain. Together they pulled Fran onto the catwalk.

"You should've let me die," Fran said with a snarl.

"I wanted to, but Stepper would've gone down with you." Janlin shook, red fury blinding her. "You would've stolen him again."

"Stolen him? Space me, Janlin, after you walked in on us, he never looked sideways at me again. Don't you get it?"

Janlin walked away, chest heaving, unable to bear the weight of what Fran was telling her. Stepper had left her after they argued about SpaceOp's Mars offer. She hated that he always ran at his family's every beck and call. He had wanted her to go with him, but she'd felt he abandoned the near-Earth colonies and *her* family. They'd bickered over it endlessly, then not spoken for months while he completed his training for his promotion.

Then, unable to bear the thought of him leaving and wanting to reconcile before he left, she'd walked in on Stepper and Fran in his bed. In the bed they'd shared so many times, for so many years.

That image still burned in her memory, and she could never wipe it away.

Didn't matter what Fran told her now, there was no going back. Stepper didn't love her. Bollocks on that, as Gordon would say. Stepper still left for Mars, still abandoned her even though she'd wanted to apologize.

After the work shift ended, Janlin lay on her bunk facing the wall, arms curled over her head, and refused any attempt by anyone to engage her in conversation.

CHAPTER FIFTEEN

THE NOISE OF shift change swelled, and Janlin swung her legs off her bunk. She sat there a long while, knowing she would miss her chance to use the head, but she couldn't bring herself to stand. Finally, when there was no time left to linger, she rose.

The Imag didn't come in for them anymore. They were expected to arrive at the assignment room on their own initiative. They all knew there was nowhere to run.

Janlin paced along the rows of slave bunks, her boots slapping the metal deck. Her body throbbed, especially her legs, but she might get a touch of the whip if she arrived late . . . which would only add to the ache.

An arm snaked out and caught at the sleeve of her grey coveralls. Janlin shook her head and tried to pull away.

"Help me die," said a girl's voice from the bunk at waist level. "I can't do this anymore."

Janlin used her other hand to break the grip on her sleeve. She knelt down, realizing it was the girl with the teardrop scar. She wasn't really a girl, more a young woman, but the dirt and exhaustion made her seem much younger. She trembled with pain and despair. Her scar emphasized the dark circles under her blue eyes.

Janlin slipped her hand over the woman's, and their fingers tangled together, gripping hard in a rough gesture of reassurance. "You've made it this far, and you know we won't give up." She pushed aside her fear of being late. If the Imag in the assignment room felt impatient today, she would pay for it, but some things were worth caring about, some weren't.

The woman's breath hitched. "Brendan threw himself into the blast furnace last shift. They've been more careful with us since, or I'd be dead too."

Janlin recoiled inside. Brendan, the handsome young engineer from Mars. "Hang in there," she said, knowing how pitiful the words sounded.

The woman turned an accusing stare on her. "For what?"

Janlin shuddered at the blunt truth. "I really don't know," she said in a harsh whisper. Only four words, and her throat felt raw, her tongue thick. She dropped the young woman's hand and ran.

She reached the assignment deck and fell into line beside Stepper just in time. She wanted to tell him about Brendan, but he grunted a warning as the Imag came through the opposite door. The alien carried his work pad in one hand and his nerve whip in the other. Fran followed him, her limp more pronounced than ever.

She looked like the walking dead.

"You, you, and you, replacing scrubber filters on deck two, lines fifteen through nineteen," she translated.

They turned and left.

"You and you, lavatory duty, deck five."

That left Stepper and Janlin. Fran stopped in front of them but did not look up. "You and you, report to outer hull deck for repair duties."

They'd wanted an assignment at the hub, where ships would dock, not the outer hull. The grav-pull would be crippling. Still, they had no intel on that area. Janlin grasped at this straw, hoping they might learn something new, hoping they were inching closer to some glimpse of freedom.

In the service lift, Stepper stared at the door as if she wasn't even there. Janlin choked on her despair. Anything they'd tried, failed, resulting in a whipping. Her gaze raked over the vidlens and jerked away.

Vibrations rattled the floor of the lift as they neared the hull deck. When the lift door opened, the stench of burnt oil washed over them. She struggled to move, each step taking immense effort.

The waiting Imag handed them a beat-up work pad uncannily similar to human datasheets and gestured at two toolboxes on the floor. This Imag wore a dirty coverall instead of a uniform, but he still carried a whip on his belt. Janlin noticed his work pad showed multiple views of the engine room. They would be watched every moment.

Janlin picked up a toolbox with a grunt and followed Stepper, who studied the work pad best he could while still slogging through the ill-lit area. Janlin scanned the room, searching for its meaning.

Metal screeched and pistons plunged in the gloom. Two orange lights, one at each end of the massive engine room, offered little guidance. Wheels with polished teeth spun wildly, flashing raw steel illumination into the shadows. Janlin saw parts on a rack that poked at her memory, but they were past it before she could place what they were for.

Stepper's face looked ghoulish in the glow of the workpad as he compared what he saw on the screen to what he saw around them. Janlin waited, the toolbox pulling on her arm and the stench and heat and noise of the room assaulting her. Finally, he turned and led her deeper yet.

The machine they were to fix was obvious, its pistons jammed, its growl a tortured whine. Stepper indicated what he needed from her, and she moved into position. She wrenched on the bolts, sweat beading until it grew too heavy and ran in rivulets into her eyes. Stepper reached into the machine to pull away the bent metal part. When sudden motion made Janlin leap back, instincts taking over, Stepper had no chance.

He screamed. The sound pierced her with terror. He was launched backwards, and fell hard. Janlin saw that the arm of his coveralls was torn above the elbow. A thick red stream of blood pulsed from the opening again and again. A fresh, sharp smell overpowered her.

Medics would already be dispatched. That is what gave the optimists hope, the fact that injuries were treated, even if sometimes the injured disappeared afterwards. It meant they were valuable alive, but they did not know if it was for something better than what they survived or not.

The Imag would have seen everything, but they would never arrive in time to save him if she didn't act now.

She dropped to her knees, instantly soaking them in oily blood, and grabbed a rag from the toolbox to press to the wound. The cloth grew dark too quickly. Stepper bared his teeth.

"Let me die," he said.

Janlin hesitated. If she did not try to save him, she would be punished. If he died, she would lose her leader, her last hope, the man who had once loved her.

If she let him go, he would be free.

She took another rag, fumbled, and twisted it until she had a makeshift tourniquet. She lifted his arm and slipped it under. He hissed, and his eyes rolled back in his head. Blood flooded his sleeve. Janlin panicked, thinking him dead, until she realized he had passed out.

She took up the ends of the tourniquet and wound them together, tighter and tighter, while pressing the other rag to the wound with all her strength. Her hands became slick; her mind slid away, everything stained black-red.

What life was this? What kind of fool was she to believe there was any hope left to them?

She let out a wordless cry and loosened the tourniquet.

"Be free," she said, hunched over him so her lips moved only inches from his ear. She sat back on her heels, chest constricted, and watched as his lifeblood drained out of his arm.

Rough hands pulled her away. Imag lifted Stepper, shouting and manhandling him onto a gurney while others applied strange medical devices to both the wound and Stepper's whole arm. The medics barked at those that pushed the gurney, and they growled back. Stepper's face, pale and drawn, was slack, eyes staring. Janlin, chest heaving, turned away. She wished they'd leave him be. It was too late to help him, why argue over his body?

Without warning she was shoved forward against a machine, and the hum of a whip charged the air. In that flash of a moment Janlin's mind broke. The Imag still didn't understand the technology, but they weren't giving up either. Those parts were probably from the *Hope*, now, and if they dismantled both ships, there would never be a way home. And someday the Imag would be successful. Someday they would Jump to Earth's system.

Janlin eyed the spinning wheels, the glint of danger, and wondered if there was time enough to die. She lunged and thrust her arm into the same churning pit of steel, clenching her teeth against the anticipated agony. The guard knocked her aside before she could complete her desperate act, and a nerve whip sang in her ear. Janlin closed her eyes and rolled.

Her open hand landed on a pipe wrench, and she swung blindly in the direction of the whip. It connected with a satisfying thump, followed by a cry of outrage. The electric whine arced through the air and clanged out into the darkness, so she swung again on the backhand.

That, too, connected, but the guard grabbed her arm in a vice-like grip. She gasped, her hand went numb, and the wrench fell to the floor. Janlin twisted, using the alien's momentum against him and hoping to force the brute into letting go. She spun, completing the move with another twist to his arm, and continued his direction of motion with a little shove.

What happened then was more than she could've wished for. Slipping on the slick floor, the guard was unable to recover from her move, and he fell headlong into a steel support post with a ringing thud. He slid down the pole with agonizing slowness and lay still at the bottom.

Janlin backed away. A moan escaped her lips, startling her from her shock. Others would be coming. This was her chance.

She looked at the machine that had killed Stepper. Just one thrust of an arm, and it would be over but for the pain. Today was a good day to die.

She ran from her temptation, her despair, her grief. She stumbled against walls, bounced around corners, sobbing as she went. Stepper was dead, and she didn't have the guts to kill herself. She wished they'd never come here, wished they'd never built Jumpships, wished the Imag had never been born.

She wished *she'd* never been born.

Janlin slammed along the corridor, gasping for air, always knowing the vast array of vidlens would track her progress, and she would be caught and whipped for her actions today.

The bowels of the ship were lit in eerie red and strangely empty of guards. She guessed guards weren't necessary in an area where slaves usually didn't go.

Lift doors stood open, and she fell into the small space.

Scanning the controls, she chose what she guessed was the opposite of where she was now, and slumped against the back wall as the doors slid shut. Who knew what would greet her when they opened again?

The pressure of gravity lessened by degrees. The lift stopped, and the doors split. Janlin let out a whoosh of held breath when all that greeted her was another empty corridor. She stumbled out and half ran, choosing a direction without thought.

A large metal shelf on wheels loomed before her, half blocking the way. Again, she saw the familiar parts, either from the *Renegade* or the *Hope*, there was no way to know which anymore. With vigour she didn't know she had in her, she began to demolish everything on that shelf, smashing them to the floor, standing on them to bend metal, breaking off essential parts. Whatever it took to keep the aliens from using what they had stolen.

A thump echoed through the hull below her feet, and she felt the shudder of the after-effect. She paused in her destruction. No sound followed, and there was no movement within sight.

Janlin scooped up a hunk of bent metal pipe and ran towards the sound instead of away. She would take whatever lives she could in payment for Stepper, and her father, and all the rest. She would go down fighting. Enough was enough.

Hatchways now lined the hall, and she put her ear to each one, listening. Based on the controls, flashing warning lights, and tight seals, these were airlocks, and the thud could be a ship docking.

She hefted the steel bar in her hand. Something on it pinched her, and she looked down at her hand. For the first time she noticed the blood caked on her arms and smeared over her fingers.

The steel fell to the floor with a clang that echoed down the long hall. Everything spun around her. Janlin shook her head, clearing it, and found herself on her hands and knees staring at the floor.

Stepper.

A few steps down the hall an alarm sounded, and the airlock door began to cycle. She gritted her teeth and reached for the makeshift weapon. It was time to die, and she planned to take as many of the enemy with her as possible.

CHAPTER SIXTEEN

AS SHE ROSE into a predatory crouch, Janlin realized she was about to act out of despair and grief instead of thinking things through. Stepper might be dead, but she wasn't. Gordon and Tyrell and the woman with the scar, they all deserved better from her. Whoever was about to come through that hatch came through an airlock, which meant there was a ship docked on the other side.

A ship.

With only microseconds left, Janlin ran back to the shelves and hid herself the best she could.

Rough grunts echoed from the now-open hatch, and Janlin peered from her hiding place. Three aliens stepped into the hall, each carrying weapons ready. They scanned up and down the hall as if expecting to be attacked at any moment. Janlin frowned, even as she ducked into hiding. Why would they be so on guard?

Maybe she'd been missed, and now a ship-wide warrant for her arrest brought in even the surrounding shuttles. Was she really that important?

She shook off the speculation. She had to get on that docked ship. To her great relief, the three newcomers went the opposite way, leaving the hatch dialled open. Too convenient, said her gut, but there wasn't much else to do but try and take advantage of it.

Janlin crept down the hall, her chunk of steel slipping in her sweaty palm. She switched hands, wiped one on her leg, and took a firmer grip. Once she reached the opening, she dared a quick glance in and ducked back out again.

It was a simple airlock, smaller than she expected. Did she really just see the hatch to the shuttle open as well?

She took another quick glance. Sure enough, open, and apparently empty. Goosebumps prickled up her arms. Taking a deep breath, she dove through the hatchway and over to the opposite side of the airlock. There was nothing to hide behind in an airlock, but she flattened herself against the wall and sidled up to the outer door.

Lights flashed on the lock, showing green and orange. Why did green always mean good to go? She recognized her exhaustion and shock coming out in one distracting thought after another, so she sucked in three deep breaths and listened with all her being, poised to fight—or flee—at the smallest sound.

Nothing.

Janlin slipped into the airlock of the shuttle. The ship could be called nothing else, based on its size and the gear she saw stowed there. Some kind of supply vehicle maybe, or transport shuttle, she figured. They had speculated about an Imag home base somewhere . . . the steel factory couldn't be it. But if she could figure out how to fly this machine, she would go where, exactly?

Again, she shook off the distraction. She could not pass up such an opportunity. Focus on getting the ship first, then on where to take it, she told herself. She would figure it out as she went.

She crept along a short passage that led into a circular room she hoped was the command centre of the ship.

Five aliens stared at her from various stations around the room.

Janlin roared a challenge as she ran headlong at the closest one, her hunk of steel swung back in readiness. She used their amazed shock to her advantage, feeling somewhat guilty, but this was no time to be holding back . . . especially since he was drawing something from his belt even as she swung.

The bar connected with the Imag's raised arm and slid to bounce off his skull. Unfortunately, that deflection cost some momentum, and did little to hurt him. The alien's weapon was brought to bear, and Janlin realized the others were shouting at him. It was no nerve whip, either, definitely a gun. The nose had a hole, undoubtedly where the projectile would emerge to splatter through her chest.

He paused, and she backed away, arms raised. Apparently, she didn't want to die as badly as she had thought, or she would simply lunge at him.

The one with the weapon gurgled and gestured at her, clearly angry, but the others continued to grunt and bark. Janlin got the impression they were attempting to keep him from shooting her.

She bent slowly, letting the pipe fall to the floor. "I'm really sorry, I must have taken a wrong turn," she said. She almost laughed with the absurdity of it. But she was on a ship, a different ship than the factory, and for some reason that gave her hope.

One of the Imag gurgled into his commlink. "Well, there goes that idea," she muttered. Soon the guards would be here to pick her up, nerve whips at the ready.

A reply rang out through a speaker somewhere, and the words were frantic and combined with the sound of . . . weapons fire?

All of them turned, eyes wide with concern, and again she questioned her perceptions. These Imag just didn't act right . . . and who was shooting at them? Janlin considered taking up her pipe and rolling into position to strike again, but too many things told her that was a bad idea. For one, there were four others who wore the same weapon on their belts as the one she'd hit. For another, she didn't feel like she was in immediate danger, nor did these aliens carry nerve whips . . . and their uniforms were deep red with grey patterns crisscrossing, instead of green and black like the guards. The strange trickle of hope swelled and ran around in her belly.

The sound of fighting came through the open hatchway. One alien called out orders, two more took up larger weapons and ran for the hatch, and another began punching buttons that brought a rumble beneath her feet.

That left the one she'd hit. He clearly hadn't forgotten about her, and still held his sidearm at the ready, but instead of anything Janlin could predict, he gestured at a seat with his gun.

Janlin hesitated only for the briefest of seconds. The ship, alive under her feet . . . the firefight . . . the fact they didn't shoot her . . . it all added up to more than she could've wished for. She dropped into the seat, and the Imag bent over to strap her in. She reached up to touch his head where she'd hit him—already a lump was forming—and he flinched. She gave him a sheepish smile.

"Sorry."

The Imag firmly pushed her arm down and strapped her in so that she was completely immobile.

"Yeah, I guess I deserve that," she said as he turned away. She was as much a prisoner as ever, but somehow it didn't hold the same sense of despair as before.

Before Janlin could follow this thought into reasoning, the two Imag returned, bursting into the control room, and the floor shook with power and the sounds of fighting were cut off. A grinding screech filled the ship. Each individual in the room struggled with buckles while still manipulating controls at their individual stations.

Three more aliens came in, one being carried by the other two. He bled a viscous fluid much pinker than human blood.

They secured him against one wall where straps were available for cargo—or perhaps this was a common occurrence that required just such a spot for the injured. One companion rushed to his own seat, but the other stayed with the downed man as the crew prepared for a rough launch. A few questions were grunted in this Imag's direction, and were answered with confidence and appeared to satisfy every query. Then Janlin watched in amazement as the crew flew under fire and what she surmised as their leader continued to administer care to the wounded alien.

Finally, the impacts that rocked the ship and made the hull shudder under her feet ended, and after a few more moments of exchange between crew and captain, gravity returned. Apparently satisfied with the injured one's condition, the captain stood, stretched, and turned to look at Janlin.

"Be no afraid," the alien said.

CHAPTER SEVENTEEN

JANLIN CHOKED ON her surprise, her mouth working without sound for a long moment. Hope blossomed and spread like fire in her veins, yet she fought the surging rise of optimism.

"How the hell did you learn my language?" she finally blurted. "How is that possible?"

Janlin stared at the alien standing over her. The being looked away, face twitching and lips pursed.

"You come, new 'ip," the leader said. Clearly a statement, not a question. Janlin tried to keep any revealing information from her face. She wasn't answering any questions without some answers of her own.

"Who are you? Why were you being shot at? What's going on?"

"You hep Gitane, Gitane hep human." Every time the alien said Gitane it came with a tap on the chest. Janlin sucked on her bottom lip.

"How am I supposed to help you? And what about all those humans still back there?"

"You . . . one. We come take one. If save many human, start war. Gitane no want war with Imag."

Imag. Gitane. War. What was that saying? Enemy of my enemy is my friend? Would it prove true in this case? Maybe, for all the similarities to Imag, this Gitane character was different. This ship was to the other as night was to day. Their boots still echoed off a steel floor, but a tough carpet of some unknown textile muted the sounds. The walls here carried paint in some areas, and in others the same material as the flooring, artfully mixed together to create a form pleasing to the eye. These aliens wore crisp uniforms, and did not smell like rancid socks. In fact, the whole place had a pleasant musk of cleanliness.

At that moment the floor rocked, and the aliens scrambled for their stations.

"What the hell—"

They all ignored her, understandably. She watched, fascinated, as they gurgled and chuffed terse phrases back and forth. The ship rocked repeatedly, and one of the aliens struggled with his controls.

Then, they all reclined their seats, which enclosed them much the same way hers did, and closed their eyes.

"Hey, this is no time to sleep," Janlin said, unable to keep her mouth shut with her panic. Strange holographic displays appeared over their eyes, like some sort of virtual reality headpiece. Janlin figured that they would open their eyes once covered and run the ship from within that interface, but she could see no movement, and nothing behind those shimmering screens.

Janlin sat helpless as the ship continued to shudder and rock under her. They must be under attack, but the not knowing for sure was the worst part. Then, a few abandoned objects lifted from their places and floated.

"Uh, guys? Gravity's off," she said in a bare whisper. Not one of them even flickered an eyelid.

Another, stronger, shudder rippled through the hull. Maybe this was it. Maybe she would die here, and it would all be done and over—no more grief, no more guilt, no more pain, no more regret—

Pressure crushed her into the seat, then tried to pull her out of it. Now grateful for her restraints, she wondered if these aliens knew how little g-force a human body could take.

She had entirely too much time to think, sitting there pinned in her chair. Questions poured through her mind, with no one to ask. Fear plagued her, and bitterness, and grief. Stepper was dead. Her father was likely dead too. Gordon still endured the

Imag slavers, forced to help them build the biggest Jumpship ever out of the scrap parts of their own ships. To get home again, they would either have to rebuild, or use the Imag ship . . . if the brutes got it to work. That left little chance of ever seeing Earth again.

Whatever the case, Janlin had to look at this as a new opportunity, even if it became only a new opportunity to seek death. Janlin struggled to breathe as the grief hit her again. It really didn't matter where they took her. They still had power over her, and even if she could get free, how would she help the rest? She understood the woman's desperation now. What was her name? Didn't matter.

Somewhere in these thoughts the pressure grew. She couldn't catch her breath, and everything narrowed to the need for air and the inability to inhale. Janlin struggled against her restraints uselessly, her mouth gaping, her chest crushed as if a loaded cargo crate sat on it. Blackness began in the edge of her vision and spread, like something evil, and Janlin's last thought was that she still didn't want to die.

CHAPTER EIGHTEEN

SHE CAME AWAKE flailing and gasping. Arms held her, hands pushed her hair from her forehead. "Stepper?"

"Okay, okay." The hands were strong, leathery, yet kind. "Good, good, you be okay."

Janlin focused on the leader's face hovering over hers and realized with a start that the alien captain bore reddish glands below her ears, indicating that she was female. But that wasn't the biggest surprise. "You can really speak English?"

"Yes," she said, and somehow, without the usual clues of a puffed-out chest or straightening of the shoulders, Janlin got the impression the alien was proud of herself. Maybe it was the lift of the chin.

"Be okay?"

This time it was a question, and Janlin nodded. "Yes," she added, realizing she'd never seen one of these creatures nod. Language was not simply words, a subject that was one of Fran's favourite lectures. "Communication is the inflection, the posture, the facial expression, and words, all together. If you are using only one, there is significant room for misunderstanding," Fran would say.

Janlin hoped she could keep the misunderstanding to a minimum.

The alien left then, pulling herself along in free-fall, although Janlin noted the door shield stayed open. Somehow, she was comforted by the small sounds that came through, and the knowledge that this crew seemed to care for her wellbeing. That, and they didn't carry nerve whips. She shuddered with the memories, content to lie there strapped to the bed and just let things play out for now.

The pressure of gravity appeared, and the alien returned, striding into the room with confidence. She undid the straps and stepped back, allowing Janlin the dignity of getting up on her own time. She got her hands under her, only to see the blood stains, now dry and crusty.

"Sorry, I'm a mess," Janlin said, fighting tears.

"Be okay. Come. Show."

"Wait." Janlin tapped a finger on her chest. "Janlin," she said.

"Jaan-in."

"Right. And you are?" Janlin pointed.

"Anaya." Thick digits tapped barrel chest.

Ah, so Gitane wasn't her name. Janlin wondered what it did mean, then. "Aa-nay-ya."

The alien chuffed. "Good. Come. Fix," she said, indicating Janlin's state of disarray.

Janlin let herself be led through the control room and into a tiny steel chamber. Anaya waved her arms and pointed at things while mixing her languages. Just behind her left shoulder stood another alien, one of Anaya's crew that had gone with her into the factory ship, and the biggest Imag she'd seen yet. Janlin stared at the hulking brute crowding the tiny room, unable to get past what others like him had done to her.

Anaya pantomimed pulling at clothes as if to take them off, then pointed at a stainless-steel cubicle. Janlin studied the cubicle and decided it must be a shower stall of sorts. When she turned back, the big male was gone.

Anaya continued with her explanations. "Wash," came up again and again, and "keen" with "hot wet" as she showed how to engage the controls, adjust them, and get clean. The instructions were directed at Janlin, and were not punctuated by the hum of a whip, so Janlin engaged her numb fingers and groped for her zipper.

Anaya, satisfied with this, backed out of the room and powered the shield door closed.

Janlin stared at the door. Did they really just leave her alone? She couldn't remember the last time she was alone, and while she longed to get answers to her questions, chances were she smelt pretty bad. Who could say no to a shower?

She scanned the room, running her fingers along every panel and depression. She wasn't sure if there was soap, or shampoo, or even a towel.

Turning away, Janlin saw that the cubicle had a water seal, like their group shower room on the factory ship. Janlin sighed in defeat, stripped off her filthy clothes, and scrutinized the controls, finding nothing she recognized. Clearly, she wasn't paying full attention during her lesson.

Janlin stepped in, pressed some buttons, pulled a lever, and, miraculously, the water came on. It had an astringent smell, and she hoped that meant she would not be just wet, but clean, too.

"Ouch, ouch, for crying out loud, ouch!" Apparently scalding was the temperature of choice for these beings. Janlin dodged the jets of water, struggling between the desire to be clean and the pain, and grateful for the distraction of avoiding being burnt while the water ran red.

After a cooler rinse cycle, a rush of hot, dry air removed nearly every bit of moisture from her body, eliminating the need for a towel. Janlin whistled in appreciation.

When she emerged from the stall her clothes were gone, replaced by a brick red jumpsuit. It held more room than she needed, but it smelt fresh. Janlin shook her head at the thought of what she must look like, but the sensation of being clean, and of wearing clean clothes, overcame any concern she had for fashion. The only thing she kept from her old uniform was her boots.

"No socks, no underpants, no bra . . . geez," Janlin muttered, although she felt more like cheering than complaining. She inspected the secret pocket in the tongue of one boot and sighed at the sight of her nano-recorder still nestled there.

She tried to activate the door, to no avail. So, she was still a prisoner. Figured.

A few seconds later the shield disappeared, and Anaya waved her arms. "Sorry," she said. "Must teach." She pointed at the control panel to the side of the doorway.

Janlin floundered, all her preconceptions blown away. She

fell back on attitude.

"Why are you kissing up to me?" she demanded. "Nice shower, new clothes . . . what's the deal?"

Anaya stared. "No understand," she said with a shrug.

"You are being too nice," Janlin said slowly, speaking each word clearly. "Why?"

"Hep Anaya, Anaya hep human."

Janlin remembered this from before. With dawning perception, she realized "l" seemed to be non-existent in their language. "I'll bet you understand more of what I say than you can speak."

"Yes." Again that pride, that self-assurance. Janlin reminded herself to be extra careful with this character. Still, she might be a little over confident, and that could play right into Janlin's hands.

"Well, I know what you can do for me . . . how can I help you?"

"Find new home." She replied so promptly Janlin couldn't help but give her that famous raised-eyebrow look. Anaya simply stared, and Janlin realized the alien couldn't read scepticism or questioning in a human's features. Made her wonder what she was missing in the alien's body language.

"How did you learn our language?"

"Human friend teach."

"Really?"

"Yes." She gave a toothy grin that was more like a feral grimace in Janlin's eyes.

"Where is this human friend now?" Janlin asked.

Anaya's smile faltered. "Dead."

CHAPTER NINETEEN

THE FEAR THAT had begun to ebb away returned in a rush.

"How?" Janlin demanded.

Anaya's fingers fluttered and her gaze travelled around the room. Janlin watched in terrified fascination.

"He . . . hot," she said, touching her own forehead.

"Sick?" Janlin asked.

"Yes!"

Janlin jumped a little at the exclamation. She wavered a little, suddenly aware of how exhausted she felt. What had happened to the rest of the humans on the other ship? Did they "steal" any others? "Who . . . was his name Rudigar?" she asked.

Anaya tipped her head. "No." She pointed at one of the chairs. "Sit pease."

She had a million more questions, but Janlin nodded and sat, strangely unable to be stubborn for the moment. Anaya went to a tiny alcove in the wall, and returned with a steaming container, which she handed to Janlin. Janlin took a sniff, then a much longer, indulgent inhalation. Now this smelled better than anything put before her in a long time, here or back home. The thought of home, and of the others still on the slaver ship, made her heart lurch, but she had to accept it was out of her hands, at least for now. She peered into the narrow bowl, shaped more like a very tall mug, trying to make out what floated in the brown liquid.

"Good. Eat."

What did she have to lose? Besides, it gave her an excuse to stay quiet. She decided to let this alien talk first. Sometimes the best way to learn the truth was to just shut up and see what the other person had to say.

Janlin took a sip, then gulped down the bowl in one go. It tasted salty, and slightly metallic, but again there was no room for complaints in this situation.

Anaya chuffed. "Good. Come. Show."

Janlin rose on somewhat shaky legs and joined the leader over at a small workstation. She watched in fascination as the alien used incomprehensible controls to bring up holo documents that hung in the air.

"Very nice," Janlin murmured.

Anaya put a hand on her arm. Janlin flinched, and Anaya pulled away. Was that sadness on her face, Janlin wondered? Regret?

"Dis no nice," Anaya said. It was clearly a warning, and Janlin wondered if she meant the way she'd flinched from touch or what she was about to show her. It didn't take long to figure it out.

Another holo image opened, flickered, and became a man laid out on a slab of steel.

The relief she felt that it wasn't her father now became shock as she studied the man. She thought he might be one of the many mechanics she'd worked with over the years as a pilot, but he was so emaciated she couldn't be sure. Victor? Vernon? She shook her head, sad that she couldn't remember.

His hair was matted to his head, his eyes sunken and marked with dark circles like some awful raccoon. A thin arm appeared, the hand shaking dreadfully, as he closed his eyes and wiped at his head. The movement was feeble. Janlin made a little sound of dismay, and her hands came up to cover her mouth.

Anaya put a hand on her shoulder, and Janlin looked up to see the skin on Anaya's forehead crinkled in what Janlin read as concern.

"I'm okay," she whispered, but it was the grandest lie of her life. Her dad was still missing, Stepper was dead by her own hand, now this forgotten man was taken by some alien fever, to say nothing of the rest of them trapped on that slave ship and all the others in places unknown. It was more than she could take.

Anaya chuffed at her, and their gazes met. Janlin realized they were a pale blue that bordered on steel grey. The alien reached out and touched Janlin on the cheek, and when her finger came away it held a drop of moisture balanced on its tip. She touched it to her tongue, and Janlin bit her lip at the sight of the blueish-purple colour of it. Still, she was touched by Anaya's kindness, by her hospitality and willingness to learn her language, even her curiosity.

"Tears," Janlin said.

"Ters," came the reply. Anaya rocked back on her heels and straightened up, looking down at Janlin with all the seriousness in the universe. "Vic," she said. "Good human, good friend."

Victor. Janlin did have the right name, but that did nothing to cheer her. Anaya chuffed something and tapped her ear, then pointed up. Victor's hologram began to speak, his eyes fever-bright and staring straight at whatever recording device had created this.

"I know Anaya will try again. Whoever might come after me, this could help." Janlin's throat closed, and the image blurred. She swiped at her eyes. She needed to see his expression to make sure he was sincere, and not put up to this.

"Trust Anaya," he said. His voice rasped, and he turned his head to cough. The whole image jumped around as he did, and Janlin realized he was holding the unit to record himself. Was he alone when he did it?

The coughing racked his whole body, and Janlin bit her lip as blood-flecked spittle covered the sheet under his chin. When he looked back, seemingly right into her eyes, his face was grey, his eyes sunken into his head.

"I won't beat this. The Imag had me in a different section of the ship, and they did tests on me . . . like allergy tests, only I think it was for this illness. Of course, that's what gave Anaya a chance to steal me away." More coughing. "She'll need to find new help. I've been with her for weeks now, and I know her motives are good ones. Help her family get free of this system so they can start again. Show her—"

Another coughing fit took him, and the image folded into itself and was sucked into the machine.

When she looked at Anaya, she was startled to see tears

leaking down the leathery cheeks. They looked pinkish. Janlin reached out, careful to make sure Anaya saw it coming, and took up the tear with her finger the same way Anaya had. Then she touched it to her lips.

Salt and water. Astounding how they were, by far, more similar than different.

"Good human," Anaya said, looking down at the device.

Janlin nodded, despite not knowing Victor well, but the pain of losing Stepper weighed on her like the awful g-forces of earlier.

At that moment a beep sounded, followed by guttural alien words.

"Wait," Anaya said, holding up her hand palm out. "Anaya go now. Be back."

Janlin sat stunned. Once again, she was alone.

The day's events came crashing down on her. The image of Victor became overlaid with Stepper lying in his own blood, pale and lifeless, and it refused to leave her mind. Despair sat deep in her chest. Here she had an opportunity, the first sign of any kind that there might just be a way out of here, and she'd let him go. If she'd had faith, held on just a few more seconds . . .

When Anaya returned, Janlin lashed out.

"If you want my help, we have to go back and get the others."

Anaya's face crinkled. "You one. We 'ook for one. You come to ship, no Imag. We go, no start war."

She must have learned the word "Imag" from Victor. As much as it lent Janlin some comfort to know that Anaya didn't want to incite war against anyone, she didn't understand the use of the title.

"Imag?" Janlin said, pointing at Anaya.

Anaya pulled back, a deep growl coming up from the centre of her chest. One of the crew, the big guy, appeared in the doorway, ready to defend his captain.

Clearly, she'd offended.

"Sorry," Janlin said, waving her hands. "Not Imag."

Anaya seemed to understand, and waved the crewman away. "Gitane," she said, tapping her chest.

Ah. That word again. Janlin had thought it was a name earlier, and had forgotten since. She repeated it best she could. "Jih-tawn-nee?"

Anaya chuffed, patting her chest with an open palm.

"Race names, perhaps?" Janlin mused aloud. It sounded like an old French word. These aliens were transients in space, on the move. But what about the planets their scans had detected?

"Anaya, why do you live in space if there are perfectly good planets in this system?"

Consternation crossed Anaya's face, but Janlin wasn't going to dumb down her language. Anaya studied her.

Janlin studied her back, took a deep breath, and let it out slow. "Where is your home? Why are you out here? Why are you stealing humans from the Imag?" she asked.

Anaya grunted. "Many . . . words," she said. Long story? "No home. Gitane, Imag, home . . . sick, no good for home." Her thick fingers deftly chose commands from the air, manipulating the hologram controls.

Janlin joined her at the console. "So, what are you planning?"

Anaya straightened. "Get 'ip, go new home. Jahnin hep . . . Gitane take 'ip go . . . out." Anaya was obviously frustrated by her lack of words to say what she wanted to, but Janlin thought she understood. Anaya confirmed it.

"Human 'ip come. Gitane hep human, you take Gitane go new home."

"So, if I help you Jump to a new system and find a new home, you will help me free my crewmates and a Jumpship?"

"Yes, free 'ip."

Maybe there was hope after all. Except . . . "I'm not sure our Jumpships even exist anymore."

Anaya grunted. "New 'ip good." An image appeared. It showed the familiar interior of the Imag flightdeck. Perched in one corner stood a ship far more familiar, and amazingly in one piece. Janlin nearly lost her mind at the sight of it.

The *Hope*.

CHAPTER TWENTY

"'IP," ANAYA SAID.

"Yes, that is my ship." Janlin faced new optimism beyond her wildest dreams while wondering how she would bear the weight of her guilt and grief.

"It might not work," she admitted. Anaya pinned her with a hard look. "The Imag have bits and pieces of our stuff . . . of one ship or both I don't know . . . and they are trying to build their own Jumpship."

The hard look cemented. "No good," Anaya growled. She flicked through more images, muttering in her own language under her breath.

Something flashed by that caught Janlin's attention. "Wait a minute . . . is that an orbital space station?"

For that she received a well-deserved blank look. But the station—ship?—had to be huge if you put things in scale. Was that what she just left?

Janlin found herself wishing—for the first and hopefully last time—that she was more like Fran. She made a fist with one hand and circled a finger around it with the other. "Station," she said, raising the single finger, then pointing at the fist. "Planet?" she asked, indicating the fist.

"Ah," Anaya said. She made some adjustments to the holographic view, and the station stood against the backdrop of the most beautiful sight Janlin had ever seen. A gas giant filled the space between them, with colours and patterns swirling on the surface. A fair-sized moon circled by, the station in its orbit.

"Station? Or ship?" she asked Anaya.

"Yes," she answered. "Imag 'ip. Imag want it all, Huantag and Jump 'ip."

Before Janlin could ask more or study the scene further, Anaya changed the image again. "Hey—" she began, but Anaya held up a beefy hand.

"Wait."

Janlin watched, wondering why Anaya showed her what appeared to be the engine room she had just lost her captain in, or one just like it. The symbols at the top of the image changed rapidly. At first Janlin couldn't figure out what she was supposed to be looking for, but as the symbols continued to shift—and the perspective too, on occasion—figures moved about the area in fast forward, and the parts that were being gathered on the floor and surrounding storage units took on a familiar shape.

"They're definitely building a Jump engine."

Anaya pointed at the nearly finished Jump engine. "Imag 'ip work? Go new home?"

Janlin hesitated. What did she tell this alien being? How much could she trust the apparent feud between them? Could Anaya just be playing good cop in order to get the information they needed?

She didn't want to say too much, yet the vision of the *Hope* kept her from simply denying any knowledge of anything.

"Who owns that station or ship or whatever it really is?" Janlin asked.

It was Anaya's turn to hesitate. "Imag."

"Not Gitane?"

Anaya shrugged, and Janlin realized for the first time that a shrug seemed to mean no. She'd have to watch that she didn't shrug when she meant ambivalence or uncertainty, because these folk would take it as a plain negative response.

"You said you didn't want to start a war with the Imag. Even if my ship still works, how would we get it from them?"

"Must try."

Right. "Of course, we must try," Janlin said, even as burning guilt surged up her gullet. She swallowed, not wanting to lose the best meal she'd had in far too long.

"What will the Imag do if their new ship doesn't work?"

Anaya's face crumpled into what Janlin took as near despair. "New Imag 'ip for war. If no go new home, Imag start war."

"On you?"

Anaya narrowed her eyes. "No. Imag hate Gitane, but Huantag have home, and Imag take home with war."

Who? Janlin gave her head a mental shake. "Who-an-teg?"

Anaya chuffed a long time at this. Janlin wasn't sure if she should laugh along or feel insulted. "Who-wan-tag. Huantag," Janlin tried. A different species, or another family name?

"Huantag live on a planet?" Janlin said, making her fist again and pointing at it. Now that she knew why these aliens were wanderers in space, it made sense that they'd want to find a new planet to call home, and the scans had shown other planets that were in that sweet "Goldilocks" zone of life.

Anaya agreed. "Get 'ip," she said, pointing at the holo. "Hep you, go new home. No war with Imag *or* Huantag."

Janlin closed her eyes, not wanting to see the disappointment her information would cause. "My ship has a big hole in it," she said, but she waved that off, knowing the shuttle bay could be sealed off. There were bigger problems. "And the Imag might have taken essential parts. Plus, I can't fly it alone."

"Need more human?" Anaya demanded.

"Oh, yes, many more." A captain or helmsman with the proper coding to gain access to the Jump commands for starters, Tyrell being the one she knew best. Besides, there was no way she would fly out and leave anyone behind . . . even Fran.

"Get human, then get 'ip." They were blunt words, spoken by someone who was used to getting what she ordered.

Who was Janlin to disagree? But there were a few considerations to iron out. "You said no war with Imag. How do we get our humans from them without causing trouble?"

"Not human with Imag. Human on Huantag."

"There are humans on Huantag?"

"Yes."

Janlin sat down, abruptly, glad in retrospect that there happened to be a stool to catch her.

Anaya opened another holo. Janlin stared. Before her hung a gorgeous water planet studded with chains of islands and tiny continents.

It looked beautiful beyond her wildest dreams.

Anaya grunted an inquiry.

Janlin rubbed her face to help her think, then stared some more. "We knew many humans had disappeared from the Imag ship, and we worried they were dead," Janlin explained. She stood again, still feeling shaky, but wanting to address Anaya and make sure she understood. "So, you want me to get the humans together on the Huantag planet, and you will get the ship from the Imag station, and we just fly out of here?"

Anaya paused only a moment. "Yes."

"Well, it's as good a plan as any we've had so far," Janlin said. "But I refuse to leave my people—humans—with the Imag. They will need to be rescued, too."

Anaya slapped a hand down on her controls, and the hologram disappeared. "No war with Imag." Her tone was hard.

Janlin had half expected that reply, and wondered what Victor's thoughts had been on the matter, but her mind was already working ahead. "Why can't you try and save the humans while getting the ship?" she said, only to see the worst scowl on Anaya's face yet. "Okay, okay," Janlin said, holding palms out in a consoling way. Once they had a crew, and a ship, they would have more bargaining power. They might just have to hold up their end by taking Anaya to a new system before returning for the others. It might be an idea to return home and bring whatever army could be mustered, anyway.

"What about the other planets in the system? Why can't you make a home there?"

Anaya stared into the distance for a long time, until Janlin wondered if she even heard the question. Finally, Anaya engaged the holo machine again, and an image of a grey planet with no visible oceans or life emerged.

The alien huffed out her breath and approached the console. With a few flicks of thick fingers, she brought up a holo of the system. "Home," she said, pointing at one of the planets. "Yiyau." She entered another command, and the holo zoomed in on the lone planet. It appeared dark, empty of water or clouds or any sign of atmosphere.

"This was your home?"

"Yes," Anaya said, her voice deep and rough. "Gitane and Imag make sick. Yiyau die. Then, big war."

Janlin thought about this while she stared at the dead planet. Anaya turned away, softly chuffing. Then she turned back to stare directly at Janlin, as if making sure she had her full attention. "Huantag fix home, no tell Gitane how."

The anger and bitterness in this was apparent, and Janlin wondered what the situation was down on Huantag. Did the humans there suffer as they did on the Imag ship?

A strange noise, akin to the squealing monkeys Janlin saw in a movie once, rang through the room. Anaya snapped to attention, her hands flying over the controls. Gurgled words passed between her and her crew over the comm-unit. Janlin watched carefully, wondering if they were under attack again.

Anaya gave a chuff, followed by curt commands, and shut down her private system.

"Come," she said, and left without looking to see if Janlin followed.

CHAPTER TWENTY-ONE

JANLIN EMERGED INTO the command centre where she'd tried to take on five aliens with a steel pipe. She grinned at the memory, and made a mental note to ask Anaya to apologize to the one she'd hit. She had trouble deciding which one it was, looking at them all busy and in the same uniform. The big guy stood out, much larger in height and girth than the others. Another one looked female like Anaya. Both of them had a smaller, softer build, with lighter skin and a rounder face. The reddish glands were hard to pick out unless you were up close.

Anaya walked behind each chair, studying the consoles and offering occasional advice. She touched the shoulder of one crewmate and gurgled a question. The Gitane lifted a bandaged arm into view and chuffed in answer. Anaya moved on, apparently assured by his answer. Janlin recognized him as the injured one, and finally saw the one she'd bonked on the head, but he wasn't acknowledging she existed at the moment.

She scanned the room, enjoying the patterns of burgundy, brick red, and burnt orange in the wall coverings. They added life and energy to the room while softening the metal that made up the ship. Doors led from the command centre, the largest being the hatchway she'd entered by. She knew Anaya's quarters and the head, with its lovely shower. Two doors on the opposite side might well lead to crew quarters and maintenance levels, if her guess was right.

After waiting awhile to be filled in on the situation as the Gitane conversed, Janlin wondered if she should be trying to learn their language. She didn't like being left out, but she was no linguist. She wrinkled her nose at Fran's scowling image crossing her mind again.

"What's going on?" she finally asked Anaya, who now sat at her workstation.

"See Imag 'ip," she said, chuffing. Janlin frowned. The chuff usually meant humour, as best she could tell.

"Are we in trouble, then?" She glanced at the chair she'd sat in for the last dogfight.

"No," Anaya said with another chuff. "Imag no see Gitane. We no big 'ip. They go fast."

"How close are they?" Janlin wasn't too sure she liked the idea of them close by. Were they searching for her? She shivered at the thought of returning to that nightmare.

"No close. We go same way, but they no see."

"We're following them?"

"Yes," Anaya said. Then she nodded, her neckless head rocking back and forth. Janlin laughed outright before she could think better of it.

"Did you just nod?" she said, incredulous. She copied the motion.

Anaya chuffed and did it again. The effect was hilarious, and Janlin found she couldn't stop. The crew chuffed, joining her, and something inside of her seemed to undo as she laughed until tears leaked down her cheeks.

Anaya leaned close to Janlin wearing her puckered-forehead worried look. "Ters?"

"It's okay," Janlin said, wiping her eyes with a chuckling hitch her breath. "Good tears."

Anaya looked more confused than ever, and that only made Janlin laugh harder. "God, I think I'm hysterical."

When she sobered, she watched Anaya work. "You said the Imag are going faster?" At the confirmation of this, she asked, "How long will it take us to reach Huantag?"

Anaya gave an incomprehensible answer, and at Janlin's look, tried to point out symbols and charts on her console that obviously were some kind of map or clock or calendar—something that would give an answer, if she had any clue what she was looking at. In space, there was no rotation of day and night to mark things by, either, something Janlin was quite used to, but it left them with no way to communicate time.

"Never mind. I guess I'll just have to wait it out." She knew she sounded like a petulant child, though, demanding from the back seat, "Are we there, yet?" The hysterics over, Janlin felt drained. A yawn split her face before she could stop it, and it got Anaya's attention.

"Come," she said, rising and leading Janlin back to her own quarters. Janlin didn't complain when Anaya showed her a slab uncomfortably similar to the bunks on the slaver ship.

Anaya left her to rest, setting the lights low beforehand.

Janlin stared at the strange room. She had no idea how long it had been since she started this "day" . . . only that it felt like a lifetime. She remembered the young scarred woman, and cringed at how little hope she had offered the poor thing. She hadn't even seen Gordon since the previous shift. The Imag kept pulling him to do wiring, often using the threat of the nerve whip if he didn't comply. All too often he'd been carried back to his bunk only to be forced to the same jobsite when he recovered.

Stepper, too, had endured his fair share of the nerve whip. The way he'd looked lately, the Imag also had him in the torture chamber with Fran. He bore new wounds and a haunted look.

"Oh, Stepper." She choked and sobbed as his grin flashed in her mind and his big brown eyes crinkled with a smile. She cried until she thought it would never stop, but sheer exhaustion eventually took her over into sleep.

CHAPTER TWENTY-TWO

DAYS PASSED, AND Janlin found boredom to be her worst enemy now. Soon she had her own clothes again, somehow cleaned of all blood. Doing her best to make use of the time, she ate their food, studied their ship, and tried to make sense of their language. Once Anaya showed her how to manipulate the holo controls, she pored over images of the Imag station, searching for clues and ideas.

She had a favourite holo, and today she sat across the room from it, just staring. Huantag. She let her mouth whisper the name. Scenarios of arriving there tempted her, but she refused to allow herself too much speculation. She'd seen how the Imag treated their captives. The fact that there were survivors living on the planet didn't guarantee anything for her dad.

Anaya appeared in the doorway with one of her crew. Janlin thought of him as "Yipho," though she knew she couldn't get the pronunciation right. Every time she'd tried, all she got was a lot of chuffing. In fact, that seemed to be the way of it with most of their words, and she'd given up on learning the language.

"Anaya, Yipho," she said, giving the name another go. Toothy displays meant as smiles were her reply. Yipho was carrying a hypodermic needle.

Janlin was on her feet before she realized it.

Anaya held up a hand, palm out, a universal attempt to placate. "Yipho give Jahnin," she said, gesturing at the hypodermic.

Anaya, too, could not pronounce Janlin's name properly, but Janlin had not bothered to correct her. There seemed to be a breakdown with "l" and the combination "t-h" sound. Maybe their tongues couldn't make the right shapes. Fran would know. Fran wouldn't take this needle, either, Janlin knew it.

"I don't think so," she said. "Not without more explanation of what's in that."

"Other human get sick," Anaya said. "Yipho make dis so Jahnin no get sick." She waved a hand at the needle and said a word in her own language. "Jahnin, pease."

Not for the first time Janlin marvelled at what Victor had taught his pupil, even the magic words of "please" and "thank you." Still . . .

"I feel fine. See, I'm not sick." She felt her forehead, stuck out her tongue, rubbed her tummy. "I'm good, really."

"No," Anaya said. "We not know it come in water or food or air . . . you get sick, you die." Yipho followed this with great interest, but no understanding in his eyes.

"You don't know what caused the illness?" Janlin said, fully worried now. "Then how do you know this will help?"

Anaya struggled for words. "Yipho good," she tried. "No hurt you. Pease."

Janlin thought it through. She was no fan of needles and would grill the med-bay staff every time they injected their crazy nano-bots. She just wouldn't blithely let people stick stuff in her bloodstream without knowing what the ingredients were.

Still, she had to trust Anaya, or she might as well jump out the nearest airlock and be done with it. Unless this was all some lovely dream—Janlin nearly laughed out loud at this thought. Some days it did feel like she'd fallen down a rabbit hole. She wondered where such an expression had come from, and in doing so didn't even know Yipho had approached until she looked up into his eyes. They were a deeper blue than Anaya's.

"Okay," she said, holding out her arm. Normally she would look away, but she watched Yipho with narrowed eyes.

"Ouch," she said in reflex. Yipho chuffed and went on his way, looking entirely too pleased with himself as far as Janlin was concerned.

Anaya studied the holo image Janlin had up. The planet

hung in the blackness of space, so reminiscent of her last view of Earth, except this marble had much more green, and a ton of water.

"Huantag looks like a wet place," Janlin commented.

"Good home," Anaya said. "Jahnin go soon."

"Tell me more about the Huantag," Janlin asked. "Why can't you live there and work with them to create a new home?"

"No Gitane, no Imag . . . go there anymore. Huantag use . . ." Here she floundered, and Janlin saw that it was due to more than a lack of words. Anaya's fists clenched. "They make us go."

"They barred you?"

"Yes." It came out like a growl, and Janlin shifted uncomfortably in the presence of such anger. Still, good to know about this bad blood between them. She needed to get a measure of what she'd be up against.

"Why do the Imag send humans there? And why do they trade with Huantag and you don't?"

"Imag no honour." Bluntly said, and Janlin was surprised that Anaya had learned such a word. She wished she had known Victor better.

"So, the Imag trade with the Huantag?" At the confirmation of this, Janlin asked the most worrisome question. "Do the Huantag use humans as slaves, then?"

"What this word, s-aaves?"

Janlin wondered how to rephrase it. "Are the Huantag good to humans, or bad like Imag?"

"Anaya no—not—know. No human ever go from Huantag."

Going in blind. Great. If the Huantag were trading or buying humans from the Imag, chances were good they weren't much different. Or they ate them for dinner. A sudden flashback to her day on Earth made her stomach churn, and she redirected her thoughts to the problem at hand. From what she had to go on, this didn't look good, and the plan still didn't clearly explain how she would get back off the planet.

"How do you know they are still alive?" She shivered at the mental images she couldn't shake.

Anaya shrugged, her way of saying "no", and pointed to Gitane writing around the holo. "Human okay," she said, and she put up ten digits, spread wide, then closed them and flashed them again, then several more times, Janlin carefully counting .

"One hundred and twelve humans on the planet," Janlin said, half to herself. "Wow. Are they spread all over? Can you tell that?"

"Here." Anaya pointed at an area in the northern hemisphere, on the largest continent. In this case, though, large was relative. This land mass couldn't be much bigger than Australia.

Janlin looked at Anaya, then at the display again. "Is that real, like looking through a window?" Anaya didn't understand this analogy, but Janlin had a good idea it was a real-time vid. It didn't have that haze of a holo, and she could see the movement of weather patterns. Fascinating technology, really.

"Anaya, you say you don't want a war with the Imag, but you're willing to steal the Jumpship from them. Won't that start a war?"

"Yes, so no war before."

Janlin sighed. "I still can't see why you can't try and save the humans while getting the ship."

Anaya's face puckered. "Too much. Getting 'ip too much . . . add humans too . . ." She let her words trail away, watching. Janlin had to admit she understood. Still, she wasn't about to let her friends and crewmates be left with the Imag.

"I think it would be worth trying. You will win them over with your ability to speak our language and a message from me."

Anaya looked sceptical.

"Your plan might not include this, but it's really important to me. I have friends there."

After a long silence, Anaya tried her nod again. "Okay, Jahnin. We try get humans too."

Janlin breathed a huge sigh of relief. "Thank you. You won't regret it."

Anaya went about her business and Janlin sat and watched the image again. This was all she had to go on, her only source of information on her destination.

What kinds of people were these Huantag? And the question of the day: what kind of people would forbid others from the only habitable planet in the system? She knew in her head she only had one side of the story, but her heart considered Anaya an ally and could see no reason for her to lie.

Janlin called to Anaya.

"When I find humans down there," she said, pointing at the image now floating above the desk, "how do we get back to you?"

Anaya gave her a long look, and Janlin really wished she could read her facial expressions better. It brought her back to the fact that she trusted a stranger in this, an alien stranger. Still, what choice did she have? She had to try for this way home, for Stepper's memory, and for Gordon and Ursula.

Anaya still didn't make a move or venture to speak, and Janlin began to wonder just what she was thinking. Everything up to this point seemed in good faith; why now did Janlin suddenly feel so . . . suspicious?

"I need to know this, Anaya. You want me to help you, to trust you . . . you have to trust me, too."

With a deep breath, Anaya went to a wall panel and removed a device that fit nicely in her grip. She handed it to Janlin. It wasn't such a perfect fit in a human's soft hands, but it was still portable, light and thin. Anaya held out her hand to take it back, and began fiddling with it. Janlin assumed she programmed it to fulfil some need. Was it a communication device?

Anaya brought it to her mouth and gurgled into it, and was quickly answered. Janlin heard the voice echo both from the device and from the control room. It gave her a thrill to know she had guessed right.

"How does it work? Can I call you?" Janlin asked as Anaya handed it back to her.

"Yes." She came around beside her and pointed first to a dial switch embedded on the side, then to a series of buttons on top. "You call when away from Huantag. Keep secret! Will work if 'ip not too far."

"So, while you're away getting the *Hope*, I can't reach you?" Anaya confirmed this. "But what if you want to call me, and I'm with some of these Huantag?"

Anaya gave one of her toothy grins and pressed a button. "This turn off. Keep power good."

"Okay. Perfect. So, you'll drop me off down there—"

Anaya shrugged a negative. "Gitane cannot go to Huantag. Imag cannot go. No people from Yiyau." She walked over to the door, engaged the shield, and indicated the door controls.

"Huantag have bigger," she said, spreading her arms wide and moving them as if around a large ball. "Stop Gitane and Imag. Gitane get 'ip, you turn this off, we come get humans."

Janlin took a wild guess. "They have shields, like these doors, that block you from going there?"

"Yes. You turn off shhhh—" It came out more like a spit, and she gave up with a frustrated twist of her lips. "Turn dis off, Anaya go, get you."

"So how am I getting down there?"

"Go there," Anaya said, and she zoomed in on an orbital space station sailing along over the ocean. "Find . . ." Here Anaya ran out of words again, so she tapped the board and brought up a smaller image to one side. It looked to be a crate of some kind, and she emphasized the need to choose one with a certain collection of markings.

"This one Huantag," she said. "That Imag. No go Imag."

Janlin couldn't agree more.

"Who owns the station?" Janlin asked. When Anaya was slow to reply, Janlin persisted. "Imag?" All she got was a hesitant pull of the mouth. "Huantag?"

Anaya huffed. "Imag and Huantag," she said, and it was an admission somehow.

"So how do I get on station?" And why was Anaya suddenly so evasive?

Anaya just stared at the holo images that floated before them. Janlin groaned.

"You don't know, do you?" Another shrug. Janlin studied the holos with her, thinking hard. "Can you show me the station closer, before it goes out of sight around the planet?"

Anaya complied, and the result was like riding a camera as it zoomed through space. Janlin blinked, a little dizzy from the effect.

"Look! Whose ship is that?"

"Imag," Anaya said without hesitation. Janlin remembered the Imag ship traveling the same way they were. No wonder they were hanging back.

"We followed them all the way without being noticed?"

Anaya chuffed. "No. Imag much faster. This new Imag 'ip. They have many. We see with tiny 'ip."

Janlin watched as the Imag docked with the station. "Why

can't you do that? Sneak in like you did with the big Imag ship."

"Huantag no trade with Gitane."

Janlin watched the view of the Imag ship as it curved around the station in its orbital pattern. Soon it would be out of their line of sight.

"Are we going to wait until it comes back around?"

"Yes," Anaya said. Despite only a few weeks spent together Janlin still knew that Anaya was holding something back. "Yes and no," she then added when she noticed Janlin's speculative look.

"What aren't you telling me?"

Anaya looked away. "Gitane 'ip go before—" and she indicated the station, using her own word for it, "—come back."

This ship . . . what? And just where was she in this equation? Janlin's heart thudded as she considered possibilities.

"Do you have a lander of some kind, a small ship to take me? I can fly it myself." That would be ideal.

"No," Anaya said with a shrug.

Too good to be true, that one. "Then what? How am I to get on station?" *And why won't the Huantag trade with you if they will with the Imag?* There was a lot more going on here than Janlin knew, and just knowing that made her uncomfortable. What else didn't she know that might be important?

"You go out. Wait for station."

Janlin stared, belatedly realizing her mouth hung open. "Out. As in space walk?"

Anaya didn't understand, but she gestured for Janlin to follow her. As they crossed the control room and headed into the airlock, every eye seemed to follow them. Janlin became more and more uncomfortable.

In the airlock there were multiple compartments of various sizes, all holding essential things for a space-faring vehicle. All along one wall were the largest of these, and they held what could only be EVA suits . . . of course.

"So, I'm supposed to just hang out in a space suit not designed for humans, waiting for a station to go sailing by, and somehow get to it and, what, ring the doorbell?"

Anaya didn't follow more than half of what she said, but there was no mistaking her tone of voice. "Yes. You go to Huantag, stop Huantag barring Gitane. Anaya go, get 'ip, come get humans. Not easy, but we must. Yes?"

Right. Put in that light, Janlin just might have the easier of the two jobs. Still . . .

"How long do I have? Oh, never mind, you can't answer that question in a way I can understand." Frustration mounted, but it gave her something to focus on instead of fear. "This one?" she said, pointing at the compartment Anaya had opened.

"Yes. Anaya's," she said, tapping her chest.

"Okay, show me how it works."

It took a long time to get Janlin suited up, and still she wondered if she really knew how to run the damned thing, especially the jet pack that was to propel her in the right direction. Through it all she kept wondering how much time she had before the station came around. She'd never paid any attention to things like that, and it wouldn't really matter what she knew if this planet was larger or smaller, or if the station moved slower or faster than the ones on Earth . . .

She stopped her train of thought with a huge mental effort. It did her no good to keep thinking in that vein. Anaya knew, and she would make sure she was on her way in good time.

Right?

CHAPTER TWENTY-THREE

THE LOCK SHIFTED and whirred, loud enough she could hear it through the suit and the roaring of her blood. Beyond, the landscape of a strange world spun below, filling her vision, giving her the sensation of being about to jump . . . and fall.

"Jahnin, go," came Anaya's voice in her ear.

Janlin's grip on the safety rungs either side of her did not loosen. Her fingers were swimming in the gloves of the suit, but the material was flexible enough that she could still hold on, and hold she did.

"Jahnin, go now."

She had to go out there. Her dad might still be down there, still alive. She imagined seeing him, getting a big hug, laughing about it all.

The station was a tiny dot in the distance, and timing was crucial. She could see the planet's surface beyond, filling the frame, revealing plenty of places for her to go splat.

"Jahnin, pease go." Anaya's voice sounded desperate.

She closed her eyes and focused on the muscles of her left hand. One by one she let the fingers loosen until only the index finger and thumb looped the handle. Then she turned her attention on the right hand.

"Jahnin!"

"Okay, okay, I'm going," she muttered. She opened her eyes but kept her gaze on the floor in front of her feet, and let go. One step. Two. All too soon she was out of floor. Before she could freeze up again, she launched her body into the emptiness before her.

"Good," Anaya said, and Janlin found her calm voice chuffing in her ear reassuring. "Jahnin—"

"I will remember, Anaya. You get out of here before you get yourself in trouble. Without you, there is no hope for us at all."

A long silence followed this remark . . . too long. "Tank you, Jahnin."

Janlin wondered at the tinge of sadness she thought she heard. Probably another misunderstanding between races, she decided, and turned her attention on her task. A little experimental jab at one button began a lazy spiral, and despite a little jab of the other she found herself looking at Anaya's ship. It looked just like any spaceship should.

For all our differences . . .

The thought had come so many times. How many lives went on in the cosmos? It must be a number beyond comprehension.

It was startling how far away the ship was already, but little jets fired and she realized that they were nudging the ship away gently. Janlin took a deep breath and nudged her own jets to life, turning her back on her ally and newest friend.

She forced her gaze past the beauty of the landscape swirling by and scanned for the station. Everything moved in slow motion, except for the station, which loomed closer on a trajectory that would—should—sail right past her. How would she do this? Panic threatened to consume all rational thought. She gasped for breath, sure now the settings weren't right for a human, or that there was some problem with the suit.

Dots danced in her vision.

Hyperventilating, that's what she was doing. She closed her eyes despite all her senses screaming at her not to, and took deep breaths in through her nose, one after another, until her heart rate slowed. When she opened her eyes, the station loomed closer than ever, large enough now that she could make out details of the ship docked at the centre of the rotating ring. The Imag ship was much larger than Anaya's.

If she could make her own trajectory match the station, she would line up nicely alongside. She would need to fire the jets just right. She understood Anaya's halting explanations now.

She wasn't shooting straight for the station, but heading for where it was going to be once she was in the same vicinity.

Still, things were moving too fast. Had she waited a moment too long to launch out the airlock? That would be fatal, if she had. She should be able to compensate, though. Anaya had told her she had more than enough power in the jets, and plenty of air for a chase if necessary. Or something to that effect.

Could she wait for another pass of the station? Did she have that much air? It seemed to Janlin to take a couple of hours for an orbit, give or take.

Questions, questions, always with the questions. She tweaked the jets, settling on her course, sure that she had enough momentum if she could simply control her trajectory.

She just might make it. Her breath came short again.

Looking for a distraction, she studied the planet's surface. On the islands dotting the ocean she could make out mountain ranges, river basins, and open range. The strangest part was the green marble look, as opposed to Earth's blue.

The station passed before her and on. Adrenaline surged, and her fingers fumbled over the controls of the jets. She would have to fire hard and long to catch it now, and she only hoped there was enough fuel to get her there.

Now she came in on the station from behind, along the edge of the ring. The place was huge! Closer and closer. The jets cut out.

"No!" Janlin cried, but a second later she realized if they fired much longer, she might end up like a bug on a windshield.

She stretched out her arms, palms out, scanning the ring for some way in. There were windows, here and there, occasionally a large one, but she saw no movement. What would an alien think if they looked out now?

All she saw was smooth metal, and no openings. The ring spun, turning on by her, but still the windows remained empty. She squeezed the trigger for the other, smaller jets, the ones that should be for slowing her down. Just a spurt, then another when she was sure they wouldn't change her course.

Ah. The ring was a moving target, and would never be a place for airlocks. She sailed along the bottom edge, feeling like a deep-sea diver under the hull of a huge ocean liner, and continued on towards the central post. All along it were openings of all kinds, big and small, and obvious docking stations, communication arrays, airlock bays . . . and very few windows.

Now it was up to her to get inside without pasting herself on the side of the hull.

"Red light each side, dark within," Janlin repeated. The sound of her own voice reassured her, and she aimed for just that set-up that seemed the closest to her existing direction.

After a few tense moments of adjustments, over-adjustments, and sheer terror, Janlin sailed into an open bay and knocked up against an interior wall. Magnets in the palms of the suit allowed her to stay put, then drag along the wall until she found another, smaller, room. The symbols Anaya had taught her were on the wall within, and she sighed with relief as the small door closed and the whoosh of air filling the room replaced the terrifying silence of open space.

Janlin scrambled out of Anaya's suit while the airlock cycled and the door into the station opened. Her hands trembled, and her legs shook so bad that she would not have been able to walk. Fortunately, here in the docking tunnel, walking wasn't required, and she gripped the doorjamb with gratitude for its solidness as she drifted in zero-g.

She did, however, resist the strong desire to drift down to the floor of the bay and kiss the metal.

She gripped the frame of the opening and peered into the tunnel. A clang came from one end, and she flinched, but she'd seen no one within the long stretch of floorless shaft. She oriented herself so that she could propel her body in the direction of the noise, and set off.

If someone came along now, there would be no hiding, because the doors she passed would probably all be open to space on the other side. It made sense—why maintain atmosphere if you didn't have to?

She just needed to find where they sorted and stored the crates for trading goods, and get stowed away for a ride to the planet.

Another clang rang out, followed by a blast of sound like an air horn. The hatchway at the end of the tunnel opened, and a disk of metal began to shoot towards her, round, and exactly the size of the shaft, filling it and leaving no gaps against the walls.

A lift of some kind, able to take people or crates from the docked ship to the central hub.

"Oh, crap."

She was on the wrong side of this one, like being caught in the elevator shaft outside of the moving elevator.

Janlin kicked out, hoping to connect with something, anything, and arched towards the side of the shaft. A glance revealed that the lift approached at amazing speed. She couldn't be sure she'd survive the impact, let alone stay conscious. Closer it came as she pulled herself along the wall, gripping with nothing but the flat of her hands at times, digging her nails into any little crevice she could find to keep close to the wall. Closer. She slipped, losing her grip, and tried to swim through the air, her heart yammering in her ears. Another glance. Her momentum in the free fall kept her going in the right direction, and the moment she touched the wall she used the slight ledge between wall panels to again propel herself. Closer. With a little gasp she reached the hatchway she'd come through and hit the command to open it. Closer. Things whirred and clicked within the door.

"Come on, you bastard, open!" Janlin said, banging the door.

The lift descended, now fifteen feet from her, now ten, now—

The hatch opened, and she swung in, flailing through the abandoned space suit still floating in the bay. She kicked one glove and it sailed out the opening only to be swept away a second later by the thick steel plate that made up the lift.

Panting, Janlin hung by one hand from the doorframe, afraid to stick her head out and have a look. Still, in the brief second that the lift passed she thought she'd seen a crate strapped to it.

How long would it take for them to offload the Imag shipment and load it on the shuttle headed for the planet? Could she possibly get on the lift when it returned?

She took the chance, hoping the alarm would sound again when the lift was ready to go. It only made sense that it would. Anything protruding out a hatchway would clearly be in the impact zone when the lift went by.

Janlin looked down the shaft just in time to watch arms in all too familiar uniforms reach out and unhook the crate before drawing it into the bay. She would only have moments to get on that lift before it accelerated, but she needed to be sure the Imag didn't see her. She inched out of the hatchway and began the drop, propelling herself to the other side of the shaft to try and stay out of the line of sight.

The shaft was about ten feet across, and she reached the other side easily, still dropping.

She sucked in a breath when another crate appeared and was loaded onto the lift. The markings on the top were just the ones she wanted to see.

But she was dropping too fast. If she landed on that lift while it still sat at the Imag's open hatch, they'd see her and raise an alarm. Her fingers scrambled at the smooth sides once again, dragging but not gripping, and she slipped away from the edge again.

The lift seemed to rise to meet her, but she knew it was purely illusion. Then the air horn sounded, and despite her flinch at the loud and abrupt noise, she thought it was the best thing she'd ever heard.

The lift began to rise, clearing the open hatchway, and a moment later she landed lightly on it. The motion created a gravity of its own that kept her glued to the surface.

Now she needed to get inside somehow before reaching the central hub.

Right.

Her fingers and eyes explored the crate for the latches. She found them, but she wouldn't be able to lift the lid without undoing the straps that held the crate in place. The walls seemed to blur by, and she noted the door to her own entry point pass like a blip on a radar screen.

Somewhere in a faraway part of her mind, hysterical screaming began. She struggled with the straps, wondering if Huantag soldiers waited on the other side of the approaching hatchway. What would they do when they found her?

She unbuckled one side of the crate and began working on the other, ignoring the questions, ignoring the screaming, ignoring the walls zooming past as the g-force made it harder and harder to move around on the lift. Another buckle let go, scraping at her knuckles as it did. She sucked on them as she worked the next one, hissing through her teeth as she abraded the other hand even worse.

The lift began to slow. Two buckles left. Undoing one more

might enable her to jimmy the lid enough to climb inside. Even then, would they check the cargo if they saw all the straps hanging loose?

She managed the third buckle, scrambling to shove the straps to one side like an over-eager kid unwilling to wait for scissors to get the ribbon off her Christmas present.

The hatchway opened above her head.

A good thing, right? Wouldn't want to be crushed between the door and the lift, right?

The straps were too tight, and she grappled with the cinching system but couldn't seem to find the right co-ordination of events to let off the tension.

She was out of time.

As the lift rose through the hatchway she spun around and set her back to the crate, crouching low and trying to be as small and still and unobvious as possible.

The lift stopped, and the hatch closed below it. Janlin felt the push of force drain away and gripped the straps to keep in place. The area was, like she guessed, a central hub; a round room with hatchways leading to the outer ring and, above and below her, to the docking shafts. Currently there were no signs of life within her line of sight, but that could and probably would change very soon.

She had to get into the crate.

Then she heard voices. Human voices.

Maintaining her grip on the straps, she shifted and peeked around the side of the crate. Another hatchway leading to the outer ring stood open, and she was just in time to watch the hatch close. She choked back a shout.

Janlin sank down, and, with an effort, brought her mind back to the problem at hand. She would find her crew later. Again, she attacked the cinch device on the strap she clung to. There had to be a way to loosen it just enough to get the lid—

An inquisitive chirp sounded behind her.

Janlin turned slowly despite the fight or flee instinct stiffening her body. Drifting . . . no, *flying* beside the crate was a strange and beautiful creature. Intelligent eyes regarded her— peaceful, calm eyes, she noted—above an obvious beak protrusion, while huge wings shifted to maintain position in the free-fall environment. Feathers adorned the creature's head, and under the wing, shoulder joint arms sprouted, ending in six fingers covered in pale skin.

Huantag were *birds*?

Janlin decided that nothing—*nothing*—would ever surprise her again.

CHAPTER TWENTY-FOUR

THE STRANGE NEW alien gestured for her to follow. Not seeing any other good options, she did, especially when the bird-like creature headed for the same passageway she'd seen the others disappear into. Janlin did a light-grav bounce down the corridor while the stunning creature glided alongside. As they descended, the gravity increased, though it didn't seem to affect the alien's ability to maintain its graceful flight. When it did land, the wings folded neatly along the shoulder and back of the arm, allowing it to walk upright and manipulate things with its arms and hands. The creature didn't seem to be wearing clothes. The resplendent feathers were all it needed for modesty, if they had that sort of thing.

At what appeared to be an open door, the alien tapped at the console to shut down the shielding and ushered her in. Janlin found herself engulfed in the embrace of Tyrell.

"Kavanagh! When you and Stepper didn't come back from your work shift, we thought you were dead!"

Tyrell beamed at her, and she stared in wonder at the once naïve and soft-skinned young man. He'd done some growing up on that slaver, and it wasn't just the facial hair. His welcome smile had a new wariness to it, an irrevocable loss of innocence.

She scanned the room, seeing many familiar faces but not the ones she'd hoped for. The winged creatures moved amongst them, tending to injuries and questions and handing out water packs. She'd have to keep quiet about her adventure for now. Who knew what these aliens could understand? "Where's Gordon?"

"He didn't get shipped with us," he said, and gave her shoulder a squeeze in reassurance. "Things have been weird. The Imag seem to be preparing for something big. At least that's what Fran said."

Janlin made a face at his mention of Fran.

Tyrell leaned in closer. "I'm worried their plans are not going to be ones we like," he muttered.

"What do you mean?"

"We've all had some weird tests done, blood work and injections. That medic with the scarred face fought them tooth and nail, but they stuck her too. Worse, Gordon's worried the Imag are nearly ready to test their Jumpship."

Janlin groaned inwardly. "It seems like a lot of us here. How many are left with the Imag?"

Tyrell grinned, taking her by surprise. "About the same number as you see here. They seemed to split us in half." He shrugged it off. "At first I was terrified, 'cause who knew what they were gonna do with us, right? But then we got here and we were shown holo-vids of a human settlement that's planet-side. I can't wait to get down there!"

Janlin's heart skipped. "Did you see any faces you recognize?"

Tyrell shook his head. "It was more of an aerial view."

"How long do you figure it took to fly here?" Janlin asked then.

Tyrell gave her a jaunty grin. "You were a flippin' stowaway, weren't you? It was only a few days, but it must've felt like more to you. You're crazy, girl!"

She'd been with the Gitane for weeks. Anaya did say the Imag ships were much faster. More proof of her honesty. Janlin just needed to decide not only who to tell about her new alliance, but when. Then she would go to work on a plan, and hopefully they could get everything in place to take down the shields quickly when Anaya returned. Janlin checked her pocket, hoping these Huantag wouldn't search them.

Tyrell frowned in thought. "Where's the captain?"

Janlin's face must've said it all, because Tyrell's bronze

cheeks went ashen. Janlin reached over and gave him a little shake. "This doesn't need to be public knowledge just yet, okay?" He nodded, eyeing those around them who celebrated their new freedom from the Imag.

Janlin stared at the tall alien approaching them. "I can't believe the Huantag would take so many of us at once."

"The who?" Tyrell asked.

Janlin's heart thumped once, too hard, and she gave him the best look of confusion she could muster. "Imag," she said. "I can't believe the Imag would take away so many at once."

"That's not what you said."

"Sure it is . . . what else would I say?"

Weak, but what else could she do? She was still so shook up—she had to get it together. Gordon would never let her get away with such a lapse. Later, when she had a chance to assess the situation, she could reassure everyone with Anaya's rescue plans.

Tyrell scratched his head, but didn't pursue it. Janlin silently thanked her luck.

The Huantag handed them drink containers and chirped an inquiry, holding up what Janlin deduced was a first-aid kit. She and Tyrell both waved off his request, and the alien moved on.

"Aren't the Birdfolk amazing? Do you think they've ever been to Earth before, and that's maybe where we got the idea of angels? I mean, it would make so much sense if ancient civilizations saw these beings and imagined them the agents of God, right?"

Tyrell went on, and Janlin let him, until she heard more voices coming down the hall, voices all talking, questioning, worried, scared. She gripped Tyrell's arm, shushing him. As the new group entered, she saw Gordon's tall figure.

"Janlin!"

"My God, you grew hair!" In fact, he looked more himself than he had in over a year. Despite the harsh conditions on the Imag ship, regular food and hard physical labour had only brought back the hulk of a man that was Gordon. Not until this forced absence did the changes hit home.

She let him wrap her in a huge bear hug. "I knew you'd make it somehow," he said, and hugged her again before releasing her to arm's length. "Where's Stepper?"

Guilt returned to crush her. There was no easy way to do this, and no better time than now, she guessed. "Dead." She said it quietly, under the commotion of reunions around them. "Why are you all here? What's going on?"

Gordon frowned. He recognized an evasion, but he let it lie, at least for now.

"We're not sure what the deal is," he said. "They just loaded up the last of us and brought us here."

Others were enjoying their own reunions and greetings, but many gathered close. With the Huantag in the room, she could not to tell of her own adventures just yet. Besides, what if Anaya didn't make it back? Why raise hopes for nothing? She'd bide her time, check out the scene planet-side, and let Gordon in on everything—later, in private.

"Yeah, Janlin wasn't even in our group," Tyrell said. "She was a stowaway!"

"What, planning to hijack the ship?" Gordon said, shaking his head at her. "You really do think you can fly anything, don't you?"

"I had to try something," she said, shrugging. "Didn't work out, though. What do you make of these bird aliens?"

Everyone responded to this, turning the conversation away from her before Gordon could ask about where she'd been all this time. Some echoed Tyrell's vision of angels while others, especially the science types, were fascinated with the unique physiology, especially compared to the first aliens they encountered in this system.

"Dinosaurs are the ancestors of birds," one man said. "Perhaps on this planet they become the dominant species and evolved into this form."

Many others chimed in with their own theories.

"They seem benevolent enough," was Gordon's comment. Janlin let some tension unravel through her.

"I am so glad to see you," she said, leaning on him.

"Blimey, girl, you've had me worried, you and Stepper both."

"I can't believe Stepper's gone, for all the trouble between us."

Gordon wrapped an arm around her and squeezed. "I knew I gave you the right call sign," he said, his mischievous smile tinged with sadness. "Bouncer: always bouncing back from anything."

Janlin could only shake her head in chagrin. She pulled Gordon close and lowered her voice. "What are the chances of these new aliens helping us?"

Gordon grimaced. "Well, there's the language barrier to get past," he said.

This brought something to Janlin's attention. "Where's Fran?" she asked.

Gordon looked away. Tyrell heard her question, though.

"She wasn't sent with us. Some say she wanted to stay, that she's defected from the human race and feels more at home with the Imag."

"Tyrell!" Gordon glared at him.

"What? She can be a real—"

"Yeah, I get it," Janlin said. "Been on the receiving end of that. But I can't see her choosing to stay with them. Not after—" She couldn't voice it, the memories of torture still too close, but they all knew what she meant.

"Yeah, you insensitive dimwit," Gordon said to Tyrell. "Don't be so eager to judge others without really knowing what they've been up against."

Tyrell had the decency to look abashed. "Sorry, Spin. Just never really saw the good side of Fran Delou."

The aliens began gesturing at seats and helping with straps. They walked with astounding elegance, wings folded to their backs. They had a strange curvature to their spines, beak-like protrusions for faces, and downy feathers of various shades. Janlin couldn't help but reach out to touch one of them as they passed, connecting with a smooth bit of arm, cool and silky, like a dolphin she had touched in a zoo once. The creature turned at her touch before she could try a feathered wing, gently guiding her into a seat and adjusting the straps.

The rest of the group seemed awed. The room fell quiet, and the aliens moved around with agile grace. They were everything the Imag were not. Janlin watched them and wondered at Anaya's animosity. She'd expected something unlikable and had hoped to avoid them at all costs. Now she felt privileged to have touched one.

The floor shuddered, and the ship rang with a clank. The aliens left, closing the hatch, and the room's atmosphere changed to one of fear.

"Rudi might be down there," Gordon said.

Janlin's eyes welled up. "I hope so." She already knew there were surviving humans down there, but how many of the *Renegade's* crew made it?

"You keep hoping, babe." Gordon winked. "Life's gonna get better than what we've had of late."

"These . . . Birdfolk," she said, almost calling them Huantag again. "They seem so peaceful."

Gordon opened his mouth to reply, but conversation became impossible as re-entry began, and Janlin squeezed her eyes shut.

CHAPTER TWENTY-FIVE

SUNLIGHT BATHED HER skin in warmth, shining from a pale green sky laced with wispy clouds. A breeze tousled her hair, making her lift her chin and close her eyes to relish it. Others crowded out onto the hard-packed dirt, so she opened her eyes and stepped forward, inhaling again and again the aromas of earth and wind and growing things. She scanned, relieved at the open spaces and lack of guards and weapons. Had she died and gone to heaven? Certainly, the sight of winged aliens gliding overhead nurtured the idea.

They all had different reactions. Gordon's mouth hung open as he turned slowly to take it all in. Tyrell whooped and danced in celebration. Jari Lovell knelt on the ground and kissed the earth. He wasn't the only one.

Janlin cried tears of joy at the viable planet, grief that Stepper would never see it, and a restless hope that her father was waiting for her here.

The aliens moved among them, handing out woven hats and containers of water. Janlin accepted her gifts, grateful that someone thought of such necessities in the heat of the day.

They stood on a high plateau stretching north and west to meet the rugged mountain range that dominated the skyline. Further southwest, a misty horizon suggested coastline and ocean, and to the direct south, the land opened to the horizon in rolling grasslands.

This scrub plain held little plant life, however, and the shuttle's scorching blast at landing seemed to do no harm to the landscape. A turn to look east revealed distant cliffs that seemed to be terraced. She shaded her eyes to peer closer. Was that . . . movement?

A cry went up, and Janlin echoed it. Figures ran from the cliff-side village, human figures: wingless and stuck to the ground and oh, so beautiful.

The light gravity made it easy to run, and Janlin laughed like a child at the long strides and bouncing leaps she could take. The grasses were more prominent here, accented by clumps of thorny bushes of the deepest maroon. She vaulted each one effortlessly, others following her lead. It was still too far to make out individuals, but she exchanged a look of hope and joy with Gordon as he matched her pace.

More and more people emerged into the scrub field from the group of buildings in the distance. The settlement was made from squat buildings the same colour as the dirt, a fine, soft tan that verged on sand. The huts were unlike anything she'd ever seen, rounded and smooth, seeming to grow organically from the very earth itself.

The first face Janlin recognized was the young woman with the teardrop scar. She ran headlong towards them with a look of consternation.

"Why didn't they tell us you were coming?" she demanded before she even reached them. She scanned Janlin, then Gordon, then the group as a whole. "Are any of you in need of medical care?" she asked, clearly bewildered that they seemed whole and hale.

"We're great," Gordon said. "We worried about you, though. They pulled you without any reason at all, and now we find you here, living the high life."

People were meeting all around them with hugs and shouts of joy amongst the waving sea of grass and the heat of real sunshine. Janlin saw three scientists, Jari one of them, exchanging excited greetings with hand pumping and much slapping of backs.

Those that met them wore hats, too, and little else. Ship wear was "modified" for the new circumstances—torn off sleeves, shortened pants, open collars.

The medic grinned. "This place is fantastic," she said, nodding in recognition at Janlin. "But usually the Imag trade the injured. You will practically double our numbers here."

"Seems they're done with us," Gordon said. "Shipped us all off except for Fran."

Janlin stood on tiptoe, leaning this way and that to scan faces while Gordon and the woman chatted. Tyrell, heads together with two pilots from the *Renegade*, turned and saw them and waved with a smile. She waved back. Many faces were familiar, but she didn't see the one she searched for. Her heart thudded from more than just the run, and she licked dry lips to try and speak.

"Come along, then," called the medic, raising her voice. "We'll have some serious building to do, and some creative cooking to finagle dinner for everyone tonight."

"Wait," Janlin called to her. "Is there a man here named Rudigar? Or Rudi?"

The young medic hesitated, and Janlin felt her gut clench.

"There's a small gravesite on the hill—"

Without knowing how, Janlin found herself on her knees. Her chest heaved and heaved. People knelt by her. She knew Gordon's voice, attempting to console, and soft hands squeezed her own.

"Come, let's get you out of the sun."

Words, sounds, heat, tears. *Don't cry*, she told herself. *Not yet. Not sure yet, right?* None of it made sense. Janlin felt all her hopes spiralling away into a dark void, and she gave herself to it.

CHAPTER TWENTY-SIX

"... JUST TIRED. I think she stowed away ... no food or drink ..."

Janlin phased in and out, listening to the low rumble of Gordon's voice in counterpoint to the medic's soft one. She really needed to ask for her name. She couldn't just keep calling her Teardrop, even if it suited her.

And then consciousness brought home the painful knowledge once again.

She wished now she was dead and gone and unknowing. What was her father's death in the grand scheme? Nothing, except to her. Her muscles were leaden, and she kept her eyes closed, faking sleep. There was still some hope that he was alive, and if she didn't rise, that hope couldn't be taken away. Yet, in her heart of hearts, she knew. Teardrop would know him, or of him. That's just the kind of guy Rudigar Kavanagh was.

"Just give her some time to rest," said the woman. Teardrop. Without meaning to, Janlin opened her eyes. She lay on a low cot, a rounded ceiling of beams and packed mud bricks over her. It was cool despite the heat outside. Other cots were set around the walls, each one empty, and a table and chair sat in the middle. Various shelving units held bowls, folded linen, and medical tools.

Janlin sat up. The voices had moved away, and for that she was glad. She certainly didn't have a monopoly on grief, but she didn't feel ready to face anyone just yet. Even as she wallowed in her heartache, it wasn't until her pain at losing Stepper surfaced that she really broke down.

Guilty over that and so many other things, Janlin dropped her head in her hands. She had selfishly let Ursula convince her that Gordon should go on this doomed mission. She had nearly killed Candice and Weston through sheer negligence. She had released Stepper from the horror of slavery and torture right before hope arrived. And now her father might lie buried six feet under on an alien hillside. Dismay overwhelmed her, but she fought off the temptation to stay on the cot.

She longed for an escape, and her gaze fell on the table that held strange-looking surgical equipment. There were scissors, knifes, clamps . . . although all shaped differently than what she'd seen before.

She lifted a knife, letting the light from outside glint off the sharp surface. She had contemplated it before. Was this her way out?

Gordon would be heartbroken, she realized. And what of Anaya? Janlin took the device from her pocket, amazed that she'd almost forgotten.

In one hand, a knife. A way out, to not care or hurt anymore. Oblivion.

In the other, a connection. Possibly a way home. Gordon still had Ursula waiting for him. How could she not struggle on for his sake?

She set the knife on the table. It could never really be an option, she knew, yet it was surprising how tempting it was. She understood her willingness to let Stepper go, in that way, understood his desire to go, and finally made some peace with it.

So many good people lost. She straightened up, slid Anaya's comm-unit into her pocket, and decided to go find the gravesite.

Janlin stepped into heat and brightness and wind. Squinting, she stared at her surroundings. So amazing to breathe the air without fear. Amazing to see the clear sky, even if it did seem more green than blue. Anaya said these Huantag brought this world back from the brink of ecological destruction. Maybe there was something to learn from these Birdfolk.

Clusters of the rounded buildings—no, shelters, Janlin realized, and temporary ones at that—were nestled under the cliffs. As she registered the huts and dirt trails, she wondered why these advanced beings housed their guests in such primitive ways. Would they be subservient here, too?

The land sloped gently away from where she stood, revealing terraces full of the adobe-style huts. Trees of brilliant green and purplish bark offered the occasional patch of shade. Over a low wall down in the valley she realized some of her old crew bent to till soil and tend plants growing there. A garden? Janlin longed for Ursula to see this place and revel in its botany. It only darkened her mood to think this way, and she held dear to her plan to get them all home again, even if it meant leaving such a utopia.

She wandered now, lost in the surreal surroundings. She imagined her dad living here. Did he garden, and draw water from that well? Janlin leaned against a wall in the shade so she could watch her own kind living as if thrown backwards in time.

Except—there were no children. Without a way to reverse SpaceOp's nano-contraceptive, there would never be any.

Janlin shook her head. Having children here wasn't part of the plan. She would not give up on going home. This place only proved they could find other planets. Once home again, they could go looking elsewhere, preferably for uninhabited planets without different races battling over possession rights.

She straightened, noticing a quiet path above the quaint village. She had to face reality so she could move forward and look beyond just surviving this adventure to find better solutions for those back home.

If Anaya played her part, it would all work out. She'd get Gordon home to Ursula. To think, she'd have done and seen none of this if Stepper hadn't—

Rounding a bend, she collided with someone coming the other way along the narrow footpath between the squat buildings. Janlin looked up into familiar brown eyes and her heartbeat faltered . . . before starting again double time to rush against her ribcage.

"Stepper," she whispered.

It seemed that everything she learned, everything she believed, every promise she'd made to herself, she forgot when she saw his face.

"Janlin?" He broke into a wide grin and took her into a tight hug, her arms squished against her sides. Then, before her breath returned, he quickly stepped back. He looked sideways at her, as if daring her to scold him for his intimacy.

"But," she floundered, wanting his arms back around her as much as she wanted to smack him for having the audacity to be alive. "Dammit, you died! I—I released the tourniquet."

"You did?" Stepper's eyebrows knitted with this announcement.

"How . . . ?"

He lifted his arm, and above his elbow ran a network of angry red scars. "The Imag brought me here under the care of *Renegade's* medic, and the Birdfolk rendered their magic on me. They did a great job, put me right back together," he said. His eyes were wide, his emotions naked to her. "Did you really let me go?"

"You asked me to!" Conflicting emotions roiled through her, but outside she just stared, numb, at the man she'd let die, the man who broke her heart, now here and impossibly alive.

"I'm glad to see you safe," he whispered. "I thought you were the one dead. I worried that you'd suffer for my stupidity."

Janlin studied him, his bare shoulders tanned darker than ever, and his eyes twinkling when he grinned at her. "Isn't it great here?" he said, waving a hand to indicate the surrounding village.

Janlin swallowed. She didn't know what to say, and so said nothing, simply staring at him as if he were truly a ghost. Then he stole any hope she might have had left.

"I am so sorry about Rudigar."

Janlin pushed past him, determined to see for herself, fleeing from the turmoil inside.

"Hey!"

She slowed, looking back. "What?"

"Didn't you just arrive with the latest group?"

Janlin didn't understand, didn't want to talk to him anymore. "Yeah, so?"

"You're clean." His confusion was accusatory.

Janlin swallowed. "Yeah. I've got a story to tell regarding that. Later. After I see his grave for myself."

Something passed over his face. "Of course. Just keep going, stay to the right . . . it's beneath that outcropping over there."

She glanced the way he pointed, and when she turned back, he was walking away.

Janlin watched until he turned out of sight. With some effort she put one foot forward, then the other, until she found a path leading away from the settlement and right to the overhang Stepper had pointed out.

The sun dropped low in the sky now, blazing and huge on the horizon. The hike left her winded and sweaty—yet calm. At least one hole in her heart was filled. Even if the man drove her crazy, a weight lifted knowing he was okay.

The little gravesite stood bathed in reddish light, the upright stones throwing long shadows onto the dry ground, shadows taller than the men and women they remembered. Seven names stood out in stark relief. Rudigar's was the third one in. A marker bore rough words chipped into the stone.

"Helmsman, Renegade. A fine man and good friend. Rudigar Kavanagh."

Janlin knelt, pain coming from both her grief and her guilt. She turned and sat beside the stone, facing the setting sun.

"I wish you'd told me," she said. "I can't believe you'd go on some crazy mission like this under Stepper's command. I bet you always knew I still loved him, even if I couldn't admit it to myself."

She brushed at the dirt, smoothing the sand and picking at small rocks. The sun dimmed and finally winked out beyond the horizon. Little creatures ran to and fro, some with fur, some with scales . . . one with both. Shapes rose and circled in the distance, and she could just make out colourful sparkling lights on towering buildings to the southwest.

Still she sat, until finally Gordon came. At first, he stood to one side, paying his own respects. Then he reached out his hand for her, pulled her up, and led her away.

CHAPTER TWENTY-SEVEN

JANLIN'S EMOTIONS BECAME suspended in the crisp evening air. She relished the light gravity lifting the body aches away, if not those of the heart. At least now she could let her father go with forgiveness and peace. He hadn't abandoned her, but had pursued an adventure in hopes of returning a hero. Her hero.

Dusk settled slow on this land, building shadows and stretching them out to fill in all the highest places. Little creatures made the grass rustle, and the breeze wove through odd-shaped leaves.

Gordon and Janlin walked together in silence, neither able to offer consolation to the other. The sounds of the gathered group grew closer, and the strange Huantag glowlights illuminated the growing dark.

"Why did you think Stepper was dead?"

Janlin glanced at Gordon, then away. "Long story," she finally said.

He slowed. "Tell me the condensed version."

She didn't want to tell him. "We should hold a memorial for my dad."

He nodded in agreement, but said, "Don't change the subject."

Janlin swallowed. "He got injured, was bleeding to death. You see the scars?" Another nod. Suddenly she was there, kneeing in the bloody pool again, her ears berated by the pounding screech of the machines around them. She tasted despair. "He asked me to set him free. I released the tourniquet. I watched him bleed."

She lifted her head, confronted her friend, challenging him to hate her now so she could feel justified to run far away until lost in this wide-open land. She saw the questions growing there in Gordon's face, but they'd reached the edge of an open area lit by larger lights and filled with people. Food crowded the tables against one wall. Celebration filled the air. Janlin looked away from his questioning and faltered, reluctant to move into the brightness. She didn't belong here, not right now.

"Wait here," Gordon said, leaving her in shadow as he moved towards the food. Janlin appreciated what he was trying to do and sank down onto a bench set against a low wall. From there she could watch without being noticed. Most faces were familiar. To one side Ron, an engineer, spoke with a tall lady she didn't know. Over at the cooking station were two young programmers she knew to be nicknamed Huey and Duey, though she was sure those weren't their actual names. They laughed and raised drinks in a toast with Tyrell.

Amazing how many of them survived such an ordeal. And now they all stood on a strange planet so far from home. There'd been over three hundred people in each crew, and what was left? Half that?

Gordon arrived at her side and passed her a plate loaded with cooked and raw foods unlike anything she'd seen. He sat beside her, lifting a blue tube and examining it before tearing off a bite. Janlin set her own supper beside her on the bench, uninterested.

"You look good with hair," Janlin said. She didn't watch him, though, but stared off into the distance. The emptiness where Ursula should be was too obvious.

Gordon chewed and swallowed. "Thanks. You should at least try some water. It won't make up for everything we've been through, but it is amazing."

Janlin accepted the bowl from him and raised it to her lips. Cool water, pure, clean, and tinged with some hint of sweetness, sent refreshing chills down into her middle.

"It is nice."

At that moment shapes appeared out of the darkness and

swooped in to land around the common area. Graceful beings strode into the light, chirping and whistling their greetings. People of *Renegade's* crew rose and waved to them, calling them over into a hut across from the cooking area.

"What's going on?" Janlin asked.

Gordon shook his head. "Not sure, although I did hear that someone sussed out a way to program a translator of some kind." He sounded peeved.

Janlin snorted. "You can't be serious."

"No, it's real," said Gordon in a grim voice. "I'm worried everyone's getting a little too comfortable."

Janlin felt comforted by his morbid emotions. Everyone else seemed so in awe of the Huantag that moved among the group. At least she wasn't alone in her mistrust of the angelic aliens. Still, it made her wonder about Anaya's bitterness. Every story had two sides, and as much as she trusted Anaya, she wanted to know what the Gitane had done to deserve banishment by these kind and gentle creatures.

A crowd gathered around the doorway where they'd taken the Huantag. A sudden cheer brought heads about, and everyone began to line up.

"What the bloody hell . . . ?"

Gordon rose and Janlin joined him, her curiosity overcoming her grief. The medic woman emerged from the hut and immediately began questioning one of the aliens with grave intensity.

Tyrell emerged a few minutes later, somehow managing to be only second in line. He caught sight of Janlin and Gordon and came at them, beaming.

"It's amazing! I can understand them!" He gestured at the aliens. "It really works!"

"What is going on?"

"Turns out Steve Netchkie was one of the first four brought here." Tyrell gave them a meaningful look. They stared back. "You know, the programmer who discovered how to use the NECs to fold space?"

"Oh," Janlin said. Had she even met the guy before?

"Anyway, he's been working with the Birdfolk to record all the sounds they make and compare it with our own words for things. Then he programmed some kind of translation software out of it. Stunning, really, especially since he designed it to upload to our own nanites. No gear required!"

Gordon gave an appreciative whistle. "Genius."

"What about the aliens? How will it work for them?"

"I don't know the particulars, but it's an upload to their own communication devices. You know, we're more alike than I would've ever imagined. Come on, get in line! Once we all have the upload, they say they have an announcement for us."

"I'll just bet they do," Janlin said. All this time humans had lived here without being able to understand their hosts . . . this could be a revealing moment.

Each crewmate that emerged stared at the aliens with fresh awe. Many, like Teardrop, engaged them in a question and answer session, and the Huantag seemed to satisfy their every inquiry. Janlin urged Gordon before her, willing to watch and wait, wondering what new view she would have of her ally's enemy when she could understand them.

Inside the hut the programmer sat at what looked to be a pile of electronic junk, nothing more than a mangled box of wires and plastic and foreign materials she guessed was the Huantag's hardware. Keys had been carved to represent the human alphabet, and the holo-display showed lines of code she hoped meant something to the man.

"Steve Netchkie." He held out a hand, radiating pleasure and success like a beacon.

"Janlin Kavanagh," she said, shaking his hand. His smile faltered.

"I am so sorry about Rudi. We are all less without his kindness and quiet humour."

Janlin nodded, unable to trust her voice.

Steve pointed out a chair at the side of the table and turned to tap away at the homemade keyboard. "He died asking for you," he said. He didn't look up from his work. "He said to tell you he was sorry, that he thought we'd be back in a matter of days. He knew you'd be with Stepper when he came looking for us."

Janlin wrapped her arms around herself and forced a deep breath through her lungs. "Thanks," she said, her voice husky.

Steve nodded and motioned towards the door. "You're good. Send in the next."

"I think I'm the last one."

"Really? Well, then, my job here is done."

They emerged from the hut to find everyone engaged in excited conversations with the Huantag. Janlin listened, and realized the clicks, whistles, and trills became understandable words in her ear.

"Well done, Mr. Netchkie," Janlin said. "It's absolutely amazing."

"Just Steve," he said, but he blushed as he looked around the crowd.

A greying Japanese man noticed Steve and Janlin at the door, tilted his head in a question, and Steve nodded an affirmative.

"Please, everyone, your attention please."

"Who is that?" Janlin whispered to Steve.

"Captain Inaba," Steve whispered back. "Those close to him call him Yasu." The *Renegade's* former captain stepped up onto a bench and faced the group.

"If you could all find a seat somewhere, it will be easier for our hosts to speak to us as a group," he suggested. Janlin could see that natural leadership and respect complemented his easy manner. Everyone moved to find a place, and Janlin joined Gordon on the ground against Steve's hut.

The six Huantag in attendance moved to where Inaba guided them, their plumage rippling in the breeze. Each bore distinctive colours and markings, and their body shapes differed just as humans did from one another.

"Welcome, newcomers," said her ear-cell. "It brightens us to see you all here."

A few chuckled at the idiosyncratic way the program chose words.

"It gives us many pleasures to speak to you and be spoken. We are the—" The translation of their own name for themselves didn't have an English equivalent, and so the program inserted the actual whistle-click he made. "Our first excitement is to say the modifications are complete on the flying clothes. Tomorrow we would test it, yes?"

Chatter erupted and the volume rose until Inaba stood and waved for silence. "For those of you who have just arrived, we were shown this flying apparatus earlier. It was designed for the

Imag, so our guests have kindly modified it to fit our different shapes better."

"I'll test it," Janlin said, rising.

"She'd be your best bet, that's for sure," Gordon said, also rising. "Number one fly-by-the-seat-of-her-pants pilot right here."

"Don't need your help, Gordon," she said in an undertone. This was her chance to gain mobility, to explore and discover the Huantag's set-ups. She didn't know how long she had before Anaya would need her.

"I am an Earth pilot," she confirmed, "and a damn good one. I'm used to flying contraptions, wind gusts, take-offs and landings, all of it. I wouldn't want anyone to get hurt trying this out."

Inaba called for a vote, and a large majority agreed to let Janlin be the first to try the alien's flying device. The Huantag watched the whole process without interruption, and Janlin wondered what they were really thinking. Their beaks and feathered faces made them difficult to read.

"Thank you for this time," one of the Huantag said. "Find us returning by morning."

They launched with a crouch and a leap, easily gaining air with their wide wings in a way that made Janlin incredibly jealous. Everyone cheered and waved, and turned to talk in excited voices about the incredible experience of conversing with the aliens. Even Gordon looked a little stunned, although he didn't seem to have much to say.

For her own part, Janlin felt quite alone in her mistrust of the angelic aliens. No one here knew their history like she did, and she wasn't about to start trying to educate them while they could do nothing but praise their new hosts.

CHAPTER TWENTY-EIGHT

JANLIN QUICKLY BECAME weary of both Gordon and Stepper tiptoeing around her. She saw the young medic talking with Tyrell and went over, leaving the men discussing the food they'd eaten that night.

"Bring her up to my hut," Teardrop was saying. "I've got some ingenious salve the Birdfolk taught us to make from a local plant. It'll clear the infection right up."

"Someone get hurt?"

Tyrell looked around and flinched. The woman's blue eyes widened. Janlin sighed. "I won't bite you, Tyrell," she said.

"Yeah, but . . . you know," he said, stumbling over his awkwardness before his face dissolved into sincere chagrin. "I'm so sorry about Rudigar, Janlin. It's all my fault—"

"It's not your fault by any stretch," she replied, running overtop his apology before the poor kid completely lost it.

The woman watched this exchange, her head tilted and face full of puzzlement. "You just arrived. How could an earlier death here be your fault?"

Tyrell opened his mouth to reply, but coughed instead. "Hmmmm, excuse me," he said, then his eyes widened. "Weird, I had a cough just like that, a little dry cough that was enough to pull me from the crew of the *Renegade*. Her father went in my place."

Teardrop whistled low and soft. "Heavy burden of guilt."

"Not necessarily," Janlin said. "If we want to lay blame, how about starting with the Imag?"

Both agreed readily.

"I'll go bring Linder up," Tyrell said. He saw Janlin's questioning look. "She got a bad gash when she fell during a whipping, and it's not healing well."

Janlin shook her head. "Bastards."

"I'll meet you there," the woman said, shooing him off. Then she turned on Janlin in almost a predatory way. "I'd like another look at you. You spooked me bad disappearing like that this afternoon."

Janlin fought to keep the amusement off her face. The medic was easily fifteen years her junior, and probably a good four inches shorter, yet she held herself with calm command that all good medics were trained for.

"Sorry about that."

"No, I understand. I also remember you getting a good knock on the head, though."

"Yep, that was me. But I'm fine now."

"For me to judge," she replied. Then she glanced around and leaned closer. "I could use a little help if you're up for it."

Janlin opened her mouth, closed it, and just nodded. She didn't want to end up working medical, but she recognized the need to keep busy. Was the woman thinking it too?

As they walked, the young woman chatted on about the various things the aliens had taught them. "They helped us set up when we first arrived, which was weird since we couldn't communicate, but these shelters were here, old and abandoned, and they brought in so many things for us to use, like the lights that we still haven't figured out. We even have a crude plumbing system that reminds me of ancient Roman ingenuity."

"How many per dwelling?" Janlin asked when she could get a word in edgewise.

"Well, those larger ones sleep six, or even eight with all the cooking being done communally. We're so used to that as a ship crew it's worked out really well here, too. I really don't have time to be learning the local plants and how to cook them. Then those smaller shelters only sleep two, and they're reserved for couples." Janlin thought the young woman coloured a bit at this admission. "They're newer, and you can see how they are all placed on the outer ring, moving up the cliff and down into what we call the sagebrush meadow."

"So, the chain of command and all the rules that go with it are out the window?"

She pursed her lips. "Not for some things, but in a situation like this, SpaceOp's rules against romance at work have gone out the window."

"What's your n—" Janlin began, but the medic burst into tears in that same moment.

"Oh, Janlin, this place is so weird and everyone is emotionally scarred from the Imag and everything, and I'm not a psychologist, I can't help them the way they need . . ."

Her breath hitched and hiccupped at each pause. Janlin gave her a hug. "It's okay," she said, fighting her own tears. They were all so tired and traumatized, and here this young woman had the medical well-being of all these survivors on her shoulders. Janlin lifted the woman's chin with a gentle finger. "We're away from those brutes, that's what matters most, right?"

She nodded, wiping at her face. "And the Birdfolk have so many great things to teach us," she said. "SpaceOp promised solutions. They promised we'd grow food in space and bring it back to Earth. They promised with the Jumpships we would find new planets, new homes, and now we have but we can't get back to tell anyone about it." She choked on renewed tears.

"SpaceOp promised more than they could give," Janlin said, wishing she could tell her it was Stepper that promised more than he could give. But that wouldn't help anything, in fact giving them less hope than ever if they discovered that SpaceOp didn't even know where they were . . . or how. She put her arm over Teardrop's shoulders and guided her onwards. "We'll just need to make things happen for ourselves."

Teardrop gave her a wide-eyed look. "I wish I had your confidence. But, you know, some are saying we shouldn't worry about getting home again, that it's better here and this way we wouldn't have to share it."

Janlin sucked in a shocked breath. "That's insane. We would perish as a species without reproduction."

"They want me to help the Birdfolk find a way to reprogram the nanos. I'm not a nano-tech! I'm just a newbie medic!"

Janlin pulled her around, face to face. "Listen, I won't give up on getting back home, and neither will Gordon. So just you never mind the talk. That's what people do when they've given up hope."

Two people rounded a corner ahead, and she saw it was Tyrell approaching with Linder. The older woman was limping, and her strained face held an off-colour tinge that made Teardrop gasp when she saw it.

"It's gotten worse real fast," Linder said, puffing with the effort of walking while in such pain.

"Okay, right in here. I've got just the thing to fix you up . . ."

Janlin leaned against the wall outside, listening to the voices within. She still hadn't found out where she was to sleep, or even the woman's proper name. Well, she had nowhere to be, so she put her back to the wall and enjoyed the heat still radiating from the sun-soaked stone. She slid down, eventually, and set her arms up on her bent knees.

The night air cooled quickly around her. Small flying shapes whizzed by the lights, accompanied by a chipping sound. Strange star patterns twinkled overhead. Janlin allowed her awe to slip in past her annoyance of the crew's general attitude. It made sense, though. Of course, people would want to stay, especially if they thought there was no Jumpship to get them home. A simple coping mechanism. Still, Janlin couldn't help feeling scornful. There was always hope . . . always. The Huantag had space flight technology, therefore a way off the planet existed. The only hitch was the Jumpship. Would Anaya be able to get the ship safely away from the Imag? Would it still be in one piece?

Janlin shifted, unable to find comfort. A smell came to her, one she felt she should know but couldn't place. She rose and began to walk, aimlessly, and when the cleansing rain came, she caught the smell-memory—that glorious aroma of wet earth and thirsty living things soaking up the moisture. She wandered on, untroubled by getting wet, watching little rivers of muddy water flow this way and that, rushing and rippling and pooling. She heard people still celebrating in the common area, no doubt under the great eaves of the cookhut or possibly dancing in puddles. A few people ran for their own hut, or perhaps to share the hut of another. The strange little balls of unexplained light seemed to dim, changing to a pale night setting for those resting.

Janlin walked out away from the village. The night sky lightened as the rain clouds cleared away. There was no moon up yet, and the stars littered the sky as profusely as they ever did from home. Different patterns, maybe, but still abundant.

She stopped. No moon. No lights out here. Yet she could see well enough to navigate around the scrub brush. She studied the shadowed landscape, pinpointing many little clusters of faint phosphoresce gathered around stones and scattered amongst the shrubbery. Janlin crouched by a pile of stones, wondering if it was safe to touch. The glow seemed to come from some kind of lichen covering the stone's surface.

"Fascinating," she whispered.

She straightened her spine and stiffened her resolve, feeling better for the walk and ready to go find a bed. As nice as it was here, they would return home and show SpaceOp that Jumpships did work and they could explore a universe of possibilities.

Still, no one would believe her story right now. She would wait. Who knew what surprises tomorrow would bring?

The peace of the place calmed her, and Janlin felt a rush of certainty. If there was anyone that could pull off such a mission, it was Anaya. Her money . . . and her hopes . . . were on the Gitane captain.

CHAPTER TWENTY-NINE

JANLIN DREAMT. SHE stood under foreign stars by Rudigar's grave, a babe in her arms, but when she knelt by the headstone it said Stepper Jordan, not Rudigar Kavanagh. She wept in renewed grief, the sense of loss too much to bear, and she snuggled the babe under her chin, the smell of new life no comfort.

She struggled for consciousness, now aware of the dream sense and seeking to end it. When she opened her eyes the linen against her face was damp with tears.

Rolling onto her back, Janlin stared at the ceiling. It looked much the same as the one she'd stared at in the medical hut, only smaller. Another's quiet breathing comforted her after the strange emotions of the dream.

She thought she'd let Stepper die, and somehow that had been a relief. New guilt washed over her. Why couldn't she let him go? She swore never to let him have an opportunity to hurt her like he had once, so she needed to just get over him. It didn't matter that they were now survivors on a strange planet . . . she couldn't let him weasel his way back into her heart.

Her roommate sighed, rolled, and when Janlin glanced over, a teardrop scar bunched up as the medic woman smiled.

"Good morning."

"Morning." Janlin rolled so they faced each other on their grass mats. "I don't even know your name. I've been calling you

163

Teardrop because of the shape of the scar on your cheek."

The woman's eyes widened. "Teardrop. It's perfect!" Her fingers brushed the puckered skin high on her cheekbone. "I like it much better than my real name."

Janlin didn't know what to say at first. "Well, I can't go around calling you Teardrop . . ."

"Sure you can," she said, sitting up and running her fingers through her hair. She yawned and stretched. "Come on, I'll show you the lower pool where we wash."

Janlin brightened at the idea of a soak. She rose from the mat and extended her arms into her own stretch. "Is your name such a bad one?"

Teardrop grimaced. "It's not bad . . . just unpronounceable."

"Oh, come on, it can't be that bad."

She shook her head. "You have no idea. I hope your nickname for me catches on like wildfire." She grabbed a cotton cloth and tossed it at Janlin, a second one in her other hand. "There's natural soapstone on the shelf behind you—can you grab two? I'll get the stuff we've been using on our hair."

Janlin thought about calling her out for changing the subject, but the thought of an actual bath was too distracting. Besides, she'd been calling the woman Teardrop for so long now it did feel natural.

Janlin glanced at the two empty mats, linen blankets pushed aside on one, folded neatly on the other. "Are we up that late?" She hadn't even heard them leave.

Teardrop grinned. "Those two are on mess hall duty, morning shift. They snuck out at first light to prep breakfast."

"A bath and breakfast." Janlin sighed wistfully. "What an improvement. Sure wish we met these aliens first."

"Not possible, since they believe leaving their planet of birth is akin to sacrilege or blasphemy or something."

"Really?" Janlin thought about this. Did it explain the strange mix of archaic with technology?

"Yeah, Captain Inaba told us this last night. He asked one of them about helping us get the *Hope* back to return home. They don't seem so keen on the idea, partly because the Imag have our ships, and partly because it's against their base philosophy."

Well, so much for help from that faction then. Janlin praised her own discretion, grateful she didn't have to worry about someone leaking her plan to the aliens.

They walked out into slanted sunlight, the air cool and scented with a promise of the heat to come. Teardrop led her down to the valley where Janlin was shocked to realize the pools were not a part of a stream or river, but low spots where water was pumped up from far below.

"Is this world so dry, then?" Janlin mused.

"Here it is," Teardrop said. "But the water table is substantial, and they have innovative ways to draw on it as required."

Janlin stared at the gorgeous pool of clear water set in a natural bowl of stone. "It's so clean, I don't want to muddy it."

Teardrop laughed. "Don't worry, you won't. The water is being filtered. Look, here."

Teardrop showed off the constructs of an advanced civilization living off the land, and Janlin shook her head in wonder.

"The Birdfolk are wonderful, full of determination to care for the world they have . . . and each other . . . even us," Teardrop said as they sank into the thermal-warmed water.

"Don't you feel a bit like we're kept pets?"

Teardrop pulled a face. "No. Why would you think that?"

"Well, they're building homes and making salves, but we haven't seen anything about how they live. I feel like the cow in the barn, never knowing what the inside of the house looks like."

"Well, that might change for you today," Teardrop said with a grin. Janlin grinned back, remembering her volunteer mission to try out the flight suits. Teardrop slid deeper into the water. "Besides, they believe in staying and making the best of what you are given, just like I said. To them, it's wrong to go too far from the planet, which is why they work so hard to keep it nice. Makes for responsibility and good caretaking, don't you think?"

Janlin couldn't believe her naivety. "If this is what they believe, they should be more interested in getting us back to our own planet than ever, not keeping us here."

Teardrop obviously hadn't thought of it that way. "You'd have to talk to the leadership circle about it. They're the ones making most of the decisions now. Maybe the Birdfolk have been told there is no going back, and so they are helping us make the best of it."

Janlin thought she'd boil the water, her blood was so hot with anger. "There is a way back," she said firmly. "I promise you, girl, there is always a way home if we want it bad enough."

She nodded. "Teardrop."

Janlin blinked. "Pardon?"

"Just call me Teardrop. Really. I love it. And I hope you're as good at finding solutions to impossible problems as you are at making up nicknames." Teardrop ducked under the water to wet her hair, thrusting up from below with vigour. She sputtered and wiped her face. "I'd really like to go home."

CHAPTER THIRTY

"WE PICK A name, and I can assign their sound pattern to that name. It'll take a while to learn the different individuals, but it should help for today."

Steve tapped away at his keys, setting things up for her and the Huantag leaning over him with great interest. Janlin stared at the creature that was going to take her flying that day. He was tall and lean, almost fragile looking, with burgundy plumage streaked with tan on top and back, and a white front. Janlin wanted to comment how beautiful he was to them, but she didn't know how, or if it would be appropriate.

"Your arms and legs are incredibly thin," she said instead, and instantly felt inane.

His chirps and whistles became words in her ear. "Our bones are light, just like this planet's gravity. We also have many lungs . . . I understand you only have two? And you have calcium in the bones, very heavy element." He studied the bundle of straps and webbed material in his claw-like hands. She hoped it wasn't worry she saw in his eyes.

"Is that going to work for me?" she asked, pointing at the intricate gear.

"Yes, yes. If Imag can fly, you small things can fly too."

Janlin wondered at the word Imag until she realized that Steve had put in whatever word he knew for an alien looking like an Imag without knowing that they were only one race of the aliens from Yiyau.

"Okay, pick a name," Steve said.

"Me?" Janlin's brain drew a blank.

"Sure, why not? You're spending the day with him."

A little thrill ran through her at the thought of the imminent flight.

The Huantag began to speak again. Janlin hoped the translation would get quicker with time and use. Her life might depend on it today.

"I am named for my height, and my family, who are all known for their diving speed. Does this help you choose?"

Janlin and Steve stared at each other, both at a loss.

"It doesn't feel right to label you," Janlin explained, "or to assign you a name common to our own. I would like to give you something more special."

"You honour me," he said with a regal lift of his head. Janlin gave Steve an appreciative look. He'd done one hell of a job on the translation program.

She snapped her fingers. "I've got it. The Peregrine Falcon was once Earth's fastest animal, diving at speeds over three hundred kilometres an hour." She flushed at Steve's look of astonishment. "My dad was really big on birds, especially the large hunting birds. He loved anything that could fly. Anyway, we could call him Falco, which I believe is part of the Latin name for the falcon."

"Falco? I like it," Steve said, tapping away. Then he leaned forward and spoke the name into his jumble of parts. Then he instructed the alien to utter his name. "There. Try it, Janlin. Call him by his human name."

She did, and the Huantag's wings expanded slightly and he shook himself, ruffling all his feathers in a show of soft decadence.

"Glorious to have you call me by name, Janlin."

Now it was Janlin's turn to be astonished. Steve grinned. "Already set you up," he explained.

"And what does my name mean in their language?" she queried. Steve's eyes twinkled.

"Little mouse bird."

"Time for flying is good," said Falco, unable to catch Janlin's indignation and Steve's amusement. "Before wind comes bigger."

"Makes sense to me," Janlin said. She followed Falco out on shaky legs. Maybe she should've told Gordon or someone about Anaya before this. What if she didn't return from this prototype test?

Before she could follow this train of thought further, she found herself being strapped into the strangest contraption of gear. Stepper, Tyrell, Teardrop, and others gathered around to watch and offer advice from time to time, but Gordon didn't appear. A twinge of worry for him distracted her from her own fear.

"Stepper, have you seen Gordon?" she asked. Wasn't like him to miss something like this.

"I saw him at the pools this morning," he said.

"I'm worried about him."

Stepper frowned. "Why?"

Janlin scowled at him. Shouldn't he know why? Wasn't it painfully obvious how badly he pined for Ursula?

Before she could confront him on this, or even ask Teardrop to look for him, Falco began to chirp at her.

"Please, you are ready. Reach your arms, good, and put these buttons in your hands, yes." Falco reeled off instructions that the translator seemed to miss half of while testing each strap to ensure a snug fit around her upper legs, torso, and over her shoulders. The impressive wings unfurled when she stretched her arms out, causing some of the bystanders to stumble out of the way, and then folded behind her when she brought them back in.

"Magnificent," she breathed.

"Is there a wait?" Falco asked. "May we go?"

Kudos to Steve for making them sound so utterly polite and dignified. Still, she wasn't sure she was ready for this.

Falco, seeming to sense her unease, again ran over the thrust controls, each one simple pressure points in the harnesses her hands rode in.

"May we go?" Falco inquired again.

Janlin swallowed. "Don't I need more room to launch, or a drop-off or something?"

"No. Push first thruster three times quick as you jump. Reach arms to open wings. Is this understood?"

"Yeah, sure. Easy as pie."

"I do not understand this word."

Steve laughed. "Yeah, I figured there'd be a few I missed."

"You can do this, Janlin," Stepper called. "You can fly anything, remember?"

His taunting made her roll her eyes even as butterflies fluttered within, as much nerves as wondering what might be possible between them in such a place as this. She adjusted a few more straps, stalling.

"You go, I will follow," Falco said. "If you fall, I will catch and bring down safe."

That gave her some measure of comfort, so she took a huge breath, crouched low, and lunged, pressing the thruster three times as she did.

The shove was both more powerful and less noisy than she'd expected. The ground fell away, the only shape staying with her that of Falco's graceful curves.

Whistles reached her, cutting easily through the wind, and her ear-cell translated. She wasn't sure replying would work as well with her breath being whipped away.

"Beautiful launch, Janlin. Low thrust power now. Stay calm, use your sense to guide movements. Try and I will watch."

Janlin cut back on the thrusters and tipped her wings to soar over the village. She thought she could hear cheers from below, and she couldn't help but grin.

She tucked her legs and fell into a dive she didn't intend, and quickly straightened them again.

"Good, good. You sense flight good, trust what you feel."

Janlin tested and played, using every button and move that she could think of while she had the safety net of Falco flying nearby. He called out suggestions occasionally, but for the most part simply followed her like a dutiful parent with a toddling child.

She finally settled into a comfortable glide, all thrusters off for the moment. Wind sighed through the strange black fibres layered into the wing structure, and a steady stream of tears ran from her eyes. Some kind of goggles might be required.

Below, the plains stretched east and south, and the mountains rose in the north. To the west lay the haze of the ocean, bright with sunshine. Most interesting to her, however, was where the southern plains dropped to meet a large river. Strange rock formations grew out of the shoreline, making her peer and squint in an attempt to discern what they might be.

"Follow!" Falco called, and he tucked into a shallow dive, speeding them towards the river and their fascinating sentinels.

Despite knowing how altitude affected perceptions of distances and size of the landmarks below, it still caught her off guard to realize just how huge the stone towers were. They evened out, Falco stroking the wind with his impressive wings and her adding a bit of thrust to her flight, but it still took a while to close the distance to the river. Below them the landscape changed to rolling hills covered in waving trees and open fields of grasses with grazing beasts and smaller flying animals occasionally seen. Beyond the river a thicker forest with a decidedly tropical look to it dominated the view. To the west the river widened and split as it met the ocean, becoming a brighter green as it met with salt water.

Janlin saw no roads cutting the forests or any urban sprawl. Where did these people live? How could they be so advanced, yet so primitive? She began to wonder if they lived in treehouses, being bird-like and all, and wondered how she would ever land in the thick jungle they seemed to be headed for.

Yet the question that haunted her worst hit far too close to home. Why couldn't Earth look like this?

Then movement caught her eye. Huantag flew in and out from the towering monoliths of rock along the river. She peered, realizing the dark areas were openings in the monoliths. A new panic set in. How was she to land, exactly? Could she steer as accurately as the Huantag, or would she end up splattered on the side of the blue-grey rock?

Falco dropped into position right above her. "When I say it, use second back thruster to slow you and glide gently in. Lower elbows as you enter opening, turning hands up, and put feet down. Follow!"

He tucked and dove ahead of her, soaring in closer. The odd buildings held hundreds of ledges with Huantag coming and going like bees in a hive. Janlin hoped they would know to steer clear of the student flyer.

Falco called and whistled, and to her relief the way cleared in front of him. He swooped straight into one of the openings, choosing a larger one to Janlin's great relief. She watched his wings fan out in a spectacular display as he backwinged and brought his legs down.

"Easy as pie," Janlin whispered to herself. She pumped a bit more back thrust, then sailed into the shadow of the building, closer, closer, remembering simulations of the Seraphs where she had careened off sides and down the landing tunnel, head over heels—

She entered the opening, twisted her arms, and tried to get her feet under her, hoping for the wonderful display of backwing that Falco had done before her. Her legs shot down and then forward, and she slid in on her back, skidding along the floor.

When she had the nerve to open her eyes, she found Huantag all converging on her, Falco chirping inquisitively.

"Okay? Good! Might be too fast, but good. Imag often tumble and roll. You did good."

He helped her up, the other aliens staring and talking amongst themselves.

"So small . . ."

"Lighter than Imag . . ."

"Thin skin easily torn . . ."

Janlin lifted her arm to reveal the scraped elbow. "Just a scratch," she said.

Falco examined it. "True, just a scrape." He whistled and chirped this confirmation to the group. "Janlin can understand you, but you do not have upload to hear her," he explained. Some Huantag ducked their heads.

"Are my wings okay?" Janlin asked, worried she wasn't the only thing scraped.

"There is some damage. We can repair it," he said to her moan of dismay. He helped her remove the flight gear and handed it to another, offering some suggestions for further improvements. Then he turned to a small individual with a focused look and dark stripes throughout his golden feathers.

"Fly to the village and tell the humans that Janlin will stay through this night so we may repair her wings and rest before flying again."

Janlin heard this with great relief. Her legs trembled, and

her arms ached with fatigue. Still, her surroundings fascinated her, and she did not want to reveal how tired she felt from one short flight. Despite her pleasure at flying, she had to admit the floor below her feet felt reassuringly solid.

Yet it did not look like any rock she'd ever seen. It appeared porous, flaky, and the walls were the same. She stepped closer and reached out to touch the blue-grey rock, only to have her hand sink into a spongy growth.

Janlin snatched her hand back with a gasp. "It's not rock!"

Falco trilled, which the ear-cell did not translate. Laughter? A new word? She decided that even with translation all this first contact stuff was exhausting.

She peered closer, daring to touch it again. It was like a springy algae growth, like a moss or thick lichen. She pinched it, but it did not break away except for a few dry flakes that fluttered to the floor.

"Buildings grow, and we program them to be harder here," he pointed at the floor, "or softer here." He touched the wall with what Janlin took as reverence. "The result has a natural . . ." and here the translation beeped.

"I'm sorry, that last word isn't coming through to me," Janlin said, tapping her ear.

Falco thought a moment. "In dark halls, or at night, buildings glow, shine, not bright like sun, but with many colours."

Janlin remembered the nightglows she'd seen in the field outside the village. "Ah, a natural phosphoresce! Very cool."

Falco patted her shoulder. "So pleased you fly. Now all of you may travel, visit, and we can sharing learning."

So much for her worries of being kept like a pet. Now she just needed to learn how the shields were run, and where the central control was. Janlin frowned. They almost made it too easy.

The other Huantag dispersed, the spectacle over. As they moved away from the opening, the same light glows they had in the village came to life, and Janlin thought she saw colour flicker out on the walls.

"Falco, how do you power these?" Janlin asked, pointing at the round glowing bulbs.

"By our sun. We took power from our planet for too long before we saw that the sun waited there for us to use for free, without harming the planet." He led her around into a room with chairs like bowls and strange apparatus protruding from high counters.

Large windows graced the one side of this room. She went over and gaped at the stunning vista below. Huantag flew everywhere, all different, all beautiful. She didn't know how they harvested the sun's power—she didn't see anything resembling a solar panel or collector anywhere.

For that matter, she didn't see any pollution, mining, or industry of any kind. Instead she looked out on a lush world of green flowing water, clear and clean, waving trees and clear skies, and lush growth undisturbed by the Huantag's lifestyle.

"Sure wish Earth could look like this." She leaned her head against the glass, overwhelmed by homesickness.

A light touch on her shoulder brought her around. To her amazement, three smaller versions of Falco stood regarding her.

"This is my group. My mate," and he indicated the tallest of the three, "and my children."

Janlin bowed. "It is wonderful to meet you."

Falco repeated this to them for her.

"May we touch it?" asked one of the children. Falco gave a sharp chirp of admonishment that translated as a firm negative, but Janlin laughed and patted him on the arm.

"It's okay." She stepped closer and reached out her hand. "Come and touch."

The one that asked came first, followed quickly by his sibling. Janlin looked for clues to tell male from female, but with their thick plumage, there was no way for her to be sure. As they explored her hands, hair, and arms, Janlin asked Falco.

"Boy or girl?" She pointed at the bravest one.

"Boy," he answered. "Both boy." Even though she was sure he felt pride in them, emotions too were hard to discern in the Huantag.

Soon Janlin squatted on a narrow bench that felt more like a perch, not surprised when that was precisely what the others did. The design left ample room for them to stretch out their wings and tails, which reached to the floor and balanced them. Falco's mate brought her a steaming plate of what appeared to be giant bugs, so she pretended to nibble and claimed a nervous flying stomach when she hadn't eaten any of it.

Janlin watched them together as a family unit, dancing that fine dance of love and nurturing clearly universal. She liked Falco, despite her determination not to. Anaya's comm-unit pressed into her leg, hidden in her pocket, and weighing on her mind.

Night fell, and the city became a fascinating display of colourful phosphoresce. Janlin stood watching at the window for a long time while the family went about their routines of cleaning up from dinner.

When the family retired, and she was finally alone with Falco again, she began her questioning.

"How do you collect the sun's power?"

Unfortunately, the translator couldn't pick up half his words, so finally he pointed at the wall. "This growth, it absorbs energy from the sun, and we direct it."

Janlin realized this would be much harder than she thought. "What about the Imag? Aren't you worried about them?"

"No. Be calm, rest assured we are safe here, shielded from any harm the Imag could bring."

"Shielded?" She put on her best look of curious innocence.

"Yes. The best sun energy is captured in space. The stations use most of that energy to operate the shields, ensuring the Imag cannot come here."

Janlin's heart sank. "There is more than one station?" she asked, pointing up.

"Yes."

"And the shields operate from those stations?"

"This is almost true. Some operate from there and some from here, depending on what needs done. Please, do not worry, we are safe."

Of course, the Huantag would expect them to still fear the Imag, so Falco would read her concern that way. Still, it was heartbreaking to discover she never needed to come down planetside at all, and devastating to find out she may need to get back to the stations to help Anaya.

It would be better if she could somehow gather the humans and return to the stations to complete her part of the mission. She wouldn't need to take down any shields then. She needed to make Falco understand that and help them. More and more, it became impossible to consider leaving them defenceless.

Janlin felt a cold chill. Did Anaya orchestrate this? Shaking off her paranoia, Janlin forced the image of a chess pawn out of her brain.

CHAPTER THIRTY-ONE

NEXT DAY, HER flight gear back on and ready to fly, Janlin stood on the launching ledge.

"You will teach the others, yes?"

Janlin blinked. "Me?"

"Yes, teach them to fly."

"Of course," Janlin said, feeling a new excitement bounding through her. "I'd love to."

"Good. Come, follow."

He leapt off the edge, spreading wings wide to catch the wind and soar off into the busy skies.

With a prayer regarding the overnight repairs to her wings, Janlin plunged from the heights of Falco's home and followed him in a dive. "Look, Ma, no thrusters required." She stretched full out and laughed with joy.

Falco led her down to the edge of the city towers. Counting quickly, Janlin estimated four to five hundred Huantag lived in Falco's building alone, and the structures lined the river for miles in each direction. They engaged a fantastic design, truly utilizing space to the best effect. She saw open markets on middle floors, and groups flying with nets, presumably to hunt for food.

The ground rushed closer, and she applied her back wing technique along with a sharp boost from the suit's thrusters, and thrilled herself with a near perfect landing except for the stumble-run she had to do to keep her feet.

"Beautiful, Janlin," Falco said despite her faltering. "You will be good teacher."

"Thank you," she said, still a little breathless. "Why are we here?"

He indicated a path leading into the trees and beckoned her to follow.

Glorious flowers bloomed all around them, spanning all the colours of the spectrum. She wondered if any of them would bear edible fruit, and her mouth watered. The breakfast she'd been offered had again looked very buggy. When it moved in her mouth, it took all she had not to spit it back in the dish. After that, hunger seemed a better option for the moment.

The trees were a mix of brilliant neon green with nearly black bark, bluish green needle leaves like spruce trees only different, and brown dead-looking things that twisted and curled as they grew. As in any ecosystem, she noted groundcover plants, flowering bushes, vines that climbed the trees, and, of course, trees. That said, nothing looked Earth-like from down here.

They came to an open meadow of waving blue grasses. Woven structures shaped into domes like their village huts, but much bigger, dotted the area. At the bottom of the frames, the blue-grey algae grew, covering the stick mesh.

"Soon you will have new home here if you choose. Down low, not high like us." He trilled, and Janlin decided it must be laughter.

"This is wonderful, Falco."

"They will take time to grow, then you will have all we have."

Janlin shook her head in amazement. Everything she'd expected, thrown out the window. Everything she'd been taught by Anaya—should that be thrown out the window, too?

Soon she flew once again, heading north to the human village. She may not have a clear plan for the future, but she'd gained her freedom and a new friend, and that was enough for now.

JANLIN FULLY ENJOYED her triumphant return, especially since Gordon was one of those who turned out to greet her.

"How did it go?"

"Did you see their city?"

"What do they eat?"

Janlin put both hands up, palms out. "Whoa, everyone. Let me get out of this gear first, okay?" She smiled at Gordon. He still appeared unimpressed. "I'm sure I can tell the story better once I'm free of all these straps."

Falco cried out from above, where he circled to be sure she was home safely. "Farewell, farewell!" he called, and Janlin waved.

"Thank you!" she cried, not sure if he'd even be able to hear her. Already he flew south with great beats of his wings.

Gordon helped her undo all the straps.

"These are fascinating buckles," he said. Janlin was just happy to see him out and about.

"Yeah, sometimes I tighten when I want to loosen, and vice versa."

"When do we get our own gear like that?" Tyrell asked.

Janlin grinned at him. "A group is coming tomorrow to help me train you, five at a time. They'll bring everything we need to adjust them to fit." She glanced at Inaba and Stepper. "We might want to draw lots or something."

"That's a good idea," Inaba said. "I will get something together once we have heard your report."

Janlin did her best to describe the glowing city, the stone towers that weren't stone, the crunchy-crawly meals, the amazing hospitality and kindness. "And the best part? They're growing us houses, too, only not towering into the sky like theirs. It'll be awhile before they're ready, but the weird algae they grow seems to be some kind of solar power collector."

"Space me," Gordon said. "Is that how they power all this lot then, too?" He waved his hand at the glowlights and cooking grills.

"Seems like."

This only brought on more questions, most of which she couldn't answer. The general consensus was that the science minds would have to travel to this city and investigate, giving them a fine chance of being bumped to the front of the line for flight training.

Finally, her gear set aside and a plate of more palatable food in front of her, Janlin sat with Gordon enjoying some peace. She'd asked everyone to just give her some time to eat before asking more questions. Now they all clustered around Inaba and three others she didn't know. They seemed to be running the show, and Stepper had a front row seat. "Who are Inaba's friends?"

Gordon followed her gaze and scowled. "That's the Leadership Circle," he said, and Janlin was surprised at the animosity in his voice. "Stepper's just in his glory now, isn't he?" he added when he noticed her questioning look. "Wants to be a leader too, no doubt, but he's forgotten all about getting home . . . forgotten some of us left loved ones behind."

Janlin watched Stepper as he interjected an opinion to the general approval of the listening group.

"He promised so much," Gordon continued. "What if we can never return?" His voice cracked on the inflection. "What if—"

"Gordon." She pitched her voice so only he would hear. "I might have a way."

He went completely still and stared at her, waiting.

"Walk with me," she said, setting her finished plate aside. They pushed off the low, flat rocks they'd sat on to get away from the bustle of the common area.

Gordon brought his food, offering her some. She nibbled on a piece of what seemed to be a root vegetable, and the taste of sweet earth filled her mouth.

"Is all of this locally grown food?" she wondered. "I've never tasted anything like it."

Gordon glanced down at his plate. "Seems right," he said. "But I worry about running into some germ or mineral or something we won't be able to handle. Has anyone thought of that?"

"We've been eating Imag food for a while without adverse effects."

"Just dammed lucky, that's all," Gordon growled.

"Wow, you are on edge."

"Yeah, I am! Everyone's so glad to be here just 'cause it's better than the Imag's sheer abuse, but they've forgotten why we're here in the first place. Even Stepper. Especially Stepper! I swear the guy's ready to settle in and play house!"

Janlin let him rant.

"What are you smirking at?" Gordon demanded.

Janlin pulled him aside, checking for onlookers. Once she

was sure of privacy, she pulled out Anaya's comm-unit.

"I wasn't a stowaway," she said, handing him the device. He stared at it, then at her, hope and confusion warring on his face. "When Stepper—when I thought he was dead and they carried him away, I attacked my guard and knocked him out. Then I ran. We were down on hull deck, so I found a lift and went in search of an airlock, and hopefully a ship."

Gordon turned the device over and over in his hands, checking every angle, but she could tell he listened intently.

"I did find an airlock with a small shuttle-style ship docked there. Turned out they were there uninvited, looking to make friends with a human. In fact, they'd done it before." She watched Gordon's face. "The captain of this ship spoke English."

Gordon's head shot up, eyes wide, and his hands stilled. "Space me," he whispered.

"No kidding. They brought me here to gather a crew while they go steal the *Hope*. I guess it's still sitting in one piece in the hangar bay of the Imag ship." She looked back at the gathering. "It's almost too good to be true how all of us are here."

Gordon frowned at this. "You trust her? She's an Imag, right?"

"Well, she's of the same species by looking at her, but she calls the ones that enslaved us 'Imag', and her own kind 'Gitane'. I think they're either different families or maybe even races."

"Why didn't you say something sooner?"

Janlin shook her head. "What if she gets caught, or can't get the *Hope*? What if the *Hope* is dismantled by the time she gets to it, or she can't get it to fly?" Gordon's shoulders sagged. "See? I don't want to get everyone's hopes up. Besides, everyone here is crazy for this place, as you've noticed." He snorted. "You, on the other hand, needed some hope. Now you have it."

Gordon threw back his head and laughed. "I did," he said, clapping Janlin on the back. "So, my friend, what's the catch?"

"What do you mean?"

Gordon crossed his arms. "There's always a catch, Janlin. Especially with you."

Janlin groaned. "How did you know?"

Gordon laughed again, and it did Janlin more good than anything else could have to see him this way.

"I can read you better than any bloke alive."

"Fine. There's a catch. But we'll worry about that later—if she really shows up with our ship. Okay?"

Gordon tucked her arm through his. "Hmm, I don't think so," he said as they wandered on through the balmy night. "For now, tell me about these Gitane. I want to know everything."

Janlin told him of Anaya and Yipho, and her impressions and conversations with her new friend. When she got to the plan they'd agreed upon, she hesitated.

"The catch, right?" Gordon was too smart by half.

"Yeah. See, the Huantag—"

"The who?"

"That's the name of the Birdfolk . . . at least that's what Anaya calls them. Huantag."

Gordon quirked an eyebrow. "Right, then, carry on."

"Well, they won't let the Imag or Gitane onto this planet, at all, ever again. They were here for a while, when their own planet became unliveable, but now they are forced to survive in space. Anaya is super bitter about this, but I wonder what the other side of the story is."

"Bloody hell, sounds like SpaceOp with Mars."

Janlin nodded. "Doesn't it, though. Anyway, the Huantag have this amazing shield technology that has prevented the Imag from bullying their way in."

"And we have to disarm it."

Janlin, not surprised at his deductive abilities, nodded. "It's the only way Anaya can come get us."

Gordon looked sceptical. "Why can't we ask the bird guys to take us out to her instead of destroying their only protection from the Imag?"

Janlin shook her head. "I've thought about that, and hedged around it a bit with Falco, but they have some pretty strict philosophy about not leaving the planet."

"From what little I've seen and heard so far, they're pretty amicable. Seems to me we should at least try and explain the situation."

Janlin chewed on her lip as they strolled along. Animal calls echoed over the constant insect hum from the surrounding desert. "Just seems weird that they would be so nice to us, and so awful to Anaya's kind."

"Maybe they have good reason to be."

"There's more. I think the shielding might be operated from the orbitals. I might have to find a way out there."

Gordon's eyes narrowed. "Then we might as well just take everyone once your mate arrives and leave the shields alone."

Janlin sighed. "And how are you going to convince anyone of that, human or alien? Look, I like what you're thinking, but we're going to need some serious big ideas to make it work. I might have misunderstood, anyway, so I want to do more snooping around before I try and steal a shuttle."

"Steal an alien shuttle? Kavanagh, you really do think you can fly anything, don't you?"

Janlin shrugged. "Only because I can." She gave him a sideways look, letting a small smile play on her lips. He just shook his head, muttering about pride and falls. "But there's even more," Janlin said, serious again. "I'm not sure if everyone is here."

"Well, Fran isn't."

Janlin grimaced. "Right. Anyway, we have to rescue them before we go. I don't ever want to return to this solar system, not for nothin'."

"Well, I have to agree with you there."

"Trouble is, Anaya is going for the *Hope*, but she was reluctant to take the time to get the humans off the Imag warship."

"Warship?"

Janlin sighed. She was supposed to be offering hope, not taking it away. Maybe she should just shut up.

"The Imag are trying to build a Jumpship of their own, but that ship also happens to be a warship destined to attack this planet. The ship we helped build."

"Oi, that's just bloody great," Gordon said.

"Sorry, Gordon, I wanted to cheer you up and I'm doing a bang-up job of it, aren't I?"

"No, better to give it all over. Two heads together, right? We'll get this all sussed out, and we'll do it in a way that shows the best of us." Gordon stepped up to one of the glow lights. "These give off no heat, have no discernible power source, yet light this little settlement to guide our way. They come on when needed, and fade when no one's around. From what you say, these folk grow their homes instead of tearing up their world to build them. I want to know more about these people before I put them in harm's way."

"Okay, okay, you've made your point, and I'm not disagreeing with you," Janlin said. She took the comm-unit from him. "But I'm not going to let Anaya down. Or tell Stepper or anyone else yet, either."

"He'll be pissed that you kept it from him," Gordon said with a grin.

"Well, tough. Not like he's always cared what I'd feel."

Gordon took a breath, hesitated, then went ahead. "He really does care about you, you know. Some would say you over-reacted when you split."

"Oh, really? And how about when I went to apologize and walked in on him and Fran having a nice shag. Did I overreact that day?"

Gordon grimaced. "No. But it has been a long time. The least you could do is try to be civil."

Janlin turned on him. "There is never a good time for me to revisit this subject," she said through her teeth.

"I know, I'm sorry. I just don't think holding out on everyone is right, and I'm not looking forward to explaining why we did it."

"I get that, but I really feel we shouldn't let this go public just yet," Janlin said. "What if someone tells one of the Huantag, and they take Anaya's device from me? Listen, once you have flying gear, we'll investigate further, see what we can find out about the alien's shielding."

"Or simply sit them down for a good long talk." Gordon regarded her for a long moment. "I want to go home in a bad way," he said finally, "but I will not do it at anyone's expense. And that means you don't need to do things you wouldn't normally do just to get me home, okay?"

Janlin gave him a sad smile. "Okay, Spin." She reached out and squeezed his arm. "You're a good man, and I respect that."

"You'd better."

They returned to the gathering. Janlin left Gordon helping with cleanup and cornered Steve.

"I heard you were one of the original brains to work out how to manipulate the Jump," she said, getting exactly the reaction she'd hoped for.

"As a matter of fact, I am," Steve said, his chest puffing up a bit. He eyed her, and Janlin hoped he didn't think she was hitting on him.

"Listen, when I was down in the bowels of the Imag ship, they had shelves of our parts. Some people have said they're trying to build their own Jumpship. Is it possible?"

Steve laughed. "They're in for a big disappointment. Steel won't function as our nano-augmented materials can. Folding space is not for the faint of heart, or those lacking the right technology."

For someone who had been a captive and slave, Steve looked mighty sure of himself right now. "So, it won't work then," Janlin asked.

"Short answer? Ah . . . no."

"And if they try to fly *Hope*?"

"Oh, they've already tried that, with me in the room as a matter of fact." His face twisted in unhappy remembrance, then changed to a smug look. "No one gave away the passwords and codes they would need."

Janlin wondered if her own codes would be enough. She'd given Anaya every bit of information she could think of to help, but until the moment came, she wouldn't know if it had worked.

She worried what the Imag would do when all their hard work resulted in failure. Anaya's plan now had a serious deadline attached to it. Once they tried to Jump and couldn't, the Imag warship would head directly for Huantag orbit. She couldn't very well take down the shields then.

Unless this was part of Anaya's plan all along. Perhaps the fact that she had Janlin's passwords, had the instructions to fire up the *Hope*, maybe that was all that was needed from her, and the entire brutal race was already in Sol's system, circling Earth. And maybe her role as destructor of the shields was a backup in case her codes didn't work. Either way, if they'd played her, all the hope she just offered Gordon was worth nothing.

CHAPTER THIRTY-TWO

"NO, PALMS UP! Twist your arms, you're coming in too fast!"

Steve whooshed past her and straight into the pile of harvested grass they'd set up precisely for such a moment. It exploded, raining straw-like pieces over Janlin.

Falco and his mates trilled, and laughter spilled from those watching. Janlin and Gordon moved forward to help Steve up, and he emerged looking more like a scarecrow than a human.

"Well, guess we have a handle for you, Steve," Gordon said, smirking. "Scarecrow it is."

Steve blushed.

"Never mind him, you had a great solo flight. We just need to work on the landing. Hold your arms out and let's inspect your wings for damage."

Janlin quickly learned that teaching someone to do something was a lot harder than doing it, even if you were really good at it. She kept her patience, though, and when Gordon took to flying as easily as she had, she recruited him as her assistant.

They got Steve in the air again, and his next landing brought cheers and applause from the watchers.

"Much better. Okay, who's next?"

Stepper came forward, and Janlin grinned in anticipation. "All right, Captain. Let's see what sort of flyer you are then."

"Be nice," Gordon whispered at her when she bent to help Gordon get Steve out of the safety straps.

187

"Of course," Janlin said, all innocence. "Why wouldn't I be?"

Gordon just snorted. Above them Steve and Stepper shook hands as the captain congratulated him on a successful training session.

"It takes some guts to take off, but a lot more to come back down," Steve said.

Once they had Stepper strapped in and the buckles adjusted, Janlin checked her gear again and launched. She gained a decent height and circled, waiting for Stepper to join her.

Living in close proximity to Stepper Jordan only made it harder to keep her feelings at bay. She'd left him twice, and was determined to never go back, but his easy smile sent her insides on their own flight patterns. She longed to confide in him about Anaya, and the possibility of going home. When they were a couple, she couldn't imagine anyone she would trust more, even Gordon. Why did he have to ruin that?

Every time her thoughts came around to those trust issues, she knew that while she may have been the one to walk away, he was the one that betrayed her, and so she couldn't trust him with her secret now.

Stepper launched into the air and spread his wings just right, but he forgot to cut the thrusters back and shot past her. Laughing so hard she could barely breathe, Janlin fired her own jets to follow him, wondering how his old fear of heights was doing just then.

"Cut down your thrust," she called as she caught up. The whites of his eyes flashed as he glanced at her, and his face was nearly as pale, but he lightened up on the jets and jerked his arms out and levelled into a wobbly glide.

"Okay?" she called. He nodded. "Right, then, off you go."

The plan was for first timers to circle the village three or four times and then head back down, with Janlin following close behind just as Falco had for her. Already she felt comfortable enough with flying that she knew she could swoop down and help someone to the ground. The Huantag who brought the gear watched this first training group as an added measure of protection, ready to launch into the air if need be.

Everything had gone so well up to this point, even counting Steve's crazy landing and Corvin's jets cutting out, that Janlin should have known something would go wrong with Stepper's flight. Even so, when his glide suddenly tipped, and his jets fired on full, it caught her completely by surprise.

Stepper shot off to the east like a rocket on a mission. Janlin swore and hit her own jets, pointing her body into the straightest line she could to try and catch him. With both of them running at full power, she couldn't overtake him—all she could do was follow. How was she going to help him down now? Her jets would run down first, being used more that day, and even the Huantag would not be able to catch up without augmentation like the jets gave the humans.

She wasn't laughing anymore.

Janlin risked a quick glance back and saw the rising shapes of Huantag coming after them. Already they seemed a long ways back. She pointed her body straight, going for the best aerodynamics she could muster, and tried to figure out what the hell happened with Stepper's unit. Did the thruster button stick?

"Later," she mumbled. "Just get him down safe first."

He began to spin, rolling like a fighter jet pulling stunts. Did one of the jets give out?

"Cut the jets, Stepper!" she screamed into the wind.

Miraculously, he did, and immediately began to plummet to the ground in a devastating spiral. Janlin tucked her wings and dove, her heart pounding. If she could get below him in time—

The spiral evened out into a nice glide, and Stepper dropped easily down to backwing perfectly as he landed on a large outcropping of rock jutting from the plains.

Janlin's fear boiled away into pure anger, her fury mounting as she flew in and landed beside him.

"What in the hell do you think you're trying to prove?" she cried as she landed. "Are you trying to get yourself killed?"

Stepper tried to look abashed, but his triumphant grin ruined the effect. "That was quite the rush," he said. He stretched out his wings, shook them out, and folded them back in again. "This is absolutely the best feeling I've had in years."

Janlin stared, so overwhelmed by her jumbled emotions she couldn't speak.

"I'm sorry if I freaked you out. I just had to test these jets and see what they could do. Don't tell me you haven't done the same."

Truth be told, she had, very early that morning before everyone showed up for training . . . but she wasn't about to admit it.

"Stepper Jordan, you are the biggest jerk I know," she said, deciding to stick with anger to push the other feelings aside. "Let's head back before the Huantag have to fly all the way out here just to find out you're fine."

"Wait." He stepped closer, reaching for her. "I'm sorry, Janlin, really I am. For everything. I know I drive you crazy, and I know you have reason to be mad, but I never meant to hurt you."

A long moment of silence passed as she stared at him, wondering if he meant it, wondering what his angle was, wondering what he wanted from her, wondering if he noticed the rush of heat in her face.

"I can't believe I let you go," she said. She sucked in a breath. "I mean, the tourniquet, I can't believe I let it go."

Stepper self-consciously rubbed his arm. "I asked you to," he said, looking away. "I failed everyone, and the pain was so intense, I just wanted to be free of it all. You know me, 'live free or die', right?"

She nodded, not trusting her voice.

"I took the easy way out." He stepped closer, took her hand, and squeezed. "But then I got a second chance at life."

She looked up into his eyes, desire rushing through her ears and chasing away all logic. If she were honest with herself, she missed him, missed what they'd had. Nothing ever was the same after that, not ever.

"I want another chance with you, too, Jannilove."

She closed her eyes, and he kissed her, at first a light touch, but quickly rising with passion.

Finally, she pulled back, both of them breathless. She reached up and cupped his face in her hands.

"Let me think about it, okay?" She wanted him, wanted to give him anything he wanted, but she also feared the pain he caused her before.

He kissed her lightly on the nose and gave her his irresistible grin. "Okay."

Trills and whistles cut the air, and they turned to see the Huantag closing the distance. Falco led the group, and when he folded into a dive, he quickly outdistanced his companions. Janlin dropped her hand and stepped back.

"Are you good, Janlin?" Falco said before he even touched the ground.

"Yes, we're good, thank you," she said, punching Stepper on the arm. "My friend here was playing a trick on me."

"It wasn't a trick!" Stepper protested, but Falco trilled, clearly understanding the situation far more than Janlin would've liked. She groaned inwardly when she realized his eyesight was likely as sharp as an eagle, or a falcon anyway. He'd probably witnessed the whole exchange, passionate kiss and all. Heat enveloped her all over again.

"I will return to the village, then, for more training. Please join us when you are ready," Falco said. *If he winks at me, I think I'll scream,* Janlin thought, but Falco simply launched into the air to join the others already on the way back.

Janlin looked sideways at Stepper. "We should get back too, don't you think?"

He nodded, watching the Huantag. "You never did tell me how you managed to get so clean before arriving here," he said then, and all her doubts and worries and mistrust slammed back into place, dampening the rush of joy she'd felt only moments before.

"I had some help. I think they were trying to butter me up, play nice instead of torturing me," she said. Janlin choked on the words, her mind reeling with the implication of her lie.

"And did it work?" he asked, looking at her now.

She shrugged. "I was so wrapped up in grief over you I barely remember what all happened. Wouldn't matter either way, would it? It all depends on Fran and what she translated." Janlin felt a different rush of emotions at the memories of her and Fran undergoing Imag torture together.

Half-truths make the best lies, and the only one who would know her story didn't jive was Fran. Janlin wanted desperately to protect Anaya's plan. What would Stepper do if he found out? She just couldn't be sure. "What do you think Fran told them?" she said, blithely changing the subject.

Stepper frowned. "I don't know, though I am really curious as to why she stayed."

"Yeah, me too."

CHAPTER THIRTY-THREE

JANLIN WATCHED STEPPER joking about his idiocy during supper that evening.

"You'd think I know the difference between on and off, being a captain and all," he said, drawing laughter. Janlin touched her lips, the memory of their kiss lingering like the coals of a bright fire.

Gordon elbowed her. "What the hell happened between you two out there?" he said in an undertone meant for her ears only.

She dropped her hand from her lips. Heat rose in her cheeks, and she ducked her head. "Just Stepper being an idiot," she said.

"Get off it, luv," Gordon said. "You're blushing like a school girl. He drew you off so you had some nice time alone together, right? So, what, then? Give over."

Janlin swallowed, grasping onto the final part of the afternoon's conversation to help cool her down. "Like I said, Stepper being an idiot. He wanted to test the jets and throw me off."

"And?" Gordon drew the word out, urging her to fill in the blank. Janlin sighed.

"And he asked me to give him another chance," she admitted.

"I knew it! Bloody wanker."

Janlin laughed.

Gordon grinned. "I can see why you'd want to, but I can see why you wouldn't." He was serious now. "Will you?"

Her own levity faded. "I don't know. He also asked me why I showed up here clean, unlike you lot, and I lied to him. Without even a pause, I just knew it wouldn't be a good idea to reveal Anaya's plan to him."

Gordon sucked on his top lip and shook his head. "And what are you going to do when it's time to tell them?"

"I don't know that, either, but I've had a lot of questions come up regarding Anaya and what she really wants from me. I'm beginning to think I've been had."

She didn't want to tell him that, but it wouldn't be right to let him go on thinking rescue was coming any day. Still, his look of disappointment crushed her.

"Besides, if I told Stepper, he'd tell the Huantag and they'd take the comm-unit from me. Seeing as it's the only line of hope we've got, I can't let that happen, not until I'm sure."

"How're you gonna get sure?"

Janlin just shook her head, unable to answer.

Gordon sighed. "None of this seems right to me," he said. Then he straightened up and turned to face her. "Will you help me with something?"

"Sure."

"I want you to take me into the city to meet Falco. Let me sit and talk with him, reason things out in my own way. You know how persuasive I can be."

Janlin knew what Gordon would be asking. "Isn't that the same as Stepper telling them? What if it doesn't go over well?"

"I won't tell them about Anaya. All I want to do is ask them to help me go looking for the *Hope* on my own."

Janlin had her doubts, but what could it hurt? Maybe they could get help, get out into the solar system again, maybe even meet up with Anaya and be able to help her. Maybe they could find out the truth of what was going on out there.

"If we could get out there and find Anaya, we could help her secure the ship. Once we return, we would be on much better ground for bargaining with the Huantag."

Gordon sat straighter, his old spark back. "Sounds like a plan B to me. If the Huantag won't listen, won't help, then we could say they've forced our hand, right?"

"Right. Okay, we'll go for a visit right after flight training tomorrow."

Gordon squeezed her arm. "Thanks, luv. And listen, if you need me to tell that wanker to leave off . . ."

Janlin laughed. "I can handle that wanker just fine, don't you worry."

CHAPTER THIRTY-FOUR

JANLIN PACED THE floor as Gordon pled his case. Falco went on about the Huantag philosophy of not leaving the planet once again. Still, something about it didn't ring true to Janlin. As much as any religion could be dogmatic and stubborn, for some reason this just seemed too . . . practiced. There was no passion behind the belief. These folk said they would be doing the humans a great injustice if they let them leave the planet, but Janlin didn't buy it.

"See, I left my own wife back there," Gordon said, indicating Falco's mate. "We want children, but if I can't get back, show her that we can travel to other planets, find a new home . . ."

Falco rustled his wings. Was it agitation? Or just getting comfortable? It was so hard to tell.

"Others have promised to stay, to honour our ways."

"Others?" Janlin said, drawing everyone's attention. "Like who?"

"Many agreed. Many more will soon."

Janlin and Gordon exchanged a look. "When did these agreements take place?"

Falco met her challenge with his expressionless gaze. "During the flight training. Soon you will all have your own suits, and everyone can be free to fly as they wish."

"That's all very nice, but are you also saying we're not free to try and return to our original home? If you truly believed that people should stay close to their homes and care for it instead of always moving on when they'd ruined the land, then you should be happy to help us return to our home. Maybe you could help us repair our planet like you did here. There's so much we could learn from you."

Falco stared so long Janlin fidgeted. "You challenge our belief, Janlin. I must think about this, discuss it with others. In that time, I will not tell the others your actual desires in order to keep you safe. Try to forget them if you can. Live in peace. Choose a new mate." This last he directed at Gordon, who shot to his feet.

"I will not!"

"Gordon, hey, take it easy," Janlin said, tugging on his arm. He'd gained weight and muscle here on Huantag, and her tug was like trying to move a boulder.

"Please try to understand our beliefs too, Falco," Janlin said, her voice harsher than she meant it to be. "We don't take new mates easily." Falco waved his mate to withdraw, and stood to meet their protest.

"This is the way of us. If you wish to share our home, then you must honour it."

"Bloody hell," Gordon said under his breath.

"You honour us with your kindness," Janlin said, jumping in over Gordon's cursing. "Thank you. Please think about what we have said, and how you can truly help us in the best way. Okay?"

Her little speech seemed to agitate him further, so Janlin made excuses for them to leave immediately, not staying the night as originally planned.

"Back to plan A?" Janlin asked just before they launched.

"Plan A it is," Gordon said. "And Janlin? Thanks for not trusting the bastards too quickly. You were right all along."

She nodded in acknowledgement. Maybe she was also right about Anaya, since her instincts seemed to tell true. Maybe the Gitane were on their way to them right now, and their desperate plan was more than necessary.

Or maybe she and Gordon would need a plan C, one where they would have to get off the planet, find the Imag, and steal back the *Hope* all on their own. Only time would tell.

She didn't mention her fears to Gordon.

"I BARELY REMEMBER any of this," Janlin said as they studied the landing complex.

Gordon chewed his moustache for a bit before answering. "You had other things on your mind."

That she had. Now, though, they needed a way off the planet, either to disable the shielding from the orbital or go out from there to find the *Hope*.

"So, what do they look like?"

Gordon gave her a blank look.

"The shuttles, dimwit. What are we looking for?"

Gordon looked back at the complex. "It's shuttle, singular, and it's right there in front of you."

Janlin scanned the area again in confusion. A large building built of the same reinforced mud-brick as their village huts stood by the blackened landing area. On the edge of the site towered a featureless plug of shiny steel . . . or what she thought must be steel. She had hoped the building, which boasted large doors on one side, held a shuttle she could steal and fly out of here. Now Gordon said only one shuttle existed, and it stood before her.

"No way . . . that alien barn silo?"

Gordon snorted. "Call it what you like. The exterior is some bio-tech material they engineer, much like our nano-tech hulls. It's tough enough for re-entry, yet Earth friendly."

"You mean Huantag friendly."

"Details. Anyhow, this is the only one, at least at this compound. I would imagine there are other landing sites, but this is the only one ever seen around here."

"Space me, I really don't remember much of our arrival. Where are the thrusters? The landing gear? The hatch, for crying out loud?"

Gordon opened his mouth to answer, but a movement to the south made her grip his arm. They lay still under the shelter of the scrub brush, eyes tracking the approaching Huantag.

They'd chosen their spot to avoid the most obvious flight path from the city, and rolled in the pervasive tan dust to camouflage their clothing. Their efforts seemed to work. Huantag circled in and landed without giving the ridge a second glance.

"Watch this," Gordon breathed in her ear.

The aliens pressed hand controls and the featureless tube blossomed like a steel flower. Ramps appeared, openings were revealed, and the Huantag moved in and out, adjusting the controls both on the machine and on the handheld controls.

"I think we need us one of those remote controls," Janlin said. "Think you can figure it out?"

"Bloody right I can," Gordon said. "I figure out the rigging, you sail, remember?"

"Don't get huffy . . . that's exactly what I keep you around for you know." She grinned, and he grinned back. This was way more fun than sitting around waiting for some alien to come rescue them.

"You'd be lost without me, luv."

"You know it." Janlin wished she had some binoculars. "So, how do we get one?" She didn't relish the idea of violence, if it could be done some other way.

They watched for a while.

"What do you figure they're doing?" Janlin asked.

"Maintenance? Prep for launch? Hard to say," Gordon said, never taking his gaze off the scene below them. "But if it's a launch, I'd sure like to be aboard."

"Stowaways, or . . ."

"A hijack situation," Gordon finished.

"I love the way you think."

They watched and waited, hoping for an opportunity to appear.

Then the two aliens disappeared into the compound.

"This is it," Janlin said, already up and moving. Gordon matched her pace, gaze never leaving the doorway of the building.

A hundred meters. Heat sucked at Janlin's energy, but she didn't break stride. The open shuttle beckoned, just asking for passengers. Seventy meters. She blinked blinding sweat out of her eyes. It felt so good to take matters into their own hands. Forty meters.

"Janlin!" Gordon grabbed her arm, swinging her around as he pulled her to a stop. Huge shapes dropped out of the green sky to land in swirls of dust all around them. Janlin cursed, covering her face with her arms.

Huantag. A dozen of the largest specimens of Huantag she'd

seen yet. One was a golden eagle to Falco's peregrine falcon.

The force of their cries made Janlin cover her ears.

"Restricted!"

"No honour!"

"Broken promises!"

The two aliens at the compound appeared in the doorway, calling out orders.

"Take them to the Council, and double our watch."

Janlin sputtered, wanting to argue that she'd made no promises, but two of the huge Birdfolk stepped forward and pointed at the sky. There seemed no way to politely refuse.

CHAPTER THIRTY-FIVE

"WE PROVIDE YOU a home, food, safety. You promise to stay. Why would you now try and take our ship, break your promises?"

They faced Aquila, a massive dark eagle that Falco said was their leader in all, and his council, all Huantag of significant size.

"The promises of one are not the promises of all," Janlin said. Her whole body trembled with fatigue from all the flying . . . and from the fear of facing what could only be a large nerve whip aimed at her side. Still, she would not smother what needed said. "If you held true to what you profess to believe, you would do everything in your power to help us return to our home planet."

The challenge took them aback. She could tell by the shifting wings, the puffed head feathers. Maybe she actually could learn alien body language.

Gordon stepped forward. "We left loved ones behind. How can you expect us to just forget them? We were supposed to find help, not abandon them forever!"

"It's not that we have no honour," Janlin continued. "It's that we have too much honour to not try getting home again. Seriously, can you blame us for that?"

Falco stepped out of the shadows of the cavernous interior room. Janlin sucked in a breath at the sight of him, wondering if he came to help or condemn.

"You must tell them the truth," Falco said, drawing the attention of the entire room. He ruffled his feathers, nearly doubling his size in his agitation.

Janlin grasped at this straw. "Yes, please tell us the truth."

This caused quite a stir, and the two Huantag that had accompanied them here appeared on either side of Falco.

"Leave him be," said Aquila. The big aliens stepped back, and everyone quieted. Falco stepped forward.

"The humans have proved to be more than the Imag ever admitted. They have a right to question. They have a right to know why their desire for home is forbidden!"

This caused another uproar, but Aquila stretched his wings, something Janlin had never seen a Huantag do inside before, and this caused instant silence to fall over the crowd.

"As much as your words hold sense, Falco, we made an oath to the Imag not to speak of it," Aquila said.

"Why? Why would we hold to such a demand? I think the Imag fear these tiny beings more than they even fear us. I also think the Imag will bring war upon us even if we do keep our oaths."

Now the noise level rose higher than ever. Aquila seemed lost in thought, and let it ride out naturally. This had to be why the philosophy felt false. At least she could take some comfort in knowing the Huantag had more than just religion backing their refusal to help.

"Falco makes sense," Aquila said as the noise trailed off. "I cannot see why telling this will cause war." He turned to face Janlin and Gordon. "The Imag made us promise that none of you would ever leave this planet. They also demanded we never tell you of this, but because we will ensure the first promise is kept, they will never know of the second being broken."

Janlin swallowed her shock and fumbled for something to keep the conversation going. "They must fear us to demand such promises of you. Why did you agree?"

"The Imag build a new warship, and our shields will only stand against so much. All we wish is to be left alone. When we learned of you, we decided to buy you from the Imag in return for their promise to leave us be. We did not think that making these promises would cause you harm, but instead help you get away from their cruelty while ensuring they would not attack us."

"Don't get me wrong, we are incredibly grateful for you taking us away from them," Janlin said. "But these Imag are bullying you even as you hide safely away from it all. Think of what they might do to others if they master the Jump technology and leave this system. You have to reconsider and let us go try and stop them."

"We cannot," Aquila said bluntly. "A human leaving this planet will be seen as an act of war. We will not put our people at such risk. The shuttle will be guarded even more closely now. You must accept that this is your home now, and let things be."

Gordon surged forward with a cry of rage, but all the Huantag spread their wings with their own cries, and presented nerve whips. The air crackled, and the smell of burnt ions filled the room. Gordon turned in a slow circle, his fists clenched, his face twisted in powerless anger.

"Come on, Gordo," Janlin said. "We're done here."

"This won't be the end of it," he warned them. Janlin shushed him and pulled him out of the room. They walked slowly down the long corridor to the launch ledge. Janlin struggled for every step, unsure if she would be able to do much more than coast to the ground and curl up in a ball.

"Janlin!"

They turned to find Falco approaching. Wary guards watched from the council chamber, but did not follow.

"I am sorry, Janlin, but at least you understand why we restrict you," Falco said. He tipped his head, his black eyes studying them both. "You must be very tired from so much flying today. Please, stay with me for tonight and rest. It is the best I can do to show you my friendship."

CHAPTER THIRTY-SIX

GRIEF WAS A funny thing, Janlin found, rearing up to crush her at the strangest times. But today, as she sat in the sun and shelled a legume-type vegetable that resembled a cross between a pea and corn, she felt . . . resigned. Resigned to her loss, resigned to Anaya's continued silence, resigned to possibly living out the rest of their lives here.

Tyrell and Teardrop went by, so lost in each other they didn't even notice Janlin. She smiled, wistful. Was it any surprise that she wanted to say yes to Stepper's request?

Shouts echoed through the community. At first, she stiffened, listening hard, but soon she realized the calls were filled with excitement. Curiosity roused her, and she left her work in the shade to walk down and join the growing crowd by the cook hut.

Inaba climbed onto a bench and raised his arms.

"Before rumours get right out of hand, let me say this as simply as I can." He couldn't help but beam at everyone. Still, Janlin wasn't at all prepared for the enormity of his announcement. "The Birdfolk have announced that they can reprogram our nano-contraceptives."

A general uproar followed this, and Janlin immediately scanned for Gordon. This would be yet another blow for him.

Inaba went on. "I'm not sure when, but they will choose two or three people, volunteers of course, and take them to their city for the procedure."

"We should celebrate!" Tyrell shouted, holding a glowing Teardrop in one arm. Shouts of approval met his suggestion.

Janlin sucked in a breath. Excitement and frustration warred within her. To stay and bear a child in this paradise of clean air and water and abundant food . . . how could she possibly consider laying this place open to the Imag? At the same time, how could she not hold up her end of a plan that might take them home to Ursula with plants and ideas in hand?

Anaya's silence was deafening, and most of the engineers had agreed that the Imag would not be successful in manipulating the Jumpship by themselves. Either that, or Fran had taken them on the Jumpship *Hope*, and there was no safe home to return to anyway. Steve had agreed that if Fran did cave to the Imag, the ships were pre-set to return to Earth's solar system, and Fran wouldn't be able to change it. So really, would it be so bad to stay?

The arguments went around and around in her head. She stared at the sky while people laughed and cried and danced around her in the face of their new hope for new life.

Someone squeezed her shoulder, and she looked around to see Gordon, his face at odds with those around him.

"Nothing yet?" he asked. Every day, he asked. Janlin sighed and shook her head. She only turned the device on for a little while at a time, but it was hard not to keep checking.

Gordon gave a decisive nod. "So be it." He turned away, as if to leave, but then turned back. "You should tell them . . . all of them."

Janlin winced. He wasn't speaking quietly or making any effort to guard his words. She shushed him, her secret safe only because of the joyful chaos around them.

"Would it make any difference? If she's not coming, she's not coming," Janlin said.

Gordon looked ready to shout, or cry, his mouth tight and his eyebrows pinched. Finally, he just turned and stalked away. Janlin let out a long breath.

Stepper walked up. "What was that about?"

"He's grieving. This is probably the worst news he could hear," Janlin replied.

Stepper regarded her. "It just seemed there was more anger

in that exchange than grief."

Janlin rubbed her face with both hands. "He is angry. What he would give to have Ursula here now . . ."

"Makes us pretty lucky."

Janlin blushed. "I should get back to what I was doing," she said.

Stepper smiled and nodded, letting her go. He really was on his best behaviour, although she puzzled for a while over a certain look of relief she'd caught on his face.

That night, Janlin stayed on the outskirts of the celebration. Both her mind and her stomach kept doing little flips at the idea of being fertile again, but the party didn't fit her mood at all. She'd searched for Gordon and been unable to find him. She let out a heavy sigh and sipped on her drink.

Many people had paired off in the time on Huantag, and for them this was a huge opportunity. Unfortunately, it made them more comfortable and less likely to want to leave. Janlin wondered if people would fight against going home if Anaya did show up.

Worse was the effect this announcement had on Gordon. As the days and then weeks had passed and no word came over the alien device Janlin carried, Gordon had become more and more withdrawn.

Janlin rose and left the common area to wander the clean hard-packed streets, away from the noise, away from any sense of celebration. Should she reveal her strange alliance, or just stay quiet now that it didn't look to be coming to anything? Did she go off and put the entire planet in danger on the chance that Anaya was there, and for some reason unable to reach her? Did she just let go of all of it, and settle into this beautiful sanctuary with clean air and abundant food and fresh water and—the biggest one—a chance to raise children unencumbered by SpaceOp and famine and an uninhabitable planet? Not one answer seemed right, so, just as she had for days upon days, she did nothing but wait.

Finally, she reached the structure she called home and leaned against the cool adobe.

A shadow moved and became a man on the far side of the walkway.

Stepper stood alone in the light of the intermittent globes.

His gaze, his silence, his presence told her everything. She could have him if she would. If she set aside all the regret and anger and betrayal and guilt, he would be hers again.

As soon as she took a step towards him, he moved too, closing the distance between them. The sounds of revelry rose and fell in the distance, the smells of packed clay and cooked meat and soaped bodies and linen cloth joined the new blooms of desert flowers and the pine-like scrub.

They stopped within reach of each other, his face half in shadow now, his expression serious.

"I love you, Janlin Kavanagh."

"I love you, too, and you know it."

His eyes widened. "No, I didn't. I thought I'd thoroughly trampled on your love until it became irrevocable hate."

Janlin shrugged, looked away, looked back. "It's a fine line, they say."

Stepper held out his hand to her. She looked at the hand, at him, at the sky. She had to know.

"Have you completely given up on going home?"

She caught the flicker of disappointment as his hand dropped to his side. "All we have is this moment. No one can take that away, no matter what else might come later. Why not treasure this little slice of freedom?"

"I'm scared to let go, to enjoy it. I feel like I'd be giving in, and I would forget all those back home that are struggling to survive. Besides, if I relax into something good, something else will come along and rip it all away. Every time I start to believe—"

Stepper stepped closer. "Shhhhh," he said, lifting her chin with one gentle finger. His touch quickened her pulse, just as it always had.

"You will never stop fighting for a way home, and I wouldn't want you to," he said. "Nothing should change that—it means you are always full of hope."

She took his face in her hands and kissed him then. He was right, and they were here, now, together. What if they could never leave? What if this was it?

"Stepper," she said against his hair. "There's something I have to tell you." He pulled her tight against him and kissed her so thoroughly her body tingled and her head spun.

"What is it?" he asked.

Janlin's mind stumbled back to reality, resisting every step of the way. "I . . ." She didn't want to start, knowing it would change everything, spoil this night of celebration.

Stepper looked at her in concern, then took her by the hand and knelt down on one knee.

"Whatever it is, it will wait for tomorrow," he said. "Tonight, I want to chase away all your fears, all your worries, everything. Just for tonight. Is that okay?"

She clasped both her hands over his and pulled him up with a little laugh. "I think that's exactly what I need."

She gave herself to the moment. *Just this once*, she thought, and then her thoughts escaped, lost to the sensation of touching, and being touched.

CHAPTER THIRTY-SEVEN

GORDON FOUND HER at breakfast.

"Have a good time?"

Heat rose on her face. "Not like I haven't slept with him before, Gordon," she said, glancing up at him to see how he really meant it. Judging by his pensive face, his big brother act would come next.

"I just can't believe you went back to him, after all the complaining—"

She laid a hand over his arm. "I know it's stupid, and I know it's not fair to you, and I don't even know if I've gone back to him or just allowed a one-night fling. Can we just let it go for now?"

Gordon sighed. "I'm sorry, Jan. It's just . . ." He sat down hard and stared into his mug.

"I know, Spin, I know. Would it make you feel any better to know that I'm going to tell him?"

Gordon's eyes widened. "Yes, that would make me feel better. So, when?"

"Soon. I was going to tell him this morning, but he was up and gone before I had a chance."

"Hmmm," was all Gordon said.

So, wanting to be true to her downcast friend, Janlin went in search of Stepper, despite feeling like an awkward teenager after a first date. She found him and Captain Inaba discussing resources of the planet and what they could produce to make themselves independent. Janlin debated using that as an excuse to leave it until later. She knew Stepper wouldn't be impressed by her decision to withhold such information from him.

That choice was made for her, however. When Stepper looked up and saw her, he made his excuses and came right over.

"Walk with me for a bit?" she asked, and he smiled and agreed. If he was going to have his moment of being hurt, let him have it out of prying eyes. He'd get over it.

"Are you . . . okay with last night?" he asked, his voice tentative.

Janlin wondered. Was she?

Yes.

It was in the way she longed to touch him, to hold his hand, to finally come clean with him about Anaya. So, she pulled him into the shade of a tree and kissed him, her heart soaring, his arms pulling her close. When they came up for air she stepped back and faced him square on.

"I'm determined not to put off talking to you about this anymore," she announced.

His bemused face was enough to make her want to start another kiss. Then she began to wonder just how to explain things.

"See, Gordon refuses to give up hope of going home, and can you blame him—"

Stepper stepped back from her. "There's nothing to hope for any more, Janlin! Can't you see that? Gordon is just going to have to deal with it."

Shocked, Janlin stared at him as the backlash of Stepper's words hit her. Gone was the soft voice of the night before. Gone was the understanding and support. "It's not true, if you'd just listen—" she started, but he wasn't having any of it.

"If it is Gordon you really want, why did you bother to sleep with me?"

"What?" Janlin shook her head, her mind stumbling away from her confession in reaction to his words. "Space me, Stepper Jordan, you are one sick puppy, you know that?"

Whether he heard her or not, she'd never know, because he walked away and rounded a bend, back to his discussion of life on Huantag.

That's when she understood his strange reaction from yesterday afternoon. Stepper worried that without Ursula around, she and Gordon would hook up. Any conflict between them was, in that light, good news. And now, for her to start her explanation with Gordon's problems was simply too much for Stepper.

"IT's OFFICIAL. I'M a complete idiot."

Gordon looked ready to make some smart remark. In fact, Janlin counted on it. But his will to even try seemed to drain away as she watched.

"What happened?" he asked instead.

Janlin just shook her head, not trusting her voice. "Come for a walk?"

They wandered out onto the plains, headed in a roundabout way to their favourite rock pile. So often they'd sat out here and examined Anaya's device, discussing possibilities, trying different settings, calling out again and again. Was that why Stepper thought she had something with Gordon?

She told him of Stepper's accusations.

Gordon choked on his astonishment. "Really, the wanker said that? Bloody hell."

"I know! And he just wouldn't listen to another word I had to say."

"So, you didn't tell him then," Gordon said.

Janlin sputtered her protest. "I couldn't get a word in edgewise before he walked away!"

Gordon stared into the distance, clearly brooding. Janlin felt like arguing, but she realized that if she'd really wanted Stepper to know, she could've just pulled out the comm-unit and shoved it in his face. That would've shut him up.

"Is he right? Do you feel that way about me?" Gordon asked out of the blue.

Janlin gaped for a moment, cutting off her immediate reaction of scorn. If he was serious—and he sure looked serious—then answering in a flippant manner would only hurt his feelings. Still, honesty was called for.

"I love you like a brother, Gordon. That's all." She watched his face. "Do you . . . ?"

Gordon shook his head, but his eyes glinted strange in the sun. "What if we're stuck here? What then?"

Janlin caught his attention, held his gaze. "I could never be your Ursula."

His face crumpled, and he turned away, occasionally knuckling his eyes as they sat in the light of the morning sun. Janlin took out the comm-unit and turned it over and over in her hands.

"I'm gonna have to take down the shields," she finally said.

Gordon shifted around, but he didn't look at her, didn't challenge her.

"What if this thing is broken or dead and Anaya's out there waiting? We have to try something! We've done the honourable thing and asked politely for help and it got us nowhere."

Gordon sucked in a deep breath. "You're right."

"What? Really? I was kinda counting on you to be my conscience."

"No. You're right. We've no other options left. We've got to take out the Huantag shields."

Janlin sat speechless for a long moment. "Okay, good. So, if you were building a shield generator and the controls to run it, where would you put them?"

"In orbit."

It sucked to see Gordon this low. "Yeah, I get that, but there would need to be something down here too. Falco even said something about it being both. Do you think we can do it from here?"

Gordon had no answers for her, and they sat awhile longer with nothing else to say. Finally, they rose to go take their duty shifts in the village.

"They'll be watching us," Gordon said as they trudged through the dust.

Janlin sighed. "I know. We'll just have to do what we can."

Everything looked hopeless, and the hurt of Stepper's latest outburst only left her feeling desperate. Still, looking at Gordon made her realize just how much harder all of this could be. Every single day that passed by tore him apart a little more.

Their feet left the raw dusty plains and found hard-packed paths.

"See ya later," Janlin said.

"Yeah, see ya."

"Oh, and Gordon?"

"Yeah?"

"Thanks for not saying I told you so."

STEPPER WAITED IN the shadows by her door that night. Warring feelings swamped her.

"I'm sorry I was impatient earlier," he said. "I know Gordon is hurting, I know you two are close, I know you feel we're giving up on going home. But I think we have to, Janni. We have to make the best of this, and fighting it will make the Birdfolk mistrust us."

"We simply cannot give up," she said, sure of that if nothing else. "I won't, for Gordon and Ursula in particular, but for all the people back on those Orbitals . . . and on Earth! . . . who still need help. While I live and breathe, I will try to find a way home."

He went very still. "I love you, I desire you, you say you love me . . . can't that be enough?" he said.

She closed her eyes and tipped her head to lean against the warm adobe wall. "It should be. I want it to be." She opened her eyes to find him studying her. "I wish it were that simple. Or that we shared the same goals."

He sighed. "Yeah, I hear that. I'm sorry that we can't enjoy this place without feeling so guilty."

"We wouldn't feel guilty if we were still trying to get help for those back home. If one or two of us could go back to the Imag, steal the Hope . . ."

"Janlin, sweetie, we won't be leaving the planet," he said, his voice grave. He took up her hand and drew her near. "There are shields in place, and rules that the Birdfolk take very seriously. They won't allow any travel off-world, that's their sacred law. They let us come here, got us away from the Imag, now we have to honour their ways."

Of course. He didn't know that she knew all this already, and thought he was breaking bad news to her. News that would convince her to give up on going home. She let him draw her into his arms, needing the comfort, wondering if somehow it could be okay to be with him, to live here, to let go of trying against all odds.

"I'm still not sure," she said, her voice muffled in his shirt. He squeezed.

"I know. And I'm sorry for how awful this is for Gordon. Does that have to destroy our happiness?"

CHAPTER THIRTY-EIGHT

THE HOUSES GROWN for them in the Huantag city were finally completed, and everyone flew in to attend the ceremony. Most of the scientists had expressed interest in living there to better study the Birdfolk's physiology. Still, many chose to stay in the village, having grown comfortable there.

They all flew together. Janlin saw grins flashing back and forth at the amazing experience of a few dozen humans traveling through the air with huge wings extended out over their backs. As they neared the city, Huantag rose to meet them and lead them out to the meadow where their new homes were. Tyrell called out to Teardrop, waving and pointing, his grin so wide it was ridiculous.

Janlin grimaced. She wanted to tell the youngster off. *Have you forgotten about Earth, and those left behind? Have you forgotten the fact that we were supposed to return with hope for those people?*

Gordon's eyes flashed and his brow furrowed. She could see the thunder brooding, and she wondered if Stepper would live through the storm when Gordon's temper finally erupted.

Janlin's eyes popped at the change in the once empty meadow. Now grand structures filled the nature clearing, some with straight walls like the humans had described for them, with shining windows and peaked roofs, others done in the dome shape like the adobe huts. In addition, the area also thronged with Huantag of all ages, colours, and sizes. An area stood ready, kept clear for them to land, and another looked to be a stage or presentation area.

Once all safely on the ground, they were led again by their guides through the crowds. Huantag children swept by in a twittering group, their wings still unformed and their plumage fluffy, legs pumping as they ran.

"They are so adorable!" Teardrop said, misty-eyed. "I can't believe how many have come to this celebration for us."

"It's quite the gathering," Janlin agreed. Their guides directed them to benches set in rows at the front of the audience. Stepper moved in close, then maneuvered to sit right in between her and Gordon. Janlin frowned at his rudeness, but Gordon turned to chat with Teardrop, and she didn't want to start an argument, so she let it go.

On the other side of the open area before them stood the first houses Janlin had seen only a few weeks before. Now, instead of just wire frames, they resembled half-boulders squatting on the ground. Within, however, she knew they held all the amenities of a Huantag household—running water, plumbing, power, heating and cooling, and shielded doors and windows.

The lighting changed, and the crowd quieted. With no preliminary speech or introduction, Huantag burst into the open area in elaborate costumes, spinning and flying around in a frantic dance that stirred Janlin's blood. Music with unusual sounds and rhythms but a solid beat filled the area. She could feel the bass notes in the ground under her feet.

Aquila stepped into the light on one side of the dancing just as the music settled into a background hum. He was the largest, darkest Huantag they'd seen, and so clearly suited to being their leader. He stood regal and tall, gaining attention despite the whirl of dancers.

"In the beginning, Birdfolk rose together, growing in knowledge and learning, but using their planet without care."

The dance whirled fast, nearly frantic, the ones circling into the middle launching into the sky to spin and tumble back to the outer rings of the dance group. Janlin glanced at Stepper and

Gordon. Both of them stared, eyes wide, and she was glad to see them as awed by the performance as she felt.

"For thousands of years this continued, until the planet could take no more, could give no more. Life began to fail. This began the Dead Time."

Dead Time. Or at least that's how the translation came across, but it fit Janlin's memories of Earth, the burnt skeletons of forests, the depleted soils, the toxic oceans rising to destroy cities, the storms that raged through what was left.

The dance slowed, and the music faded. As each row of dancers reached the middle they stopped until they all stood still, crowded together at the centre, the only movement feathers ruffling in the wind.

"Finally, we applied all our learning and skill to this planet, letting go of many things we thought were important in the struggle to care for our dying home."

The huddled group rippled, and raised their arms in unison to wave back and forth.

"Life returned, slowly, slowly, and we promised to never let foolish things distract us again."

From the centre emerged a spray of water, a glorious fountain lit by lights from below. The dancers fell and bowed to the bright fountain, and rose to dance in celebration around it, many rising on full-spread wings to create a multi-tiered dance.

"Space me, but that's beautiful," Stepper said. Janlin agreed.

The music changed, and Janlin searched for its source. It sounded like horns and drums now, low and sonorous, though she couldn't see any musicians. She suspected it was all produced electronically.

"We began to expand outwards, building homes on orbitals with great plans of moving ever outwards. But in doing this we forgot our home, our promise to our planet. We looked outwards instead of in."

New dancers appeared, circling to the outside but never rising up. In fact, these Huantag wore thick, padded costumes of burly shoulders, sunken heads, and masks all too familiar.

"Imag!" said many voices around her in recognition. Even the wings of those dancers acting as Imag were hidden away in the bulky costumes.

"The Imag came, stretching out into surrounding space, for

221

they had also stripped their planet into Dead Time. We welcomed them," the circle took the new dancers in, all swirling together, "but they did not understand the changes they needed to make to keep our home safe."

The Imag dancers threw out their arms and Huantag fell away from them, tumbling to the ground and drawing gasps from the crowd.

"We turned our vision back to our home, finally understanding that to move away would be our undoing. The Imag nearly brought us to a new Dead Time, and would not listen to our pleas, so we sent them away for the safety of our planet, and for our very lives."

They showed it all, the Imag pushed away, the continuation of the nurturing that brought the fountain back to life. At this time the Huantag's source of lighting was extinguished. Darkness enveloped the area. Then the lichen spore pulsed and glowed from both the new buildings and benches and naturally through the trees in the surrounding forest. The effect was stunning.

"From this we learned to always care for our own place, and to not run away from our problems."

The dance finished in a spiralling display that expanded out over their heads. The lichen seemed to dance too, a nebulous array of light and colour pulsing with the music. The dancers spread wider and wider out, until the music came to a crescendo and faded to a pleasant background melody that Janlin realized had been present throughout. Aquila moved into the centre, spreading his great wings, and children of all ages rushed into the stage to surround him, trilling and singing in a way that the ear-cells did not translate.

Stepper slipped his hand over hers. "Aren't they amazing?"

She nodded, letting his hand rest there. The longing to have a family, to stay here forever, became overwhelming.

"It brightens us to greatness to have you share our story. Soon we will find a way for you to have children again, to live in peace and harmony on our beautiful home."

She imagined a home with Stepper, imagined passionate nights and loving days like they had when they first met. She imagined being pregnant, raising children. If Anaya had tricked her, and they were stuck, would it be so bad to settle down and enjoy it?

Janlin longed for just such a life, but a glance past Stepper to Gordon's tear-streaked face brought the true reality of things back with frightening force. She squeezed Stepper's hand, her mind roiling. She would continue to hope on Anaya's return. For Gordon, for Ursula, for the survivors on Earth eating each other in desperation, for those in the stations fading away from lack of food. Once she had proof there was a way home, then she could bring Stepper on board.

She sat weeping with the beauty and hope displayed before her, waiting for the ceremony to end so she could somehow comfort Gordon.

CHAPTER THIRTY-NINE

AFTER THE CEREMONY Janlin grabbed Gordon by the hand, ignoring Stepper's attempts to engage her in conversation, and pulled him in the direction of where she'd seen Falco.

"If you're trying to piss Stepper off, it's working," Gordon said. He'd dried his eyes, but he looked hollow, his gaze burnt by salt tears.

"Stepper can wait. We're going to sign up for one of these new houses."

Gordon blinked. "Really?"

"Really. This is a great way to snoop around more," she said in an undertone as they moved through the crowds viewing the new homes.

They found Falco with another Huantag discussing the possible positions that the humans could have in the community. He ended the conversation when he saw their approach with a bob of his head, and the other Huantag moved away.

"Janlin. Gordon. Did you enjoy our performance?" His eyes were bright, reflecting the lights decorating the paths.

"Very much," Janlin said. "It is a reminder of the Dead Time happening back home on Earth, and it gives us hope we can repair our own home planet someday."

Falco's flinch told her what she needed to know, even if he covered it well. "The story must be told again and again—so we do not forget, our children do not forget, and our children's children do not forget."

Gordon jumped right in. "Listen, mate, we'd like to learn from you, try to settle in better. Could you help me get into one of these homes? I'd also like to work and learn with an electrician or communications tech or something like that."

Falco bowed slightly. "If that is your work specialty, then this can be done."

He asked them to wait, and launched up to soar around over the crowd, displaying his absolute comfort in the sky as he dodged other flyers. Another rose to join him and they returned together.

"What about me?" Janlin asked Gordon as they watched the two approach.

"You're welcome to crash here anytime, of course," he said, "but wouldn't us living together make Stepper uncomfortable?"

"Well, yeah."

"Then why not find a place with him, give the whole thing a go? Make it look like we really are getting comfortable. It might give us more chances to act later."

She had to agree it made sense.

Falco's friend was shorter, more rounded, with pure white plumage marked with touches of black on wing tips, head, and down his back.

"This is Gordon, and Janlin," Falco said, pointing to each in turn. "We will need Steve to set up my friend's name in your translation database. For now, he will teach you how to set the power systems for the next batch of homes."

"You're building more?" Janlin asked.

Falco drew upright, his eyes wide. "Of course. When children come, you will need more space for family groups and schools. Is this not good?"

Neither of them answered, and Falco blithely continued. Gordon agreed that learning the Huantag's power systems would be an interesting job, and Falco walked them over to the smallest style of dwelling in the meadow. "This would be perfect for you. Would you like to see how the power is set up before we cover it over?" Gordon nodded. "Janlin, please wait for my partner to return before you come inside. He will have important steps to show you both inside and out for the operation of your building."

"Sure, go ahead. I'll be there soon," she said, giving Gordon a smile and a nudge. Falco guided him into the building.

Stepper called out to her from the doorway of a smallish shelter done in an Earth-style look.

She joined him, and he pulled her inside with a grin. "Here? Or should we stay at the village? I do like the pools there."

She couldn't help but smile as his excitement. "Maybe we need both."

"Ah, brilliant idea!" he said, giving her a warm kiss.

"Gordon is looking at taking that one, we could just bunk there when we're here until more shelters are completed."

Stepper got a funny look. She knew that look, and she didn't like it. "I still can't believe you aren't interested in him," he said. "You guys seem attached at the hip."

Janlin could only shake her head. "You really have forgotten all about Ursula, haven't you?"

"Space me, you think I'm blind? Ursula isn't here, and you're just waiting for him to get over her."

"Stepper!"

"Well, it sure seems true! You are always hesitating, always missing when I go looking for you, and then you two come wandering back together . . . what am I supposed to think?"

"You're supposed to trust me!"

"I want to, Janlin, but your actions just keep making me look like an idiot."

"I make you look idiotic?" Her voice rose, and his did too, until they were both slinging ever-more brutal insults.

Falco and Gordon had emerged from the other house, and other Birdfolk hurried over. "Please, we do not accept this violence," one of them said.

"Sorry," Janlin said, to both them and Stepper.

"Whatever, Janlin." Stepper turned and stalked off.

"Janlin?" It was Gordon.

"Just Stepper being Stepper," she said.

"And you being you, I'd imagine," Gordon replied, and he couldn't keep the little smirk from his lips.

"Yeah, something like that. I guess I've been as much a jerk as he has."

"Well, now, don't take on too much of the blame."

"He thinks I'm just waiting for you to get over Ursula. I'm afraid nothing I do or say will ever convince him otherwise."

Gordon sighed. "You're probably right."

Falco approached and did his little bow. "Gordon, the building is done and ready for you to live."

He looked over at Janlin. "Is this normal action for humans, to love one day and the next day hurt?"

Janlin gave a dry laugh. "Well, it's normal for Stepper and me. I wish you could see Gordon and Ursula, though . . . that's a completely different story."

CHAPTER FORTY

MANY SETTLED INTO the scientific community, now officially named Kavanagh Meadows after Janlin's dad. Gordon proposed the name to the other residents without Janlin's knowledge, and they all agreed, surprising her with a beautiful naming ceremony that doubled as a memorial for Rudigar Kavanagh.

Janlin travelled between the two communities, but Gordon never returned to the mud brick village, and Stepper never showed his face around the Meadows. It actually made things a little easier for her. And while she still didn't tell Stepper about Anaya, she did make an effort to spend more time with him, sharing meals and baths and a bed until it started to feel like it really could be something.

Janlin took on menial work washing dishes and food-gathering, content to do her part. But she also checked for word from Anaya and continued scouting for intel on the shields. Meanwhile Falco's friend, dubbed Lari for the Latin suborder of the gull family, taught Gordon the basics of Huantag electronics.

"Absolutely fascinating," Gordon told her one night as they shared a simple evening meal of tubers and grains. "This mossy stuff absorbs nearly ten times more energy than it needs to live and grow, and the Huantag tap it, even store it in a type of fuel cell set up. Through tapping it, they can control the growth and use it to both construct buildings and produce power for anything and everything."

Janlin only half listened. "What of their communications? Are they going to let you into that?"

"I'm working on it. Have you had any luck?"

Janlin hadn't. She'd wandered the city, holding conversations with any Huantag that had the time and interest to do so, without gathering anything of interest. "I think the shielding setup is on a top-level need-to-know basis only. The rest of them live on comfortably knowing the shields are there and not caring how or why or where they're run from."

Gordon sighed, pushing his half-eaten meal away. "I'd give anything to share that with Ursula," he said, indicating the food. "Or at least hear her voice again."

Janlin sat up as if struck.

"What?" Gordon asked, eyebrows knitting.

But she bent and ducked her head under the table, undoing her left boot. She dug a finger into the small tear in the tongue and came up victorious.

"Gordon, I can give you Ursula's voice," she said, holding up the nano-recorder. "If you're sure you want it."

Gordon's face twisted between longing and grief. "I do. Bloody hell, as much as it won't matter a smidge, I do."

Janlin dialled up the duet from so long ago, and they both cried as they watched a younger Gordon sing with his lovely wife.

JANLIN SAT OUT in the common area of Kavanagh Meadows, working with Elwood and Perry of the *Renegade* crew on some flight gear adjustments they were planning to propose, when the sky darkened with a large group of Huantag. Aquila landed in front of Janlin.

"We seek Gordon," he said.

Janlin, already on her feet, frowned at the lack of greeting and the harsh tone. "He is working with Lari in the city," she said.

"No, he is not. Gordon left a message for Lari. He threatened that he would destroy all the Birdfolk in our city if we did not reveal the location of our shielding devices by nightfall . . . to you, Janlin." The fierce leader glared at her, his black eyes never blinking. "Now we cannot find him, or any way that he could possibly do as he says he will."

"He wouldn't," Janlin said. "He's just desperate to go home. Don't you see? Even kind and generous men like him will go to great lengths to be free. You say we are not allowed to fight the Imag and try and get our ship back, and so we will fight you."

He stared, the silence growing thick. Finally, he drew up to full height and made his pronouncement. "All humans must return to the outer village. You will be detained there, unwelcome to learn or work with us any longer." Elwood and Perry both gasped. "Your flight gear will also be taken, for it is not safe to us for you to fly."

Janlin groaned. "This will only make things worse," she said, but they were done listening to her. Aquila launched into the sky, calling orders to escort any human found amongst Huantag back to the village and set a perimeter guard rotation.

"What about Gordon?" she called out, but he already flew too fast and far to hear.

"Please prepare to fly," one of the remaining Huantag said over Elwood and Perry's arguments and questions. Janlin dropped her own gear and took off at a run. The Huantag shouted for her to stop, and then made piercing calls that did not register in her translator.

More Huantag flew in, so Janlin dodged into the woods surrounding the meadow and hid behind and half under a huge boulder, trying to figure out what she was going to do. She had to avoid capture in order to help Gordon. She worked her way through the dense foliage parallel to the pathway, hoping she would get lucky.

If she had any clue what that recording would do to Gordon, she'd have crushed the nano-disk under her heel to ensure he never had a chance to see it.

Now, the only chance she and Gordon had was to stay free. Maybe they should start guerrilla tactics, doing little things to breed fear and make the Huantag realize they couldn't cage the humans here against their will.

She could smell the river and hear the rush of water. She pushed through and saw Gordon standing on the beach. A number of Huantag landed around him with their wings spread wide.

"Dammit, Gordon," she said under her breath. "You weren't

supposed to get caught." She'd have to do what she could on her own, then.

She turned to go deeper into the woods, ready to go to ground, when Gordon's cry of rage and fear reached her ears. Without a thought she turned back, charging through the trees to the riverbank.

"Enough," she shouted as she emerged. "No more nerve whips! You are not Imag!"

The Huantag that circled Gordon backed away and a few more landed to block any chance of her escaping. Gordon lay twitching in the rocks, his body locked rigid. Janlin ran to him, taking his head into her lap. Her hands came away red—he'd smacked his head with the fall.

"Sons of bitches," Janlin hissed. Gordon's eyes sought hers, tears leaking down into his ears, his mouth pulled back in rictus.

"Thank you for returning, Janlin," one of the Huantag said. "Now you will all go back to your village so that we may be sure of our safety."

CHAPTER FORTY-ONE

THE HUANTAG WERE true to their word, returning all travellers to the village and setting a vigilant guard around the clock to ensure no one went exploring. If she saw one land, Janlin would approach to beg for a word with Falco or Aquila, but the Huantag refused to speak with her, launching into the sky whenever she got close. Once, frustrated, she kept going, but that brought a flurry of stones from above until she gave up, returning bruised and sore to the village.

Everyone in the village cast her sullen looks, or just turned aside when she approached. The Huantag told Inaba and the rest of the leadership circle that they would review the situation in thirty days' time, but not before. Janlin and Gordon became outcasts, rightfully blamed for their loss of freedom.

Janlin went about her routines the best she could, avoiding everyone as much as possible, but most especially Stepper. When she couldn't avoid him, Stepper just looked through her as if she didn't even exist. She told herself it was for the best.

She worked hard to comfort Gordon, not caring what anyone else thought of the time they spent together, but Gordon remained grim to the point of being unbearable to be with.

Teardrop, of all people, became her pillar of strength through it all. The medic found Janlin at her father's gravesite one evening, red-eyed and miserable. Being a sweet young woman with more maturity than most, she didn't accuse or pry, just shared a basket of food and commented here and there on inane things like the weather.

Routine took over, as it will, and raw as she felt, Janlin was grateful for something to fall back on. People began speaking to her again, though Gordon did not fare as well as she did on that front. She continued to monitor the comm-unit, but not with the same vigilance or hope.

As Janlin and Teardrop walked from the mess hall one morning, clay mugs of flowerbud tea in hand and hair still damp from bathing, a *Renegade* crewmate waved them down.

"Iphie, you've got a new patient," he said. "Some cold or flu—not that you can do much for that, eh?" He grinned and went on his way, work gloves in one hand and a long-handled hoe in the other.

"Iffie?" Janlin teased, but Teardrop didn't rise to the bait.

"Iphimedeia," she said absently. "My mother was a Latin freak. You can see why I like the nickname." She closed her eyes, her face pale.

"You okay?" Janlin asked.

"I've been worried about this." Teardrop turned a watery blue gaze on Janlin. "I don't have anything left to fight infection. If bronchitis or pneumonia starts spreading, many could die very quickly." She took off in the direction of the med-hut.

"Whoa!" Janlin had to step double-time to catch up. "Maybe it's just one person with a cold, Teardrop. Aren't you blowing this a bit out of proportion?"

"Maybe. I can only hope." Teardrop lowered her voice, and Janlin had to strain to catch the words. "We were supposed to come into new environments with every possible precaution. The Birdfolk's version of a common cold could kill us all in a matter of days—and so could their version of a 'cure'. I'm amazed we haven't had a problem sooner."

"Why didn't we catch anything from the Imag, then?" she said, even as she remembered the holo of Victor on his deathbed.

"A ship environment is usually a lot cleaner place than a planet, at least in our experience."

"True."

Teardrop stopped, Janlin taking two more steps before she even realized. The woman's eyes rounded in dismay. "At its height, bio-terrorism found ways to infect people with nano-germs that could be programmed to wait before emerging to do their damage."

Janlin's heart quickened. When Anaya found Victor, he'd been in a separate part of the ship. He said something about tests they did on him.

"Do the Imag have that kind of technology, Teardrop?"

The young med-tech shrugged even as she resumed her half run, half walk. "I have no idea, really. That would be a question for the science types, I guess."

They approached the now familiar med-hut.

"Wait outside," Teardrop ordered.

"What? Why?"

"Just in case." Teardrop slipped inside the dim coolness, and Janlin stepped into the shaded doorframe. Tyrell sat chatting with an older red-headed lady. She bore dark circles under her eyes and a pale, feverish look.

"Sandy, right?" Teardrop said cheerfully, giving Tyrell's shoulder a squeeze before sitting beside them.

"Sandy Beckett," the woman confirmed. "Ron got tired of listening to me complain and thought you might be able to help."

"Of course. Let's have a look at you." Teardrop inspected her ears, eyes, throat, and glands on her neck. She asked basic questions about eating, sleeping, soreness, and fever. Janlin admired her calm bedside manners, considering her shaky panic outside.

"Ron . . . I can't remember his last name," Teardrop said.

"Ron Westmoore. We're bunking together."

Tyrell nudged Teardrop, and she absently swatted him away.

"I'm afraid you will need to remain here," she said, all business. "I'll be restricting all visitors, too." Tyrell's flirty smile faltered. Sandy groaned.

"She's contagious, then?" Janlin asked from the doorway.

Teardrop shook her head. "I can't say for sure, but chances are good. I'd rather err on the side of caution." She patted Sandy's shoulder. "I'll see what I can make up to sooth your throat."

Before she did anything, Teardrop pushed Janlin out the door. "Go find Ron, and anyone else they've been hanging about with . . . but especially Ron. Have them come up here right away."

Tyrell came up behind her. "What can I do?"

"Sit down," Teardrop said, pushing him back into the hut and going to a shelf to start pulling out jars and containers. "Sorry, Tyrell, but you're now part of my little quarantine. Janlin, see if we can use a different hut for first-aid, and look for volunteers to run it."

"Are you sure I should go?"

"You didn't come in, and you haven't been here long." Teardrop returned to Sandy's side with a spoon and a bottle, but first she reached out and squeezed Sandy's hand. "It's probably just a cold or some common thing," she said, "but it's my job to take every precaution we can to keep others from getting sick."

Janlin nodded at the three stark faces and left at a run. Did her throat hurt? *Psychosomatic*, she told herself. *Don't even think about it.*

For the first time since landing she thought of Yipho's injection, and his strange satisfaction in administering it. At the time Janlin saw it as some sadistic pleasure, but now she wondered if he'd used Victor's blood to create an anti-viral. Isn't that how it was done, centrifuging the blood to use a small dose to inoculate? Maybe they could do the same sort of thing once Sandy got better, although Janlin admitted she didn't even know if you could do something like that with a bacterial infection like strep. And if it was bacterial, most should recover just fine. The trouble was complications could occur, and then only a decent antibiotic would help them.

Janlin thought of the med stores on the *Hope*. If Anaya . . . . But there was no sense riding on "if" just now.

The thought that hit her then made her stumble to a halt. What if the injection Yipho gave her *was* the bug?

"Hey, what's the hurry?" Gordon stared at her over an armload of what appeared to be tree roots. "Did you hear something?" he demanded.

"No. Listen, do you know Ron—uh—Westmont, Westmoore, something like that?"

"Sure. Saw him this morning. He said his mate Sandy wasn't feeling well."

"Yeah, Teardrop's worried about it spreading around. Now

I'm worried it's too late for her quarantine to work."

Gordon's eyebrows shot up. "That doesn't sound good."

"It isn't," she called over her shoulder. "I've got to find Ron. If you see him, send him to the med-hut."

Next thing she knew, Gordon was keeping pace, his duties abandoned. "Janlin, I ate breakfast beside that guy. How serious is this?"

Janlin shook her head. "I don't know for sure. Did you eat from the same spoon? Drink from his drink? Then you might be fine, as far as I know. This could get dangerous, though. Teardrop's really worried."

Gordon grabbed her arm and stopped her in her tracks. "We must get off this planet."

For the second time that morning Janlin found herself calming someone else when her own panic simmered just under the surface, ready to boil over.

"We've tried." She put her hands up, palms out, to still his immediate reaction. "I'll also try calling again. If the comm is dead or broken, or for some reason Anaya can't get through to us, then we have to drop those shields. We're screwed until we either get her in, or she figures something else out." She kept her voice steady and firm. "We'll just have to survive this. Teardrop will do everything she can, and she has a lot of faith in the Birdfolk coming up with things to help."

"No. I'm done waiting around for Anaya or the Birdfolk or anyone. I think it's time we took matters into our own hands."

Janlin rolled her eyes at him. "We've tried that too, remember? Though it would be nice if we could get our hands on the med stores of either Jumpship," she said.

"It would be nice if we could find a Jumpship," he said.

"But we can't return home if we're carrying some awful virus, Gordon," Janlin said. Gordon stared at her in new horror. "That's why we're going to need to figure out a cure, and that means trusting in Huantag ingenuity . . . or . . ." Was Yipho's injection a cure?

"Or what?"

Janlin shook her head. She hadn't told him about the injection she'd received on the Gitane ship. "One thing at a time," she said. "I've got to find Ron."

Just as she found Ron and instructed him to find his hut

mates and report directly to Teardrop, Janlin saw Stepper striding towards her. He had Inaba, Linder, Steve, and Corvin with him.

"Janlin, we require some assistance—"

"Right, you've got perfect timing. We need to discuss the quarantine and which hut to assign to first-aid while the med-hut is off limits."

Stepper's face reddened even as his eyes widened at her speech, but the others seemed to take it in stride. Inaba moved forward.

"Please explain your use of the word 'quarantine', Ms. Kavanagh," he said.

"Well, at this point we're not sure of anything, but Teardrop says it could be a common flu virus or a strep infection, but either could be dangerous considering our lack of antibiotics and other meds."

Inaba nodded. "The medic has the right idea, then. We should limit contact and wash carefully. It might also be a good idea to check the mess hall crew for sore throats."

Stepper passed a shaky hand over his forehead. Did he seem pale? Janlin narrowed her eyes and he straightened.

"It's important we act quickly on this, and keep people calm, but Teardrop also hoped the Huantag could help."

"The who?" Stepper asked.

Damn! "The birdmen, bird-folk, whatever you call them," Janlin said. Her heart tumbled along a little faster. Stepper frowned at her, but the others were already discussing the best way to explain a viral infection to the aliens.

"I've got to get back," Janlin said, hoping her flounder would be lost in the moment. She turned and walked away, back stiff, and when she couldn't stand it anymore, she glanced back. Stepper stared after her. She hurried around a bend, putting a wall between them, and cursed her slip. Stepper knew her too well, and would not forget that she'd called the aliens by a strange name he'd never heard before.

CHAPTER FORTY-TWO

As JANLIN CLIMBED up the trail to the med-hut again, she saw Gordon sitting against the wall by the entrance, head on his knees.

"What's going on?" Janlin asked when he looked up at the sound of her approach.

He looked stricken. "For the moment, I'm the guard," he said. He turned red-rimmed eyes up to look at her with desperation. "Two more sore throats have been brought in, and all of those from her hut are sick too."

Janlin did the math. "What about Tyrell?"

"What about him?"

Janlin grimaced. "He was in the med-hut when Sandy was brought in and became part of the quarantine."

Gordon groaned, wiping a hand over his face. "I'm scared to even stick my head in there." He climbed to his feet. "Janlin, I want to go home. Tell me again how we're gonna do that?"

Janlin took a breath, let it go. "She'll do it, Gordon. She will, and she will return for us. I have to have faith in that. I can't imagine it's an easy task stealing a huge space ship out from under a bunch of Imag, and the warship could be anywhere. The trip here seemed to take weeks, though I had no way to communicate time with Anaya."

Gordon hung his head. "I'm glad you believe in Anaya still, because I trust your judgment."

"It's all we've got."

"But I still believe everyone else deserves to have the same hope. Why are you holding out with this?"

Because of Stepper, Janlin thought. *Because of everyone, and the way they'll look at me when I try to explain it, and the way everyone loves the Huantag—or at least did.* Maybe things would be different now, although she got the sense no one would understand until they met Anaya. Not even Gordon did, really.

"Holding out on what?" Stepper came around the corner of the med-hut wearing a grim look of determination.

Janlin swore, a rush of dismay filling her.

"Hey, Stepper. Heard you leader types made a sort of government today," Gordon said. Stepper never took his eyes off Janlin, but Janlin loved Gordon for trying to distract him.

"We did. Now if you two wouldn't mind filling me in on what you were discussing . . ."

Heavy silence thickened the space between them, the day now so hot the air shimmered.

Janlin knew Stepper would never forgive her for leaving him in the dark on this. She should've just left the settlement right off and gone in search of the Huantag's shielding controls on her own.

"I didn't come here with the others," Janlin said. She couldn't meet his gaze. "I came with a different group of aliens."

Stepper blinked. "Different how?"

Janlin relaxed just a little. At least he was giving her a chance to explain.

"They're an opposing family group or race or something of the Imag. They look a lot like the Imag, but they are called Gitane."

Stepper wrinkled his nose. "How can you possibly know something like that?"

"The captain of the ship I came here on, she had learned our language. She'd made friends with a *Renegade* crewmember before. They were trying to get help from us without inciting a war with the Imag, so she recruited me to gather the crew here while she steals the *Hope* from the Imag. All I have to do is take down the planet's shields and she'll come get us." Then she showed Stepper the comm-unit. "I've been waiting for word."

"This is ridiculous," Stepper said, and Janlin bit down on her disappointment. Why had she expected anything different?

"It's our only chance to get home," Gordon said. "Whatever—"

"Can't you see? It's a set-up." Stepper grabbed the comm-unit, inspecting it with a scowl. "We take down the shields for the Imag and they can walk right in and take the planet. There is no 'Gitane'." He snorted in derision. "I can't believe you fell for this."

"Anaya's not like that," Janlin said, forcing the words out. "She's risking her own crew—"

"How so?" Stepper demanded, overriding her. "It sounds like you face all the danger. You have to take out the Birdfolk's only source of protection, which is of course against their will. You're the one risking your neck, and ours, and the generous owners of this planet! And what about the *Renegade* crewmate, what happened to him?"

Janlin shook her head, denying her own doubts she'd tried so hard to ignore. "He got sick . . ."

Stepper's eyes widened.

"No, it's not like that. If you could meet her, talk to her . . ." She glanced at Gordon, but how could he back her on this? "She just wants a chance for a new start, a new home planet. You built Jumpships because we couldn't seem to fix the mistakes we've made on Earth. The Gitane are just like us."

Stepper stared at the comm-unit in his hand. "We wanted to find new worlds . . ." He seemed dazed.

"And Anaya's people do too. There's no way she's on the side of the Imag. She's coming to rescue us!"

Stepper stuck his face right in hers. "What if I don't want rescued? We have what we were searching for right here."

Janlin snatched the comm-unit from him as Gordon pushed in between them. "How can you say that?" Gordon's quiet tone made Janlin shiver.

"They healed me beyond my wildest hopes," Stepper said, exposing his spider web of scars and flexing his fingers. "They have a beautiful world, and they're willing to share it with us, if you two would quit causing problems. They were even willing to help us reverse the nano-tech birth control. We could live free of SpaceOp and the famine and—"

He never saw the fist coming. Blood spurted instantly from

Stepper's nose as Gordon pulled back for another go.

"Wait! Dammit you two—!" Janlin dove between them, hanging off Gordon's muscular arm. He shook her off, breathing hard, his grey eyes like sharp steel. Janlin spun on Stepper.

"You thoughtless asshole!" she said. "It's never about anyone but you, isn't it? It doesn't surprise me you'd ignore the plight of your own race, but how could you say that to Gordon?"

Stepper, his hands holding his nose as blood flowed between his fingers, groaned. "Try to be reasonable. There's no possible way back."

Janlin wanted to hit him herself. "My friend is out there making it possible," she said, her voice full of warning. "And Gordon and I will not give up. I will do whatever it takes to fulfil my part of our plan so that her efforts aren't wasted."

Stepper's arm snaked out and snatched the comm-unit from her. Her wordless cry of dismay was drowned out by the crackle of breaking parts as Stepper smashed it against the wall of the med-hut.

"You will not threaten the friends we have here," he said. "You've already screwed things up bad enough." Blood flowed freely down his face, making him look demented.

Sounds of reaction made Janlin realize they'd drawn a crowd. Teardrop stood in the entrance of the med-hut, eyes wide. Two of the Leadership Circle watched, gazes flicking between Stepper, the smashed device, and Janlin.

Gordon moaned and fell to his knees. With the greatest care, he gathered the pieces of plastic and electronics in his big hands. When he looked up, it was to nail Stepper with a look of pure hatred.

"Your grasping for power over others has really gone too far, Stepper."

Janlin recognized Gordon's words as a deep truth. It explained Stepper's actions all along—his choosing a Mars assignment that didn't include her, his building the Jumpships without authorization, his creation of a governing party here that included him but didn't ask for input from the group as a whole. She turned to the gathered onlookers.

"I didn't want to tell you of this because I didn't want to raise false hope. There's no telling if my friend can secure the *Hope* from the Imag." Latecomers gasped at the idea. "And I really wasn't sure of how to broach the subject with the Huantag."

"The who?" asked Inaba.

"That's the name of the Birdfolk. Huantag. It's the name of the planet, too. Unfortunately, they wouldn't listen to Gordon and me about helping us get off planet safely without putting them in danger because of some promise they made to the Imag. And now, because we tried to go against that, they've made us prisoners here. There's no doubt they're not going to like this plan either, since they wouldn't trust my friend's good intentions." She tried to find a straightforward way to explain it all. "There's so much misunderstanding going on."

She helped Gordon to his feet. In his big hands, he cupped the destroyed comm-unit.

"Did anyone here know Victor?" she asked.

"I did!" said Linder.

"So did I," said Teardrop. "He was a good friend."

Janlin nodded and took a deep breath. "I have a story to tell you."

CHAPTER FORTY-THREE

As JANLIN SPOKE, Gordon sat against the wall and began to painstakingly reconstruct the comm-unit. Teardrop sat in the doorway to the hut, tears glistening in her eyes as she listened. Stepper also leaned against the wall, head back in an attempt to staunch the blood flow. No one offered to help him.

"Victor recorded himself not long before his death. 'Trust Anaya,' he said." Janlin scanned her audience. "I do! I trust her, and believe that if we follow the plan she set forth, we have a chance to go home."

"The Birdfolk are so peaceful, though," Linder said. "Even after Gordon's outburst. How can we rightfully undermine them, let alone threaten their entire planet's safety?"

"Yeah, chances are if this friend of yours does steal the *Hope*, the Imag will be hot on her tail. If they find out we've taken the shielding down . . ."

Agreement rippled through the crowd. The threat was clear, and Janlin understood both sides of the argument. "We've asked them for safe transit to orbit, but they made a deal with the Imag. They took us in on the understanding that we are not to ever leave again, or it will be taken as an act of war."

"Then they can't go back on that without being prepared to go to war," Inaba said. "And that goes against everything they believe in."

"It doesn't though," Janlin argued. "They must see we need

to return to our own planet—that they are right in the sense that we should never have left it in such a mess. If we took home some of their ideas, maybe we could make our own comeback like they did. If they would just help us a bit, we could do the fighting for them."

At this thought everyone spoke at once, talking over each other, and finally Teardrop shouted. Janlin started. She had no idea she had it in her.

"Before we do anything, we should ask the Birdfolk for help with this infection," Teardrop suggested. "We may still have a long time to wait before this friend of Janlin's returns, and this is far more urgent."

"And I'd imagine everyone will want to hear Janlin's story before we put it to discussion," said Inaba.

Janlin stifled a moan. She knew everyone had a right to know what was happening and have a say in the decisions made, but her impatience sometimes sent fair play out the window, especially when she thought it was perfectly clear what was right for everyone.

She looked again at Stepper and realized how wrong she could be in making those assumptions. Stepper saw this as home, a place of peace, and didn't want to see it threatened. He thought he was clear on what was right for everyone, to just live peacefully here and give up on going home.

The crowd dispersed, urged away from the med-hut by the leaders once they understood the gravity of Teardrop's concerns. Stepper continued to sit, back against the hut wall, bloody shirt held to his nose with an arm propped on a bent knee.

Gordon muttered new curses as he turned shattered pieces this way and that. Janlin knelt beside him.

"Anaya won't give up," she said, pitching her voice so Stepper would hear it too. "Neither will we. I'm certain the Huantag have communication devices of some kind we could play with."

Gordon nodded, though he didn't stop trying to fit the pieces into place. A tear dropped onto one, and he quickly wiped it dry with exquisite care.

"I want to go home," he said, his voice a bare whisper that rasped over a broken heart. He looked up, and the pain of hopeless longing welled in his grey eyes. "I promised Ursula . . ."

He covered his eyes with one big hand. Janlin wrapped her arms around him from the side. There were no words she could offer her friend, nothing but her belief in the promise of a stranger.

She looked over to find Stepper focused on them, his mouth turned down in pain and anger and—somehow—bewilderment. Janlin stared back over a chasm of regret and new anger.

A FEW HOURS later Falco came winging into the village, circling until he spotted Janlin waving. He landed a few feet away from her.

"Janlin, there are many sick in our city," he said. He struggled for breath. "I wanted to warn you to stay away, even if your guards fall short in numbers."

"We've got sick people here too," she said. "Is there anyone looking for a cure? There is a chance we brought this illness, and you may only find a cure through our blood."

"I will pass this idea to the council." He moved to go.

"Wait!" He turned back only half way, his wings partly spread and knees bent to launch. Did he fear the illness? Whatever it was, she wasn't done with him now that she had someone listening.

"Why did you shun the Imag?" And the Gitane, but that wouldn't translate. "Why didn't you try and teach them, help them with their own world?"

Falco's head twitched side to side, but he still answered. "You know the story. They caused great destruction and refused to follow our rules to protect the planet. They argued that we'd fixed things and didn't need to worry so much. They felt they could go back to their old ways." Then he fixed her with his intense gaze. "Why do you ask this?"

Janlin considered. "I met someone before I came here. I considered her a friend. I may be wrong about her, but she felt you did not give them enough of a chance." She made sure she had his full attention. "I have a feeling she knows a way to cure this illness. But the bitterness at being turned away from the only inhabitable planet in the system may prevent her from wanting to help."

"This is Imag?"

"No . . . Imag-like, but not Imag. Gitane." How did she

explain? She was so sick of the confusion, the communication breakdown, the questions and doubts spinning in her head. "If you would contact them, be willing to work with them—"

"No, Janlin. That will never be a good choice. I will report to my superior, let them know you have this illness too. It is just as I suspected, and now we can take the proper procedures to end it."

Falco pulled into his full height and expanded his wings. "We may have been wrong to let Imag extract our promise, but the council says there is no going back."

"I need my flight gear," she said as he turned away.

He didn't reply for a long moment before clacking his beak-like protrusion in a way she'd never seen before. "I left your flight gear in the place where you and Gordon meet." Without warning, he stuck his face right in hers. "Be sure of your choices, Janlin." He turned away and launched into the sky.

She watched him fly away. "Sometimes that's impossible, Falco."

She turned and ran all the way down into the sage meadow. The guards above her circled, but did nothing more. Many times, she and Gordon had sat out here watching them fly overhead.

At first, she thought Falco lied, but then she saw the tuft of fabric hidden beneath the boulders. She stood sweating, chest heaving, and stared at the tiny speck that was Falco returning home.

Then she looked up at the circling forms above her.

It would have to wait. At least she had a new opportunity to work with.

CHAPTER FORTY-FOUR

THE QUARANTINE DIDN'T work.

More fell ill over the next couple of days. Despite Teardrop's warnings, Janlin helped her nurse the sick. Janlin noticed Teardrop lagging and pale, and attempted to put her into a cot, too.

"I can't, Janlin," she protested, and Janlin could hear the rasp that gave away the sore throat.

"You can and will. There is nothing more you can do, and you won't be helping if you're sick."

Tyrell agreed. "Come lay here with me," he whispered, and Teardrop gave in. Janlin brought them both flowerbud tea.

"You two just keep an eye on Sandy and Ron from there, okay? I'll be back in a while."

Sandy and Ron rarely woke any more, only tossing and muttering in feverish delirium. Janlin gathered the bedpans that needed scrubbed and headed for the river. Turning at the door, she was heartened by Teardrop's drooping eyes. If she just got some rest, she would recover more quickly.

After cleaning and delivering the bedpans back to a sleeping group, Janlin walked the deserted paths down to Inaba's hut. She called out a hesitant greeting, worried by the profound silence that wrapped the entire common area. It seemed like just a few days ago that they'd danced and celebrated here.

"Inaba?"

"Don't come in," came the answer from within the hut.

"It's okay, I've been nursing the sick," she said as she entered the hut. The Japanese man sat wrapped in blankets, yet still he shivered. Janlin frowned. The day had its usual heat. Why didn't he sit in the sun and get warm?

Then she saw that he sat very close to another cot, occupied by a sleeping form.

"Is there anything I can get you?" Janlin asked, keeping her voice low.

"No," Inaba said. "Unless you can bring us a miracle."

"I had hopes for one," she said, thinking of Anaya and the broken comm-unit.

"I suspect this may be the Imag's plan," he said.

Janlin blinked. "Sorry?"

"The Imag could not rely only on you succeeding in taking the shielding down, so they set an alternate plan in action. One or many of us were probably infected with this on purpose. I speculate that's why we were all brought here."

"Brought here to die," Janlin whispered.

"And to infect the Birdfolk."

Janlin closed her eyes. Where was Anaya?

"How is it you are not sick, Ms. Kavanagh?"

She remembered Yipho's injection.

"Truthfully, I don't know what to believe anymore," she said. "The aliens I travelled here with injected me with something. It was either the disease or the cure. Could I be the carrier without being sick?"

Inaba looked sad. "It is quite possible."

Janlin watched him tug at his blankets and shiver. "Why don't you come sit outside in the sun for a bit?" she said.

He looked down at the sleeping form beside him and considered. "Maybe just for a few moments. I am so cold . . ."

She got him settled and sat beside him. "So, I'm either a carrier, a live biological bomb, or I am proof that my friend saved my life." She told him of Victor's illness, and how he had been separated from the rest of *Renegade's* crew and subjected to a series of tests before Anaya stole him away. "I'd like to believe in Anaya."

"So, you need to remove the Birdfolk's shielding in case she waits without being able to tell you she's here."

Janlin nodded. "I am worried that the device was already out of power or broken before Stepper's actions. But taking down the shielding has proven to be more difficult than I thought it would be. And what if I'm wrong? I could make a very bad situation much worse."

Inaba sighed. "If we are to die anyway, then the risk is worth it, yes?"

Janlin stared in shock. "Do you think it's that bad?"

He didn't answer.

"Okay, so how do I do this?" She gestured at the sky to indicate their imprisonment. Hawk-like Huantag watched by day, owl-like ones by night.

Inaba just shook his head. "I do not know, Ms. Kavanagh. But I fear all our lives rest in your hands now."

FALCO FLEW IN again that evening. He looked and sounded awful, his plumage ragged and his step unsure.

"I am sent to collect things to make a medicine." Once he explained, Janlin led him to the med-hut and asked him to wait outside.

As she stepped into the relative cool, she instantly registered the awful scene at Sandy's cot. Teardrop turned, an anguished expression on her face. Ron sobbed, his head buried in the blankets over Sandy.

"She's gone, Janlin. Just like that. Gone."

Janlin pulled Teardrop into a hug. "You did everything you could, Teardrop. We all did." She pulled Teardrop aside and told her Falco waited outside.

"They want to study swabs and blood samples," Janlin explained to Teardrop. "I think they are working to find a cure."

"We will sterilize everything carefully," Teardrop said, pointing out the materials and a case to store them in. "Do your hands, too, and the case. In fact, wipe down everything before you take the samples, and then again when you're done."

Janlin shushed her at that point. Teardrop's obvious pain when speaking made Janlin wince when she heard it. She held up a stick of some sort of plastic. "Is this what I take swabs with?"

Teardrop nodded and held out her hand. "I will do my own throat, and you hold the case open. I don't want you to touch it."

Janlin wanted to point out that if she was going to get sick, she would've by now, but she simply did as she was told. Teardrop struggled to get her feet under her, staggered a few steps, and dropped to her knees by Tyrell's cot. He hadn't noticed Sandy's passing, and that made Janlin more worried than anything else.

"Pass me the syringe."

Janlin brought the case, watched her draw blood without any reaction from Tyrell, and closed the case on the completed samples.

"Wipe everything—"

"I know, I will," Janlin assured her. She set the case aside and helped Teardrop to her cot. "Just rest, and try not to talk." She wrung out a cloth and laid it over the woman's forehead.

Teardrop closed her eyes and sighed. "Just tell them—ask them to hurry, okay?"

She was asleep before Janlin stood.

Once outside again, Janlin bit her lip. Who would care for the dead? The breeze ruffled her auburn hair, now long enough to tie back if she had something to do it with . . . or some time to think of such inane things.

Janlin approached Falco and handed him the case. From the corner of her eye she saw anxious faces peering from doorways and shaded corners.

"If any of you are well enough, we could sure use some help," she said.

Falco whistled, and she could hear the harshness of it under the translation in her ear.

"I have tried to bring help, Janlin. No one will come, and too many are sick too quickly."

Janlin sighed. "I understand."

He turned to go, but before he could launch, Janlin called out.

"If you would give me access to some communication equipment, I might be able to get help."

"Might, Janlin?"

Yeah, might . . . that was the problem. "It would be better than the alternative," she said, letting a warning note through in her voice despite not knowing if it would register in his translator. "If you don't help me find a way to communicate with any ships that might be out there, then I'm going to find a way to bring down those shields, Imag warship be damned."

"Please, Janlin, be patient. We will study this and make medicines," Falco said. He crouched and launched, the case cradled in his arms.

Before he was out of sight, Stepper accosted her.

"It's you, don't you see? They planted it in you, and when we're all dead, you can go take the shields down and they'll just move right in." He stumbled a bit, righted himself, and glared through a fever haze at her. "I did the right thing breaking that device."

"Stepper, you look awful."

"You've betrayed us all, haven't you?"

"Are you really saying I would intentionally murder everyone, to say nothing of a Hauntag genocide?" Janlin's mouth worked, and she longed to spit away the awful taste that rose in her throat. Doubt ate at her. Did they give her the cure . . . or the disease?

Stepper stared at her in horror. "The Birdfolk are sick, too?"

Janlin cursed. No one needed that kind of information right now. "They are working on a cure. I just delivered samples they requested. It's going to be okay, Stepper."

"You can't know that. Even if you didn't know, it was you they sent it with. Why else are you healthy?"

"Because Anaya helped me," she said. Thoughts tumbled through her too fast. "If we can reach her, she could—"

"See?" Stepper said. "She even wants you to report in, let them know how well things are working."

"No, you're not seeing it right," she said. She focused her attention on Stepper, willing him to listen, to understand. "Victor got sick, and one of Anaya's crew gave me a shot against the same illness. You might be right about it being from the Imag, but Anaya's crewmate created the cure."

Stepper sucked in air.

"They could make more," Janlin said, ploughing on. "They could make an inoculation or antiviral."

Stillness settled over Stepper. Even the wind seemed to die in that moment.

"Space me," Stepper whispered. "Whether inoculation or infection, you really are the carrier."

"Not necessarily," Janlin cried. "Besides, that doesn't matter anymore. What matters is finding a cure, and Anaya might have it."

Stepper shook his head, denying the possibility.

Janlin couldn't stop. "We've been trying to contact her all along. I'm worried the Imag may have taken them. But if Anaya succeeded, then she could be waiting in orbit, with our ship and the cure, and now I would have no way of knowing."

Stepper winced. "Maybe they could fix the device so you don't have to take the shields out. You have to make sure somehow . . ."

"How should I ask for that?" Janlin said, cutting him off. "By telling them, 'we're sorry we made you sick, now we want to talk to those you barred from your planet? Oh, and by the way, they're probably the ones that sent the infection?' I'm sure that will go over really well."

It was too much. Janlin couldn't decide what Anaya's true intentions were, and talking with Stepper just fed her own doubts that she wanted to discount but couldn't deny.

She shuddered, head pounding in the heat of the midday sun. "I can only hope to somehow prove you wrong." She started walking away, but she heard the derisive snort from Stepper.

"Give it up," he said.

She turned back. "And when you're on your deathbed, Stepper? Will you be more interested in possibilities then? Or would you like me to reserve a spot beside Sandy right now?"

He paled. "She's dead?" A hand went to his throat. "Sandy was the best programmer we had," he said finally.

"Get some rest, Stepper. We're not beat yet."

CHAPTER FORTY-FIVE

As JANLIN CLIMBED the hill towards the med-hut, she probed at her throat for telltale signs of swollen glands for the hundredth time, with no sign . . . nothing.

Whatever Yipho had done, she had to believe it had saved her the awful disease sweeping through the humans and Huantag alike.

"Have they figured anything out? Did they let you ask about contacting your friend?" Teardrop stood at the door, one hand on the frame, the other holding a rag over her mouth.

"You should be lying down," Janlin protested.

"They just came and took Sandy." Teardrop swallowed hard. "I'm worried Ron will be next."

"I delivered the samples. Between the Huantag and Anaya, and human resilience, we will win out, I'm sure of it." Janlin moved to hustle Teardrop back to her cot.

Teardrop held up a hand. "You shouldn't come in. It's only by some miracle—"

"It's not a miracle," Janlin insisted. "Otherwise it wouldn't be so important to find those who gave me the injection."

"Still . . ."

Janlin could tell Teardrop didn't want to take any chances, and appreciated that.

"I won't tell you what happened until you're horizontal," Janlin said. Teardrop sighed, and it was all too obvious to Janlin that it tired her just to stand. "C'mon, shoo, into bed."

It was far too easy to win, and soon Janlin sat beside Teardrop's cot, relating how she sent a message to the Huantag, and of Stepper's belief that she was the carrier. "Is that possible, to be the carrier and not be sick?"

Teardrop reluctantly admitted it was.

"The Huantag are struggling with this illness, too," Janlin finally told her. Teardrop groaned.

"This is not good, not good at all."

"Hopefully the Huantag will come up with something."

Teardrop didn't reply, and her eyes were closed. Janlin shifted, unwilling to sit idle but unsure of what more she could do.

"This is bio-terrorism," Teardrop said, not opening her eyes.

Janlin leaned forward. "Not something natural? Are you sure?"

"All happened at the same time, and it's so deadly. It was triggered, not natural."

Janlin caught her breath. Did that mean the Imag warship was in orbit? If it was, how could she possibly justify any attempt to take out the shields?

She watched helplessly as Teardrop struggled to breathe. "Can you use me somehow to make a cure? If Anaya's medic gave me a cure, would it be accessible that way?"

But Teardrop shook her head. "It would be too weak. Plus, we don't know what we're fighting . . . don't have the right equipment to find out, either."

"Dammit, we need Anaya."

"I wish I could've met her," Teardrop said.

"You will meet her, soon, I'm sure of it," Janlin said, but she studied the pale figure stretched out on the cot and sucked her bottom lip in worry. Anaya had no way to contact her, and no way to get access to the planet. If the Huantag would allow her a way to communicate, especially with a possible cure involved, everything could be solved. But the Huantag had their own political red tape to navigate, and this illness didn't seem willing to wait. She had to go to Falco and make him understand.

"Water." Teardrop did not open her eyes, but her hand reached. Janlin took the hand, frightened by how hot Teardrop's skin was as she held it gently but firmly. Janlin took up a cool mug of water and brought it to Teardrop's lips.

Each tiny swallow brought a flinch of pain, and Teardrop opened her eyes as it brought her around again.

"Janlin," she croaked. "You shouldn't be in here." She tried to rise, to tend her duties as she saw them, but she couldn't even lift her head.

"I know, you've told me before," Janlin said in a whisper.

"Janlin . . ."

"Shhhh, just rest. We'll get word from the Huantag soon." Janlin's resolve hardened. "Just hang in there, girl."

Teardrop wouldn't release her grip on Janlin's hand, however, so she sat with Teardrop the day through, feeding her sips of water, talking when consciousness came, crying when it slipped away.

Through it all she kept her back to the still form beneath the sheet that was once Tyrell. There would be time to tell Teardrop later.

THAT EVENING NO Huantag flew the sky above the village. Taking the chance, and hoping she was wrong about why the skies were empty, Janlin went to her flight gear and launched into the sky.

No one challenged her.

She turned and flew to the city. As she drew near, the empty skies and silent city made her chest tighten with waves of fear. She flew along the building fronts, calling to Falco, to anyone, hearing only her cries echoed back at her.

Finally, she circled around and went to Falco's ledge. Inside the hall, no one appeared to greet her, and when she turned into Falco's home, she found only more emptiness. She peered into the side corridor in Falco's home that his mate had always appeared from. Dare she enter such a private place?

"Falco?" she called. No sound answered her but the sigh of the wind. She took a step, and another, past an empty room, until she stepped into a larger chamber.

There on a large circular cushioned area she found the bodies of Falco, his mate, and his two sons, each one lifeless and cold.

Her return flight held remnants of an old familiar nightmare, memories of Earth and the pregnant girl's slashed throat interlacing with Falco's family group all dead in each other's embrace.

She landed in the common area and ripped off her flight gear, uncaring whether or not it would ever work again. Once free of it, she slumped against a wall in the too-silent village, unwilling to move or even think. Exhaustion took over and she let go, falling into a fitful doze.

Gordon found her a few hours after dark.

They walked around the settlement, checking each hut. Gordon carried out three more dead before they'd completed the rounds.

"We're going to have to dig a communal grave," Gordon said as he laid out the bodies. "I can't keep digging individual ones."

Janlin swore softly. She took up a blanket and laid it over the still faces. "I'll help. Makes sense to dig in the cool of the night."

Gordon grunted his agreement. They worked in silence at their grisly task.

"I'm glad to see you still up and around," Janlin said, hoping she didn't tempt fate by saying it.

Gordon gave her a look so full of despair she gasped with the power of it.

"I have a sore throat." He shrugged. "I figured lying around resting wasn't working for these poor souls, so I just kept going."

Janlin swallowed her horror and tried to answer in a calm, reasonable voice. "Well, we're done for now, and it can't hurt to get a bit of sleep, can it?"

They walked down to the pools, washed up, and headed back up the hill to the med hut.

"Stay out here, I just want to check on Teardrop."

The interior was pitch black, with no one to care. Weariness overtook Janlin like a weight that made her want to forget the globe lantern and sink down onto an empty cot. She fumbled with the alien design until finally light filled the space, and she turned to see Teardrop's gaping mouth and staring eyes.

Janlin cried out.

"What is it?"

Gordon appeared at her side. She whirled on him, adrenaline firing her weary body, and pounded on his chest, forcing him to back up out the door. "No! Get out of here!" she screamed at him. "Get out! I can't bear to see you die too!"

Gordon backed from her angry fists, eyes wide. "She's dead?" he said. "Our little Teardrop?" He shook his head, not willing to believe it, not willing to accept it.

Janlin turned and stumbled into the hut to fall at Teardrop's side.

"I'm sorry I left you alone," Janlin whispered. "I'm so sorry, so sorry." She reached to close the lifeless blue eyes and give the medic some respect in death before she lost all control and lay sobbing into the blankets of the sweetest woman she had ever known.

CHAPTER FORTY-SIX

THE NEXT DAY dawned hot, a gruelling heat that sucked any resistance the sick could muster. Janlin stood in the doorway of the now-empty med-hut. Nothing moved, and a wind swirled the dust into a little twister. Janlin shivered even as a bead of sweat trickled down between her shoulder blades.

Anaya must be waiting. Janlin had to lower the shields, even if it meant opening the planet to the Imag. If the Imag sent the disease, they wouldn't do anything while the virus still existed. That would give time for Anaya to come and help. Did that make her a traitor?

No. She did this to save her people, not to hurt anyone. If they knew Anaya like she did . . .

The sun scorched her, and she turned away. Her eyes adjusted too soon, revealing the empty mats and discarded bits of lives left behind. Too many lay under white sheets, awaiting burial.

Except for her. She felt fine.

A burst of bitter laughter startled her, and she whimpered when she realized it came from her own mouth.

Footsteps on gravel echoed through the still heat. Janlin dashed to the doorway. Inaba leaned on a wall across the way, his face pale, black circles under his eyes. Janlin let out a little cry of dismay.

He nodded. "No one has recovered."

Janlin hung her head. "Among the Huantag, death travels even faster." Janlin sank against the wall. "This is ridiculous," she said a moment later, straightening up. "I have to go take down the shields in case Anaya is there, waiting."

"What will you do, Janlin Kavanagh?" His voice rasped, and he blinked slowly, as if the struggle to open them again was nearly beyond him.

Janlin went to him and took his arm to guide him to a piece of shade to rest. "I will think of something. If I can't, I will search this planet until I find a ship, then fly this system until I find Anaya, and the truth."

Inaba's steady gaze regarded her. "So, you still have doubts."

Janlin pursed her lips. "Of course. It's been weeks, but the device is broken. They could be waiting, wondering why I don't answer their calls. Or something could have gone wrong. Or I was taken for a fool, and they are simply waiting for us to all die."

"Removing the shields could be what they wait for."

"I know. But if we are dying anyway, then there is no reason not to try, is there? Isn't that what you said?"

Inaba bowed his head.

She helped him back to his hut. He was alone there, now, just as she was at the med hut. He sat on the edge of his cot, unwilling to lay down. Janlin understood. It would be an admission of defeat, and Inaba was not ready to surrender.

"Godspeed, Janlin Kavanagh," he said then. His soft voice bore pain both physical and emotional. He put his hands together, palms flat, and made a little bow. Janlin attempted to return the gesture, her hands clumsy, goosebumps prickling her upper arms and neck. Inaba acknowledged her effort, and then turned to lay down on the cot, his back to her in dismissal.

Janlin turned away. She bit her lip, even as she wondered why she bothered to fight the tears. Out in the burning heat, she walked through the deserted settlement, the only one hale among so many sick.

A huddled form propped up against a hut wall stirred at her approach, calling her name. Another form slumped beside him, little flies crawling on exposed skin. Janlin shuddered.

"I'm sorry, I can't help—" she began, trying to be polite but knowing the best way she could help was to get moving on her plan.

"No, I'm sorry," the figure said. She realized he held a knife from the cook hut in one hand. He lifted his head, black hair falling away from pale sunken skin, and Janlin took an involuntary step back.

"Stepper?" She recovered from her dread and went to kneel by him. She touched his cheek. His skin felt like paper baked in an oven.

"Life is short." His head lolled, and his staring eyes glazed over with pain. "We shouldn't fight."

Janlin tried to take the knife, but he had too solid a grip on it. "Now's not the time for this," she said.

"I'm a jerk, but I really do love you."

Janlin looked away. Emerging from the hut across the way two stooped figures stumbled and struggled with a blanket-wrapped burden. It could be nothing else but a body. Janlin swallowed against a throat thick with dust and regret.

"Just survive a few more days, you hear me? Whatever you have to do, just don't die." She tried again to take the knife. "You don't need this."

Stepper gave her a macabre grin, eyes bright with fever but intelligence and understanding still shining through. He did not release the knife.

"I wish we had another chance."

Janlin stared at him for a long moment, then pulled off her left boot and pried out the nano-recorder. She took up his free hand and placed it there, curling his fingers around it and squeezing tight.

"You kept it," he said, just as he had that day in his office millions of light years away.

"I did. The nicest gift you ever gave me, and I never could make myself get rid of it no matter how mad I was at you." She took his face in her hands, made him look at her. "Make a notch every day when you wake. Count, and stay alive, and I'll be back with help."

His head slumped forward, and she could tell by his shaking shoulders he wept.

She ran.

Hut to hut, body to body, some alive, some not, eyes all staring with fever, skin all pale and hot, mouths gaping in the dead, no one to care for them, no one to chase away the flies and wrap them gently to be laid on a pyre or buried in the ground, no one to bring water to those still struggling for one last breath . . .

Janlin wiped at her eyes, sweat and tears blurring her vision. The settlement seemed to waver around her, and she grew more afraid with each body she encountered.

Every hut, every path, she scanned both living and dead, not finding the face she dreaded and hoped for. Finally, she spun in a circle in the central common area.

"Gordon!" she cried.

"Janlin?" came the reply, and she choked on tears of relief. She followed the sound to find Gordon sitting in the shade of a wall, Anaya's comm-unit in his lap. He pushed a button, brought it to his mouth, and spoke.

"Mayday, mayday, this is the crew of the *Hope* calling for help. Please respond." Janlin gasped.

His arm dropped. His voice held no urgency, and after her initial rush of hope Janlin realized he must have performed the same actions before, perhaps hundreds of times.

"Gordon," she began, but he held up one long finger that somehow silenced her. He focused on the device, gently pulling it apart, switching one interior component with another before snapping it back together.

Again, the comm-unit came to his mouth. "Mayday, mayday—"

"Gordon!"

His eyes popped wide open, and eyebrows shot up his forehead. "What?"

"I need to take that with me," she said, pointing at the device.

Gordon frowned, and her heart clenched with fear at his fevered confusion. "Where? Why?" Then he let out a little sigh. "Doesn't work anyway. We're goin' tits up, luv."

Janlin sat beside him. She squeezed his knee where the SpaceOp issue pants had torn, his skin scabbed and hairy and far too hot to the touch. "I know, Spin," she said. "But Anaya's device might come in handy. So would you, if you feel up to coming."

Gordon blinked, straightened. He gave a little nod and handed her the device. "Where?"

"It's time we went back to the landing site and get one of

those shuttles running. I'll fly out to the orbital station and see if I can find the shielding controls . . . or Anaya."

Gordon laughed outright, and Janlin flinched away from him until she realized he didn't laugh at her or her idea.

"Space me, girl—you really do think you can fly anything, don't you?"

Janlin grinned. "Keep your voice down, idiot. There are still people who don't agree with this."

Gordon sobered and shook his head. "Why? There's no one to hear, no one to care anymore. When do we leave?"

"Now." Janlin scrambled up, sought out a few water containers left hanging by the cookhut door, and filled them at the tub sink inside. Gordon rose and followed her, holding each water jug as she filled them. His hands shook so bad she made him drink a full one before they left.

"Are you sure you're up for this?"

Gordon pursed his lips. "Bloody right."

Janlin watched the way he leaned on the wall, listened to the way he shortened his sentences, only saying what he had to. Still, she wanted—no, needed—Gordon at her side. She might be able to fly anything, but he might be the only one who could figure out how to start an alien ship. And once she found Anaya, she wanted him treated right away.

Janlin swung the water jugs over her shoulder. "Here."

He looked in surprise at the device she offered him. She knew he'd keep trying to call out until he stumbled upon the right combination of internal hook-ups. It gave him something to live for.

They descended out of the settlement and onto the scrub plain. Janlin stopped to look back at the hill where her father lay. Gordon leaned on her shoulder, gave her a little squeeze of comfort.

"I'm glad he never lived to see this day," Janlin said, and turned away.

CHAPTER FORTY-SEVEN

"SOMEONE'S FOLLOWING US," Gordon said. He hunched over, hands on his knees. The last time they'd stopped, he'd ended up slumped on the ground.

"I know," Janlin said, encouraging him to keep walking with a hand under his arm. "We're almost there."

She glanced back in time to catch the third heat-hazed glimpse of the man following, then faced forward again. Ahead rose the shuttle building, the steel barn silo waiting beside it. No Huantag graced the skies, and Janlin found she wished for their presence, even if it went against her needs just then.

"I can't do it, Jan. I can't walk another step."

"Good."

"Good?" Gordon asked, confused at this unexpected response.

"Yeah, good, 'cause we're gonna crawl now." She dropped low. Gravel crunched as Gordon landed hard on his knees.

"Here." Janlin handed him the last of the water. "Drink it all."

He didn't argue. The heat of the plain added to his fever, and Janlin didn't want to leave him.

Janlin wriggled up the slope on her stomach to peer over the top.

She glanced back over the plain behind them. There was no sign of their pursuer. "Dammit," she said under her breath.

Janlin suspected it was Stepper, and hoped she was wrong. He seemed too sick to be sane, let alone capable. Everyone was so sick—even Gordon, and he was one of the last to succumb. It especially bothered her that whoever followed attempted to stay hidden.

Gordon laboured up the slope and collapsed beside her. "What's the plan, boss?"

Janlin edged up to scan the landing site again. Dust coated her tongue, and gravel raked her knees and palms. The shuttle still stood right where they'd seen it last time, all done up tight and smooth.

Nothing moved but the waves of heat. "Come on, let's get out of this sun," Janlin said, hauling Gordon to his feet.

"Great idea," Gordon said, slurring his words. He started stumbling down the slope they'd just climbed.

"No, no, Gordon—this way."

"Huh? Are you insane?" He peered up at the sky, one eye closed to the brightness.

Janlin just took his arm and guided her friend up over the ridge and out onto the flattened area.

"What are we doing, Janlin? We're not supposed to be here." Gordon sounded tired and beyond caring, yet he still made the effort.

"Just stick with me, Spin. Hopefully things will all make more sense soon."

They stumbled across the open area and tried the door to the hangar-style building. Of course, it didn't open, but Gordon broke open the panel and only played with the interior for a few moments before it slid free. Inside, cool air welcomed them into a large empty space that could clearly accommodate the shuttle outside.

"Right, see if you can find anything that looks like communications, and keep a lookout for one of those remote controls for the shuttle." She would prefer to communicate with Anaya sooner rather than later. It also would help matters to make sure the Imag were not around. "And make sure she's on the up and up," she growled. Gordon turned his head at her words, but carried on with his perusal of the workbenches and storage areas without asking.

"There's nothing that looks like communications here, luv,"

Gordon said. The cool interior seemed to have helped him a little, but not enough.

Janlin hunted for just one thing, and found it just as he gave his bad news.

"Gordon, come on!" She rushed to the doorway and began pushing all the buttons on the handheld one after another. Finally, the shuttle blossomed with a hatchway and ramp.

"Nice work," Gordon said. His eyes sagged shut, and he wavered on his feet.

"All right, just get on up this ramp and you can have a nice rest."

"Fix comm-unit, too," he said. He leaned on her hard, too hard, and Janlin stumbled under his weight.

"Gordon!"

He straightened and she almost went down before she could regain her balance.

"Space me, a little warning next time maybe?"

"Janlin, give me your nano-recorder," Gordon said, suddenly quite lucid. Janlin could only stare at him in horror.

Gordon took her by both shoulders and shook her a bit. "The little disk, has that bloody duet I did with my wife. Come on, cough it up. I can use it to fix the comm-unit!"

"I don't have it."

Now it was Gordon's turn to stare. "What the bloody hell do you mean, you don't have it?"

Janlin gripped her forehead with one hand. "I mean I don't have it. Come on, maybe we'll find something in here."

She moved into the ship, banging her way along a hall and into an open area.

"Okay, let's see what we have." Janlin turned slowly, taking in the foreign bridge, her lips moving in a silent plea for something familiar to guide her. Like the shuttle's exterior, the inside was smooth and shiny, without any hints as to where the controls might be. "They must be holographs," she muttered to herself. "How do I activate them?"

Gordon followed her in and slumped down, his back to a wall, Anaya's device once more in his hands. A slight click echoed off steel, and he gently, lovingly, cradled the separate pieces. Janlin wanted to shout at him to help her, but it wasn't fair to him. He could barely stand as it was. She should just be grateful he arrived on his own two feet.

She turned her attention back to the confusing array of nothingness around her. She pushed at steel panels, felt along every edge, prodded and pulled at the rare protrusion.

"Nothing works!" Janlin banged on the console—if that's what it was—without any result, not even a crack, just sore hands.

"Try the handheld," Gordon mumbled. Janlin peered around to see him still propped against the wall, legs splayed, head hung down over the device in his lap. His fingers, the only part of him that moved, reassembled pieces yet again.

At that moment a crash made her spin around, and Gordon's head snapped up, eyes wide, face pale, too pale, with dark rings circling his eyes.

Janlin wished for a weapon as she tried every button and combination of buttons she could think of on the handheld. She threw it down in frustration and let her fingers slide over smooth steel, seeking for clues in vain. Sounds continued to echo from the air-lock.

"We are such space heads," Janlin whispered. Gordon would never have let her enter a dead-end place without some kind of guard on the door, or a booby-trap, or . . . something. Having his brain fried by fever did not work in her favour.

Janlin was not military trained, but she was the one with a clear head. The blame was all hers.

Janlin began tugging every little notch her fingers could find. Wall. Floor. Inching along in desperation as sweat broke out over her whole body.

"Come on, come on." There was nowhere to hide, no way to surprise, nothing to shoot with, strike with, or even throw.

Another bang. Was it their pursuer? Or Huantag? Maybe they weren't aware of the trespassers? Maybe it would be a friendly surprise, something to laugh about later?

The uncertainty might drive her insane.

Quietness settled, making her own breathing loud. Gordon grunted, and the snap of the device being closed up again ricocheted through the small metal space.

Janlin spun around, a wordless cry escaping, as he brought the comm-unit to his mouth yet again.

"Mayday, mayday—"

"Gordon, no!" Both voices were too loud. There'd be no hiding their presence now.

Gordon gave her a demented stare, but before she could console or comfort or ease the broken device from him, the undeniable sound of someone approaching made them both freeze.

"Damned traitors," came the slurred voice. "Betrayed us, now you're trying to run away, aren't you? Bitch. Not leaving without me."

Stepper dammed Jordan. That's who had followed through the scrub plain, unable to avoid detection yet trying to hide.

He had the nano-recorder.

Janlin relaxed a fraction, watching the hatchway. Stepper appeared, and his eyes narrowed when his gaze fell to her and Gordon.

His nose wrinkled in distaste. "You can't run." His eyes unfocused, and he blinked, leaning on the doorframe of the hatch. "Made us sick, now you die too. Karma."

Janlin's gut twisted. "Stepper, do you still have the disk I gave you?" she asked. She kept her voice steady, nonchalant.

"Pretty little toy. Got all your men on there, don't cha?" He pulled it out of his pocket and tossed it into the air. It fell as he spoke. "Don't you think this is a bad time for worrying about stupid crap like this?"

Janlin moved to catch it, trying to watch him and the tiny device at the same time. She didn't know Stepper's game, but she knew he was feverish and delusional. If he decided to go angry on her, it could be touch and go.

She caught the nano-recorder. "Thank you for keeping this safe," she said directly to Stepper before turning to give it to Gordon. He nodded and went right to work.

She turned away, going back to her search. The ship had to have onboard controls and communications. All she had to do was find them.

"Janlin!"

Gordon's shout gave her enough warning to avoid Stepper's lunge, the blade he held just grazing her shoulder.

"Christ, Stepper!" She gripped her arm, felt the wet heat. Her hand came away smeared with blood. "You mental malfunction," she said, backing away from the blade, shiny red, as he continued to advance. "I'm trying to save you!"

Stepper spat vindictive curses. Janlin shied away, stunned by his intensity. Blood soaked her sleeve. He had never been this malicious, this nasty. She saw clearly that nice Stepper was not and never would be enough to make up for mean Stepper.

Gordon moaned. Something snapped inside of her.

She rushed Stepper, fear washed away by terrible hopelessness. She knocked his blade away and struck his head with her own, watching through black spots with great satisfaction as he crumpled. Then she scooped up the blade and began kicking, stabbing, slashing, and smashing every square inch of the control room, half methodically, half mindlessly.

A weight slammed into her, the blade flying free of blood-slick fingers before she crashed into the wall. Something popped in one knee, and she screamed.

"See what you make me do?"

Stepper's voice, hot in her ear, made a film of red descend over her vision. She twisted, throwing him off. Her knee exploded with pain. "Why didn't you just stay dead?" she screamed at him.

He went still, his eyes wide, before they narrowed again. "That's just it, isn't it? When I had my little accident, you let me go. It was so much easier that way, wasn't it?"

Janlin felt every muscle tighten, every nerve coil, as she listened to him. His words hit too close to the truth, because she needed to let him go and couldn't.

She let him rant, let her own anger build. Then, when he was finished, she let the spring go, her fist connecting with a crunch, and Stepper went down hard.

"Wow." Gordon's voice cracked, and Janlin came back from some faraway place. Her hand hurt, bad, but it was nothing compared to her knee . . . or her heart.

"Are you all right?" she asked.

Gordon didn't answer, but she heard the click of the device being reconstructed yet again, and looked to see him raising it to his mouth.

"Mayday, mayday—"

The device crackled.

Janlin fell over herself getting to Gordon's side. "Anaya?" she cried.

"What are you idiots thinking, taking down the shielding now?"

"Fran?" Janlin's voice broke on the inflective. Her head spun with confusion. "What are you talking about? Where the hell are you?"

"Oh, I know all about your plans, Janlin," Fran said, caustic as ever. "And here I am in the lovely Imag warship ready to invade the planet, and you fools remove the only thing standing in their way."

Janlin sputtered denials into the comm-unit even while her face flushed with guilt. Still, that may have been Anaya's plan, but she hadn't done anything yet. Then she stopped short, the view of smoking console panels and sparks arcing through the air making her reconsider. Had she done so much . . . by accident?

"Trap," Stepper said. He rolled, holding a bloody nose, but he didn't attempt to rise.

She refused to believe what Fran insinuated. "Fran, everyone's sick down here. I need help contacting a friend with medicine. Fran?"

Only static answered her. Janlin slid to the floor, broken in and out, all her hope gone.

She'd done her part, and now the Imag would win. She couldn't stop the vision of Anaya standing triumphant on board the warship, chuffing at the human's stupidity, biding time to land and take control of the planet once its inhabitants were all conveniently dead or dying.

"You were right," she said to Stepper. "I was a complete fool." Janlin looked to see his lips fading to blue as his mouth widened, gasping for breath. "Don't die, you son-of-a-bitch!"

She rolled closer, her knee sending shockwaves of pain so bad she nearly blacked out, and laid her head on his chest. His breath came slow, and his lungs wheezed. Janlin slumped against him. "Oh God, I've been a fool."

The radio crackled.

"Jahnin?"

Everything stilled. Her fluttering fingers, her pounding heart, her ragged breathing, all of it seemed to come to a complete incredulous stop.

"Anaya?" she whispered.

Gordon stretched his arm to her, his eyes round. She fumbled for the device, held it to her mouth. "Anaya, is that really you?"

Chuff. "Yes. How 'ip go? Can no make go."

Janlin wanted to laugh and cry all at once. "Thank you, Anaya," she said, her voice rough with emotion. Then her mind kicked into gear. "Anaya, we need help, many of us are sick, Huantag too, people are dying . . . what did you give me? In that needle . . . do you have more—lots more?" She took a deep breath. "And the Imag are here, too! I did my part, but now the whole planet is vulnerable and it's my fault!"

Chuffing, long-winded, filled the room.

"What the hell is that?" Gordon asked.

Janlin wanted to laugh and cry all at the same time. "It's laughter. Gitane laughter."

"Imag busy now, best time for us to take 'ip." Sounds of weapon fire echoed across the link. "But 'ip not go. Pease, Jahnin, need make 'ip go." All sounds of amusement had disappeared.

"You're still on the Imag ship?" Janlin let her head fall back in despair.

"Yes. Need make your 'ip go now!"

Between them, Gordon and Janlin tried to explain the start-up process the best they could.

Again and again Anaya said, "Yes, did this as Jahnin say." Her voice took on a ragged edge as they reached the final step.

"We need Stepper's code!" Janlin twisted around and stared at his still form. The captain and his second were the only ones to have that final access, though there were ways to circumvent them . . . if you were on the ship and had plenty of time.

Gordon grabbed the comm-unit. "Hold the comm-unit close to the panel," he instructed. Then he clearly said, "Janlin, J-A-N-L-I-N."

They waited through a long moment of silence. "No work," Anaya cried. Weapon fire drowned out her next words.

Gordon began running through every possible word he thought Stepper might use. Janlin shook Stepper. His lungs rattled loud enough to hear, and his skin had paled to a waxen veneer. She tugged and loosened his shirt collar. She gripped it for comfort, before swinging an arm back and slapping him as hard as she could.

He moaned, his eyes blinking.

"Stepper, what is your password for the *Hope* command console?" Janlin said, still holding his collar. Her face was close to his, the smell of him strong. "Come on, Stepper, your password." She waved at Gordon to pass her the comm-unit.

Stepper's eyes closed, then opened, peering at Janlin. "Jannilove," he said softly, like a caress. He slumped again, his eyes rolling back.

"No, Stepper! Stay with me! We need your password for Anaya!" Cursing, she brought the comm-unit to her own mouth. "Anaya, go find a human named Fran. She is on the Imag ship, and she's the only one that can help you. Anaya?"

There was no reply.

Gordon gently took the device from her. Janlin laid her head on Stepper's chest. His heart raced, weak and stuttering and too fast.

"I can't find another way," came Fran's voice. "I need some ideas for taking this ship out."

Janlin stared at the comm-unit. Gordon's relief was palpable, even over his confusion. "Fran, what the bloody hell are you talking about?" he asked.

"That you, Gordon? Always with the funny." She sounded vague, distracted. "Done working for these a-holes. Worse than SpaceOp. So, I want to take out their ship. A little payback. Any ideas?"

"Tell her to get to Anaya," Janlin said.

"Fran, can you get to the *Hope*? We've got a friend on board. Help her get launched and come get us."

Fran's derisive laughter echoed through the room. Janlin ground her teeth.

"You guys are delusional if you think I'll leave now. The Imag told me—you'll all be dead of some virus soon. I'll probably get it too, so I might as well do some good before I go."

Janlin groaned. Every moment pulled at her as precious time slipped away like Huantag sand.

"You're right, we are sick," Gordon said. "Except Janlin. Her friend, who's on the *Hope* right now, has a cure."

"Janlin, of course," Fran said, her voice deadly hard now. "She'll be awfully lonely, then, once I blow up this alien tub of crap."

"No, Fran, you're not listening. If you help her get the ship running, you can bring us some meds. I don't know how much longer Stepper can hang on!" Gordon held his throat and let his head fall back. Janlin wanted to scream at Fran, but that'd be the worst thing to do, she knew.

"Fran, please believe me," Gordon said through clenched teeth. "If you blow that ship up you remove any chance of ever going home."

Fran laughed again, a demented sound that made Janlin shiver. "There's . . . nothing to go . . . home to, especially if I fail." Little gaps were coming between her phrases, as if she focused carefully or was too busy to keep track of her thoughts. "The Imag have turned this tub into a rudimentary Jumpship and will probably head Earth's way before too long . . . as soon as they've taken this poor planet." The sound of tools at work continued over her voice. "No, better that I give these bastards some payback and make sure they never leave this system. Are you going to help me or not?"

Janlin and Gordon stared at each other. Gordon raised the comm-unit again. "Help Anaya fire the *Hope* first . . ."

"No wait," Janlin cried. She held out her hand and Gordon, with a look of uncertainty, slid the unit to her.

"Fran, you're right, there's no time if you're to succeed." Gordon stared at her in horror.

"Never thought I'd hear you say that, Kavanagh."

"Well, it's my fault the Huantag are in danger. I can't just leave them wide open to invasion."

Fran was quiet for a moment. "I've wracked my brain for a way to blow this sucker up. You got something?"

Janlin looked to Gordon, like she always did for this kind of help. "I don't bloody well think so," he said, shaking his head. "There has to be another way."

Janlin sighed. "Gordon, if you can think of a way to get us the meds we need, convince the Imag to not only leave the Huantag alone but give us our ship back, and protect Earth from their eventual arrival, then I'm all ears, my friend."

He hung his head, and Janlin swallowed hard before calling Fran again.

"Not really coming up with much. Give us a sec."

Gordon looked up, his face twisted with grief and anger. "I wish I could fry each and every Imag with their own nerve whips," he growled.

"Nerve whips . . . Fran, what sort of fuel do they use?"

"A pretty common mix, nothing unexpected in there. Mostly hydrogen, like us."

"Nerve whip."

"What good would that do?"

"Nerve whip and water? Make a spark in the fuel tank."

"Huh. It just might work." Fran's voice was thoughtful.

"But listen, you've got to go help Anaya first. Maybe she'll have a way to take them out that's safer for you."

"No, the only way this will work is if I get right into a tank and set a line—you know that."

"But—"

"No buts," Fran said. Her voice dropped to a whisper. "They're coming. I think they've noticed I'm missing from my usual post. I've only got so much time . . . thank you, Janlin."

A final click, and the unit went dead.

"Fran!"

Both Gordon and Janlin cried out at the same time, but there was no response.

"We have to get that ship running for Anaya," Janlin gasped.

Gordon took the unit and began calling for the Gitane captain, trying different settings as he had before. Janlin checked Stepper, who looked entirely too much like a cadaver for her liking.

"Outside," Gordon gasped.

"Why?"

"If she's successful, we'll see it." He hauled himself to his feet as Janlin navigated her injured knee under her. They shuffled out of the shuttle and onto the landing pad, one sick, one crippled.

It took them some time to get into the open field. Gordon stood, ignoring Janlin's urges to sit and rest. He tried the comm-unit a few more times, with no results. They watched the sky.

All too soon thunder rumbled through the air, and they craned their necks to see a fireball pushing rolling clouds of blackness across the sky.

Gordon fell to his knees. "Ursula." The comm-unit slid from his fingers into the dirt.

Janlin watched the destruction as if from a great distance. The threat of the Imag was gone, but the settlement and the Huantag were dying with no hope of a cure, and Anaya and the *Hope* were destroyed.

There was no going home.

Every time there seemed no hope to be had, she'd found a way to go on. Every time she dared hope, it was ripped away.

Now she was done.

She limped away from Gordon. He would be dead soon anyway. She would find a cliff and throw herself off it. No one could blame her, could they?

Ten steps, twenty, thirty. Then she turned back, turned and faced what she would lose. She looked to the expanding black cloud in the sky and saw Huantag lifting to investigate. She looked back at the cliffs, where her father lay six feet under and so many that deserved more waited under white sheets. She looked at the shuttle, laid open to her wrath and hopeless hope.

She looked at her friend crumpled in the dirt. What could she do?

She returned to Gordon, scooping up the comm-unit from where he'd let it fall and shoving it in her pocket before guiding him back to Stepper. She would stay with them until the end, refusing to think beyond that. To do anything less would be wrong.

CHAPTER FORTY-EIGHT

AFTER A LONG, gasping, grief-stricken cry, Gordon fell asleep, a fitful fever-wrought doze full of incoherent mutterings. Janlin wished she had water to bathe his forehead.

She moved to Stepper's side. Here, even water seemed fruitless, although his bloody face distorted his features so she couldn't tell just how bad he was. Janlin tore a piece of her shirt and moistened it with her own spit to carefully cleanse the blood away.

Stepper stirred, moaning. "Shhhh," she said, gently blowing over his face to dry and cool it.

His eyes opened, blinked shut, opened again. "What's happened?" he asked, still not aware of her.

"Nothing. Just rest."

"Water?"

Janlin bit her lip. "I have none."

Stepper rolled his head side to side in a denial. "Something's happened, something bad. I can hear it in your voice." His focus settled on her fully. "Jannilove," he said, a sad admission of all they'd lost in one single word.

She couldn't reply. Tears sprang to her eyes, choking her, and she could not bite her lip hard enough to make them stay put.

"I was wrong," he whispered, eyes closed again. "I heard the alien, heard . . ."

Tears dropped off her chin, and she hitched in a breath. "Doesn't matter," she whispered back.

His lips parted, and he made a vain attempt to moisten them. "Does," he said. "I let you down, let you go, angry young man not so young anymore . . . too full of himself." This took too much, and he panted for a bit. Janlin's tears continued to flow, her sobs caught inside her in an attempt to hide them from him.

"If I live, will you give me another chance?"

Janlin shook her head, even though he couldn't see it. He didn't need to know how badly her heart was broken. He'd never change. It was over anyway. Soon she'd be alone.

"Janlin?" His voice rasped. "Please . . ."

Choked with the grief for all that never was, and all that would never be, Janlin took up his hand.

"We're all out of chances, Stepper," she said softly. She wouldn't lie to him, even if he would die soon.

He let his breath out in a big sigh and closed his eyes. His face relaxed, his head falling to one side. Janlin pulled him to her, lifting the wasted shell of him easily. She rocked him, cradling him to her, washing his face with her tears.

A FAINT CRACKLE of sound brought Janlin out of a vague unconsciousness. Her throat burned, her eyes refused to function. Was she sick now, finally? She held the thought as a morbid hope of release.

Another crackle brought her further to herself, and she pushed up to look around. Gordon lay as if dead, but then twitched, throwing his head from side to side with a cry.

"Gordon," she said, her voice rough.

That crackle again, and she focused on the sound, so close, finally registering the voice coming from her pants' pocket.

"Jahnin?"

Janlin gasped, practically ripping the pocket in her rush to pull the device out.

"Anaya?"

"Jahnin, 'ip go!" Anaya's voice held triumph.

Janlin stared at the comm-unit. "I thought you were dead!"

Anaya chuffed her pleasure. "Word from man, make 'ip go."

Word from man—Jannilove! That was the password, his cherished nickname for her.

279

"Anaya no dead. No talk—'ip no talk . . ."

Janlin could hear her friend's frustration with the gaps in vocabulary. "No communications after the Imag ship blew up?" she supplied.

"Yes," Anaya sighed. "Come get you now."

"How do you know where we are?" Janlin asked. The news left her somehow drained.

Anaya explained that the device had a locator beacon. "No work before, you . . . gone. Now back. Is good."

Janlin looked over at the man who had repaired the device for her. "Yes, is good, but I need help fast. Medicine like Yipho gave me."

"Come soon."

Anaya signed off for re-entry, and Janlin stared at the device in her hand, knowing that if she hadn't picked it up and kept it active, none of this would be happening.

She looked at the two unconscious men either side of her. Janlin grit her teeth and lurched to her feet to limp outside as the sounds of a landing shuttle reached her.

The moment the shuttle hatch opened Janlin limped and hopped inside. She found Yipho and pulled him to his medkit.

"This, now," she said, fumbling to try and remove it from the wall herself.

Anaya, having followed, gently pulled Janlin's hands away, grunting a mix of languages. She pointed with one hand and patted the medkit until Janlin realized that the entire crew, including Yipho, was carrying cases that looked suspiciously similar to the medkit.

"Oh, sorry," Janlin said. "This way, then. Please hurry!"

Janlin gestured towards the shuttle and held up two fingers, then pointed towards the settlement. No one responded or even looked at her. Yipho's mouth hung open. In fact, they all stood staring about them in what could only be complete awe.

"Later! Later you can be amazed," Janlin shouted. "Tell them to go!"

Anaya barked her orders, and her crew moved.

"What about the village?" Janlin asked.

"See?" Anaya said, pointing. To Janlin's surprise, a very familiar Seraph circled for landing in the distance. Anaya chuffed. "We have more crew, too," she said. "Find Gitane with

Imag, get them free."

"That's fantastic, Anaya," Janlin said. "I had moments of doubt, but you really did come through."

"Get human, go 'ip, find new home, yes?" Anaya looked around her, her eyes shining.

Janlin's gaze looked to the distant Huantag city. Anaya took her arm and turned Janlin to face her.

"Find new home, yes?"

Janlin pinched her lips between her teeth. Did she dare say what she was thinking?

"Jahnin?"

"Have you ever considered working on the planet you have?"

The far-away sparkle dimmed, and Anaya focused a steel gaze on Janlin. "No new home?" The tone wasn't exactly threatening, but close. Janlin could hear words like betrayal, broken deal, liar—all words Anaya didn't know—echoing in that tone.

Janlin flinched, looking away. "The Huantag have amazing technology, and they've fixed up this planet." She dared a glance at the Gitane. Anaya stared out over the plain, so Janlin took a deep breath and continued. "If you shared your medicine, helped them recover from the sickness, they might help both of us repair our worlds."

Anaya's gaze snapped to Janlin, her brow furrowed. "Why do this? Huantag no care for Gitane!" She thumped a fist on her chest for emphasis.

"So, make friends. Give them a reason to feel grateful to you. Let them know you're not Imag." Anaya's frown turned to a scowl. Janlin ploughed on. "Listen. The Imag sent this sickness among us and then traded us to the Huantag in an effort to kill them off. Then they could take their planet without having to fight for it. They even made the Huantag promise to keep us here, never letting us leave the planet, on the threat of war. Meanwhile they planned this biological war all along. Is this a Gitane way?" She took a deep breath, wondering if the next step took things too far. "If you aren't bothered by the fact that the Huantag are dying in huge numbers and might be wiped out altogether, then I don't want to take you out into the universe."

"You promise!"

"Sure, I did. But the Huantag are dying. You can have this

planet all to yourself, so I've kept my end of the bargain by finding you a new home planet." Janlin dropped the flippant tone and turned to face Anaya full on. "They're dying, Anaya! Don't you care about that? If you don't, I would prefer to leave you here to do just as the Imag were going to do." Janlin opened her arms to the landscape around them. "This will be all yours, since the Huantag will soon be dead in staggering numbers without your help."

Was she getting through? Anaya stared at the middle distance again. Janlin let the alien sift her thoughts for a few minutes. She kept glancing at the shuttle, itching to go see Gordon and Stepper, make sure they were okay, but she couldn't give up on this.

"Help the Huantag, and they will likely help you in return. That's the kind of people they are."

Anaya blinked and sucked in a big breath. Before she could speak, Yipho and a crewmate emerged from the Huantag shuttle carrying Gordon. Janlin hobbled over to him, pleading with every limping step for the universe to cut her a break and let him live.

His eyes were closed, with a breathing cup over his mouth and nose. One touch to his forehead, her other hand taking his, and his eyes fluttered opened.

"They stuck me," he said, his words slurred.

"Yeah," Janlin said around a big grin. "Yeah, they did." She patted Yipho's arm, nodding and smiling and wishing she had some way to thank him. Did Gitane hug?

Anaya pulled Janlin back while giving orders to her crew.

"That's going to work, right?" she said to Anaya. "He's going to be okay, right?"

"Yes, Yipho good. It work."

Janlin struggled to breathe past the overwhelming relief. "Tell them, thank you," Janlin said to Anaya. "Thank you," she said to them directly, hoping the tone carried the sincere meaning even if the words were foreign. Anaya added words that made the stretcher-bearers chuff and raise their chins with pride.

They returned to the Huantag shuttle. Janlin stared at the hatch, her proposition to Anaya forgotten. Soon Yipho emerged, followed by a second stretcher. She couldn't bring herself to ask.

Anaya called out to Yipho, and he answered with a nod and a toothy grimace.

"He okay too," Anaya said. "But very sick."

Janlin nodded, not trusting her own voice.

They boarded the Gitane ship and settled the men into their version of med-bay. Janlin had a moment of memory for her father, which led to Teardrop and Tyrell and Sandy and Ron and Victor . . . Janlin sucked in breath after breath, overwhelmed by the sheer weight of loss.

Anaya stood at the open hatchway, staring out over the planet's scrub plain. Janlin considered going back to her original agreement. Would it be so bad to take the Gitane to a new planet somewhere? It would be what humankind would have to do . . . unless they could get help from the Huantag.

The Huantag were right. People are tied to their planet of origin, and they needed to make the effort to correct the mistakes they'd made instead of just running away. Human and Gitane alike. She had to hold firm. But if Anaya didn't agree with Janlin's new sense of honour, it might make getting the *Hope* away from them a bit tricky.

Janlin straightened her back, gripped her resolve, and went to stand beside the alien she wanted to call a friend.

"I'm glad the Imag threat is gone," Janlin said. "Although I'm confused about how it all happened. We told our shipmate on board you were there. She could've gotten free!"

Anaya faced Janlin. "Anaya see Fran. She want to die a big hero."

Janlin gripped the hatch frame for support. "You . . . talked with Fran?"

"Yes. With no Fran, we no get on 'ip. She hep."

"But she wouldn't go with you . . ."

"No go. She want war with Imag, no return."

Fran had done what no one else could. "She is the true hero of today," Janlin said, her voice rough.

Anaya turned back to the view, and Janlin joined her, staring out over the golden landscape of stark beauty. Could she have done the same in Fran's place? So many times she'd longed for a way out, contemplating suicide as the only answer left, and later congratulating herself for not giving up, for not giving in. But this—Fran's action was one of courage beyond anything she was capable of.

"Thank you for your sacrifice, Fran Delou," Janlin said to the sun and wind and sand. She wondered if she could ever match it. Wondered if any of them would ever stand on Earth soil again. Wondered if she had some last thing to say to convince Anaya, now that she'd made her stand, some last bit of leverage to convince her.

She had nothing. It wouldn't be worth standing on Earth if she knew she'd made the last surviving Huantag pay for it. She would die here along with them if that's what it took.

Anaya chuffed, soft and gentle. "Okay, Jahnin. You right. Help Huantag too." She lifted her comm-unit and gave orders, and they turned to take their seats in the shuttle. Moments later the Gitane shuttle rose from the settlement to fly on to the Huantag city.

Anaya nudged Janlin. "You hero now, Jahnin. To Gitane, to Huantag, to Human," she said.

Janlin lost all grip on her emotions then, weeping for those they had lost and the hope of going home.

CHAPTER FORTY-NINE

JANLIN WAS RIGHT there when Gordon's eyes fluttered open.

"Uh . . . bloody hell," he croaked.

She checked the monitor, then laid a cool hand on his forehead.

"It'll get better quickly, I'm told," she said, holding his head up so he could sip water. "The fever's down, and your breath doesn't rattle like a marble in a can anymore, so that's good."

Gordon's hand gripped hers. "Where?" His eyes roved around the strange surroundings.

A grin split her face. "This is Anaya's ship. We're special guests. She's taking us to the *Hope* right now."

Gordon stared long enough and strangely enough to make her concerned. "Gordo?"

He blinked. "*Hope*?" His voice was a raw croak.

"Yes." Janlin fussed about the room, unwilling to face his cadaver-like stare. Survivor guilt crept in, even as she limped on her still-sore knee. "We'll Jump as soon as the ill are stable." Or gone. They had continued to lose the sickest for a while.

"Home?" He blinked furiously, tears popping out to flow back into his hair.

Janlin squeezed his big toe, her other hand now full with things for the recycler. "Rest. I'll let Yipho know you're awake."

Gordon heaved a big sigh and swiped away the tears with one big hand. "Ursula," was all he said, and his eyes closed again.

Janlin stood in the doorway choking on tears of relief. Gordon would make it. They would go home, and they would bring help, but it had come at a horrible cost.

"CAPTAIN INABA!"

They were back aboard *Hope*, Anaya's shuttle safely stowed in the bay with the Seraph, and preparing to Jump home.

He turned and gave her a sad smile. "Please, call me Yasu," he said. They clasped hands, sharing an unspoken exchange of grief. "It's good to see you."

She nodded, unable to figure out just what to say in such a moment, it all just felt like such babble.

"You did well to trust, Janlin," he said then, surprising her. "Don't lose sight of that in your guilt and grief."

FINALLY, THEY WERE ready to Jump. Despite assurances, Janlin wondered how they could be sure of the *Hope's* condition . . . or how they would be on the other side. But she put all these fears away when she understood how nervous Anaya was.

"Just think, you'll go down in history as the first of your kind to Jump."

"An if humans no 'ike me?"

"There will always be haters," Janlin said with resignation. "Most of the time it's people acting out of fear. As people get to know you, they'll see how amazing you are, and it'll be fine."

Anaya chuffed. The remnants of her people were now helping the Huantag rebuild and recover from the Imag virus. They would be safe while she took this leap into the unknown.

Gordon appeared, back on his feet and possibly more eager for this day than anyone else aboard. While still a shell of his former self, he had regained enough of his joviality to greet everyone cheerfully.

"Anaya, I'm still trying to figure out how to thank you for all this," he said. "One day I'll manage it, some great idea, and I'll probably need my wife's help to figure it out."

Everyone chuckled, and the mood was high. After all they'd been through, they could finally go home.

"Captain on the bridge."

Immediately the mood of the room changed. Stepper stalked in, his shoulders riding high, his mouth a straight line. "Status."

They went through the flight checklists carefully. Some people sat at unfamiliar stations, filling in for those lost, and Stepper's terse tone made everyone flustered. Finally, it was done.

"Ready all stations?"

"Aye, Captain."

"Wait!" Everyone turned to stare at Janlin. She swallowed, wondering why exactly she had to draw attention to herself. Was it so important?

"Kavanagh?" Stepper demanded.

His anger steeled something in her. She looked around the room and saw the anguish and horror they had all experienced reflected at her. She also saw the strength, the resolve, and yes, the hope, and she straightened up in the face of his anger in a way she never would have before.

"This Jump is for all those we leave behind," she said into the questioning silence, a silence that held for several heartbeats as they all remembered faces that wouldn't return with them.

Stepper loosened his clenched jaw and gave her a nod.

"For all those we leave behind."

JUMP

The End

ACKNOWLEDGEMENTS

THIS STORY BEGAN in the sweaty New England heat of St. Anselm's campus, where the Odyssey Writing Workshop is held. Our assignment was to create a slam piece of flash fiction to read aloud at a public book store event. I was at a loss. How to be so brief? Calie Voorhis gave me simple, yet brilliant, advice: take one powerful moment, just one, and write that.

So I did. And promptly "saw" the whole story behind that moment... what led up to it, and what followed (well, mostly). So began a thirteen-year journey to publication, with that scene still a cornerstone of the story. Much gratitude goes to the entire Odyssey family for their continuing awesomeness and mighty inspiration.

Then there's IFWA... how to encompass the profound effect this group has had on me, professionally and personally, for twenty-five years now? Small splinter groups often grow off the main group to be more manageable, and such a group named SAW helped with many versions of this tale. Sherry, Ann, Tereasa, Susan, Randy, Val, Gerald, Mike, Anna, Renee, Celeste, Al, Calvin, and many, many more have all helped create the writer I am today.

Special thanks to my publisher Margaret Curelas. Thank you for remembering Janlin, asking for her story back, and reviving a dream. Dear Reader, please know that any mistakes between these covers is on me, because Margaret also did a wonderful job of editing.

I have to give big credit to my family, especially my kid, for being so patient with an introverted reclusive writer person like me. And sometimes even later in life you meet people who become your world. Thank you, Wayne, for bringing my dreams new clarity and hope.

And most of all, thank you, dear reader, for the opportunity to share with you a story about spaceships and the crazy people flying them. JUMP

ABOUT THE AUTHOR

Freelance editor, fiction author, and wood artisan, Adria Laycraft earned honours in Journalism in '92 and has always worked with words and visual art. She co-edited the Urban Green Man anthology in 2013, which was nominated for an Aurora Award. Look for her short stories in various magazines and anthologies both online and in print. Adria is a grateful member of Calgary's Imaginative Fiction Writers Association (IFWA), and a proud survivor of the Odyssey Writers Workshop. You can see her carvings at the Hidden Art Show for the When Words Collide book festival. Learn more about Adria at adrialaycraft.com, or follow her YouTube channels Carving the Cottonwood and Girl Gone Vagabond.

Lightning Source UK Ltd.
Milton Keynes UK
UKHW011632160919
349872UK00002B/324/P